RANDOM
HOUSE
LARGE
PRINT

Lost and Found

Also by Danielle Steel
Available from Random House Large Print

Silent Night

Turning Point

Beauchamp Hall

In His Father's Footsteps

The Good Fight

The Cast

Accidental Heroes

Fall from Grace

Past Perfect

Fairytale

The Right Time

The Duchess

Against All Odds

Dangerous Games

The Mistress

The Award

Rushing Waters

DANIELLE STEEL

Lost and Found

A Novel

RANDOM HOUSE
LARGE PRINT

Copyright © 2019 by Danielle Steel

All rights reserved.
Published in the United States of America by Random House Large Print in association with Delacorte Press, an imprint of Penguin Random House LLC, New York.

Cover design: Lynn Andreozzi
Cover illustration: Tom Hallman based on
© Tim Fitzharris/Minden Pictures/
National Geographic Creative (water),
© Robert Glusic/Photodisc/Getty Images
(road/mountains)

The Library of Congress has established a Cataloging-in-Publication record for this title.

ISBN: 978-1-984-89042-9

www.penguinrandomhouse.com/large-print-format-books

FIRST LARGE PRINT EDITION

Printed in the United States of America

10 9 8 7 6 5 4 3 2 1

This Large Print edition published in accord with the standards of the N.A.V.H.

To Tom,
My beloved cowboy,
so greatly loved,
bigger than life,
so vast, bigger than the sky,
forever a part of me,
with all my love,
until we meet again.

And to my so greatly
loved children,
Beatrix, Trevor, Todd, Nick,
Samantha, Victoria,
Vanessa, Maxx, and Zara,
with all my heart and soul
and love for you forever,

Mommy/DS

"You're not old until your dreams become regrets."

—Anonymous

Lost and Found

Chapter 1

Madison Allen lived in an old brick firehouse in the West Village in downtown New York, a few blocks east of the Hudson River. The firehouse was a hundred years old. It had been a departure for Maddie, after living on the Upper East Side most of her life. She had raised her three children in a comfortable although not luxurious apartment, in a serious-looking prewar building. Buying the firehouse downtown had been an act of independence for her, and it had become a labor of love. She had bought it fifteen years before, when her youngest child, Milagra, had left for college. Her older two, Deanna and Ben, were twenty and twenty-one when she bought it, and still came home for school holidays. Two years later, they had moved into their own apartments, and never came home to live again after they had graduated.

Deanna moved into an apartment in Chelsea and got a job as an assistant designer for a successful contemporary fashion brand that was popular with young women. She had gone to Parsons School of Design and had real talent. She was fiercely competitive with other designers and single-minded with her love of fashion, always focused on her own success. She was less intellectual than her brother and sister. Ben, her younger brother, had a keen instinct for business and had done well. Milagra, the youngest, had been writing since she was fifteen, and her first novel was published by the time she was nineteen. All three of Maddie's children were very different from each other, with their interests in design, business, and literature. Unlike her younger siblings, Deanna had a killer instinct.

After graduating from Berkeley, Ben had decided to stay in San Francisco, in the world of start-ups. He swore he'd never come back to New York to live, and he hadn't. He loved the outdoors, California life, and the high-tech world. He was a kind and loving person, a good husband and father, and caring son, although Maddie seldom saw him, and rarely contacted any of them. She didn't want to intrude on them now that they were adults, and most of the time waited to hear from them. Sometimes it was a long wait, so she called them. But she held out as long as she could.

Milagra had gone to UCLA, taken post-graduate writing classes at Stanford, and moved to Mendocino in northern California. She needed isolation to write her books, and silence. So Maddie heard from her the least often.

Maddie would have rattled around her old apartment alone, like a marble in a shoebox, if she'd stayed there. When she moved downtown, her children had been shocked, and objected strenuously. They felt awkward in their mother's new and somewhat unusual home. But she was firm about it and knew it was right for her at the time and they would adjust to it eventually. And as she knew they would, they grew up and left.

The firehouse still had its original brass pole that the firemen had used to slide down. She had someone come in to polish it every few months, and had tried sliding down it once herself. It was scary and exciting and fun, though she had come down faster than she'd expected. Buying the firehouse had been a happy event for her, and a new adventure. She'd loved it then and still did.

And the statement she made with the move was not as harsh as her children had claimed or feared. There were four floors, with two good-sized rooms and a smaller one that shared a bathroom on the top floor and were set up as bedrooms for Ben, Deanna, and Milagra whenever they wanted to come home. They had hardly ever used them, and now, fifteen years later, never stayed there at all.

With a successful start-up to his credit in his life as a young entrepreneur, Ben had no time to come home. After he sold the business and started a second one, he was even busier. He had a knack for discovering a need that no one else had thought of, and capitalizing on it. Married now, at thirty-five, with three children of his own, Willie, Charlie, and Olive, six, five, and three, he rarely came to New York, and stayed at a hotel when he did. His wife, Laura, was from Grosse Pointe, a suburb of Detroit, and had friends and relatives in Chicago, but she came no farther east than that.

They had full and busy lives in San Francisco, and a beautiful house with a spectacular view of the city in Belvedere, a tiny island of high-priced real estate in Marin County, twenty minutes from San Francisco. They were so heavily scheduled between Ben's work, the social schedule Laura arranged for them, and all the activities for the children that it was never a good time for Maddie to come out, even for a brief visit. The few times she had she'd felt like an intruder. Her grandchildren scarcely knew her. She saw them once or twice a year for a few days, and could barely keep up with their after-school activities, computer lessons, karate, soccer, swimming classes, and ballet for Olive, along with their constant playdates and the other activities their mother organized for them. Laura kept everyone busy, and successfully kept Maddie at bay, although Maddie never complained. Her son was happy, which was good enough for her. She would have liked to see more of him, and to live in the same city, but it hadn't worked out that way. Maddie was generous about it. She always tried to be tolerant of their differences from her, and had encouraged them to follow their dreams, and be independent.

She had sensed on the day of the wedding that she had lost Ben to his new in-laws. Ben and Laura spent Christmas in Grosse Pointe with Laura's parents, and her siblings and their children. Her parents' home on the Big Island in Hawaii was an easy vacation spot for all of them. Ben and his family went there for most school holidays, or to Mexico, or Aspen. Nothing Maddie had to offer could compete. She had no country home, and a busy work life herself. They could have stayed at the firehouse with her in New York, but she recognized that, as Ben's family grew rapidly, it would have been too cramped, even dangerous for such young children, with the narrow circular metal staircase and the fire pole. She was hoping to get them to New York on their own when they were older, but that wouldn't be for a long time. And Laura's goal in the meantime was to be important in the San Francisco social scene and show off her husband's success. There was no time or room for Maddie in all that.

Milagra lived in an entirely different universe from Ben, in windswept, foggy, rugged Mendocino. She had bought a small crumbling Victorian house after she sold her second book, and she restored the house herself. She never drove the three or four hours to San Francisco. She wrote eerie, haunting gothic novels, which weren't bestsellers but enjoyed a steady, moderate success, enough for her to live comfortably. She had a solid following of faithful readers who loved her books. Her work was dark and strange, and her isolated life in Mendocino suited her. She had started writing at fifteen and had nearly been a recluse ever since. Milagra didn't need people around her to be happy. In fact, she preferred her solitude so she could write. Even a friendly phone call felt like an intrusion to her, so she didn't give her number to anyone, and called no one. Most of her contact with her mother was by email, when her internet was working. She had internet access where she lived, most of the time, but poor cellphone reception, which suited her perfectly. She was always working on a book, and at thirty-three she lived alone, with three large dogs and two stray cats. She hardly ever saw her brother, but emailed him from time to time. She never wrote to Deanna. They were just too different. She hadn't been to New York in six years, since she'd bought her house. Maddie visited her whenever Milagra was between books and allowed her to.

Milagra had gotten her name when Maddie had almost lost her several times before she was born. They named her "Miracle" in Spanish. She was a solitary person whose life was her work. She had nothing in common with Ben and his wife, Laura, and Milagra always told her mother that they had nothing to say to each other when they met. She had even less in common with her older sister, Deanna, who was hardworking, hard-driving, and fully engaged in the fast-paced world of fashion in New York. Milagra had always thought her sister aggressive, and said she scared her. Deanna had bullied her as a child and ordered her around, always convinced that she knew best. Deanna had always called Milagra "the weird one."

Deanna was married to David Harper, the executive editor of a highly respected publishing house. As a designer, Deanna made more money than he did, and she added glamour to his life. She had always had a sharp edge, even as a child, and an equally sharp tongue. But she and David were a good match. She ran their life together and her career with an iron hand. They had two daughters, Lily, seven, and Kendra, nine, and Deanna was as ambitious for them as she was for herself. They went to one of the best private schools in New York, and were just as busy as Ben's children with after-school activities. Kendra was serious about ballet, and Lily took hip-hop lessons. They both took violin and piano. Deanna had their lives carefully mapped out.

All four of them retreated to their house in the Berkshires on weekends, where David could read manuscripts, Deanna could work on designs, and the girls could take riding lessons. The girls were taken care of by a nanny, which gave David and Deanna a break from their stressful high-powered lives during the week.

Deanna never invited her mother to spend weekends with them. They entertained in New York but never included her there either. Deanna had always been critical of her mother, and thought she was too much of a freethinker, and a little eccentric. The firehouse had been the first sign of it, in her opinion, although it suited Maddie perfectly, much more than an empty, lonely apartment uptown would have, once they'd grown up. David and Deanna lived in a co-op in the East

70s, between Madison and Park. The apartment had been photographed by **Architectural Digest** and Deanna had decorated it herself. Maddie's neighborhood in the West Village was warm and friendly, with small restaurants, fun shops, and people wandering the streets in good weather on the weekends. Maddie went for long walks along the river, which both invigorated and relaxed her. Her contact with her oldest daughter was often tense. At thirty-six, Deanna was outspoken about whatever she didn't like, and she thought that her mother living in an antiquated firehouse was Bohemian, made no sense, and was even embarrassing. Why couldn't she live in an apartment uptown like other people her age?

It made perfect sense to Maddie, and when she restored the firehouse, she set it up for her convenience, with the guest bedrooms on the top floor for her absentee children. The floor below it, the third floor, was made up of her own bedroom and a small sitting room she spent her evenings in, reading or doing research relevant to her work. Her living room was on the second floor, along with a renovated kitchen large enough to eat in. She never entertained, but she could have, at her table for ten. And on the ground floor were two small offices, one for herself and the other for her assistant, Penny. The large space with twenty-foot ceilings once used to house the fire trucks was her photography studio. Once she moved in, she was able to live and work in the same place for the first time, and her clients loved coming there. It was sparsely but stylishly decorated, she had wonderful, eclectic taste, and great style. She had a collection of antique fireman's helmets from around the world on one wall, which fascinated people. Everything about the place was interesting, unusual, warm, and charming, like Maddie herself.

Maddie had backed into her career by accident. Blond, tall, and lithe, with an exquisite face, she had done some modeling after college at NYU. Her parents were both high school teachers. She hadn't figured out her own career, all she knew was that she didn't want to be a teacher like them. They were underpaid, overworked, and disillusioned with the public school system. She modeled as a stopgap, for the money, and it paid well. She hadn't enjoyed modeling but she liked the freedom it gave her. She had her own apartment on the East Side in a decent neighborhood. She hated the cattle calls, the pressure, nasty magazine editors, and bitchy, competitive girls, but she was able to live on what she made, and only planned to model for a year or two. She had majored in art history in college, which didn't pay her rent when she graduated, and her parents weren't able to help.

Within months, she was noticed by a well-known French fashion photographer, Stephane Barbier, who lived and worked in New York. He hotly pursued her personally and professionally. She fell in love with him, and he convinced her he was madly in love with her too.

Six months into their passionate relationship, she discovered she was pregnant with Deanna. After long nights when Stephane drank too much and smoked furiously, they decided to get married at city hall. Her parents would have objected to the hasty decision, but Maddie's father was dying of cancer by then, and her mother was too devastated to pay attention to what her only child was doing. Maddie settled into life with Stephane in utter bliss. It wasn't how she had intended to start her life, with a shotgun marriage, but it all seemed to be working out. Once her pregnancy showed and she couldn't model, Stephane put Maddie to work as one of his studio assistants. She became an avid student of everything he did. She loved watching him during the shoots, and continued working for him after the baby was born, eventually becoming his first assistant on every shoot he did. When Deanna was four months old, believing that nursing would keep her from getting pregnant, Maddie got pregnant with Ben. Stephane was ecstatic when their son was born and acted as though Maddie had really done it right. Deanna had been a fussy, difficult baby. Ben was a ray of sunshine, always laughing and smiling, almost from the moment he was born.

The marriage held up for three years, until Milagra was born after a difficult pregnancy. Maddie was eight months pregnant when she discovered Stephane's torrid affair with a nineteen-year-old Polish model, the star of the hour, and all the infidelities that had come before her. Their life unraveled rapidly, and by the time Milagra was born, Maddie's world was crashing down. Stephane was drinking too much, and his career was slipping by then. When Milagra was a month old, Stephane told Maddie he was leaving her and going back to Paris with his new love. Maddie's mother had died the year before, of cancer like her father, and she had no one to turn to. At twenty-five, Maddie was abandoned with three young children, and no way to support herself. Her parents had had nothing to leave her. She had to live by her wits and hard work, and would have to pay for childcare while she did. Stephane told her bluntly that he couldn't afford to pay child support, and left. She didn't want to go back to modeling, although she could have and would have if she had had no other choice. Instead she took a job as another photographer's assistant, for a salary she could just barely manage to exist on to feed her children, pay for day care for the kids, and pay her rent. He was a young, earnest photographer, just starting out in the business. True to his word, Stephane sent her not a penny from Paris, and she heard that he was having a baby with the Polish girl. She filed for divorce, and rapidly discovered that she knew much more about photography than her new employer did. In a bold move, she decided to work as a fashion photographer herself. The money she made increased quickly beyond subsistence level, and within two years she became more successful than Stephane had ever been. She was willing to work hard, long hours, and collaborated well with the major fashion magazines. They loved her work.

She and the children never heard from Stephane after he left and less than two years after he moved back to Paris, he died in a motorcycle accident. His death didn't change anything for her or the children, except the idea that the children had a father who might want to see them again someday. By the time he died, he was no longer with the Polish girl. She had left him for someone else and taken the baby with her, and his career had tanked after he went back to France. When the money and his prospects ran out, the Polish girl did too. He had left behind in the world four children he had done nothing for.

Maddie was alone in the world with three children. She worked harder than ever, and became one of the most sought-after fashion photographers in New York. The lean years were over for her then. She had a life and a successful career she loved. It allowed her to spend time with her children, except when she had to shoot on location. She had a housekeeper who took care of the children when she had to go away, but she was with them as much as she could be in her off hours.

Maddie managed to balance her life efficiently, and eventually broadened her work to include portraits of important people and celebrities. For her own satisfaction, once her children were in college, she expanded her scope further to include major newsworthy events and moving human portraits at the scenes of wars and natural disasters, showing old men and women, devastated young children, lovers in each other's arms, some women holding dead children and others giving birth. She went to elections, riots, demonstrations, earthquakes. She took the high-risk assignments she wouldn't when her children were younger, out of a sense of responsibility to them. She was in love with the human condition, sometimes at its worst, seen through the camera's lens, whatever caught her eye, grabbed her heart, or fascinated her and the people who saw her photographs, and bought them.

In recent years she did less and less work in fashion, although she was still very much in demand. Thirty years into her career, she could pick and choose who and what she photographed now.

The firehouse was the perfect setting for her. Her clients loved coming there, exploring it, and listening to her talk about it. Maddie had a warm, modest, humble way of dealing with her subjects. It put them totally at ease and the photographs she took of them were extraordinary and looked straight into their souls.

Ben was very proud of her, although from a distance. Milagra paid little attention to her mother's career, only her own, and Deanna always had some caustic comment to make or criticism to offer about her mother's work. Maddie was used to it, and tried not to let it upset her, but sometimes it did anyway. Deanna knew just where to put the knife and when to turn it. At times, Maddie wondered if Deanna was jealous of her, even though that seemed unlikely since she was successful on her own. But Deanna had a fierce competitive streak with everyone. To Deanna, life was a race she had to win, no matter who she had to kill to do so. She'd had a sharp tongue all her life, and only her husband didn't seem to mind it. He liked how ambitious she was and admired the results. She pushed him hard too, and her daughters.

Deanna dropped in at the firehouse occasionally, usually unannounced, at a convenient time for her, with total disregard for her mother's schedule. She acted as though Maddie were a housewife taking photographs as a hobby, rather than one of the most important photographers in the business. There had even been two museum shows of her work, which only impressed Deanna briefly. Her husband, David, was more generous about his mother-in-law, and realized how talented and respected she was. But even he couldn't curb Deanna and rarely tried to. Maddie had never been able to either, and she sympathized with David. Her oldest daughter was a force to be reckoned with, and she was just as harsh with her own children, although Maddie was sure she loved them. Deanna was very much her own person, and, at thirty-six, nothing was going to change her. And Maddie was too wise to try.

Although Maddie felt guilty whenever she thought it, in some ways it was a relief that Deanna didn't make time to see her more often. Deanna was too busy and thought she was too important herself to spend time with her mother. Deanna had her father's dark hair and good looks, although none of his irresistible Gallic charm, and none of her mother's gentle softness, which made all her subjects fall in love with her.

Maddie was a kind, compassionate woman and it showed. She was strong, and had worked hard for her success, but she never imposed her own will on others. She had earned everything she had fair and square, while being an attentive, loving mother, and she was never demanding of her children's time. They were all adults now, and she respected the fact that they had busy lives of their own. The reality was that, except for a few old friends she rarely saw and her work, Maddie was essentially alone, and she didn't mind. Her photography filled her life and satisfied her. She used her time well. Work had occupied her every waking hour since her kids had grown up. And with the passage of time, and busy lives, she and many of her friends had drifted apart. Close friendships were difficult to maintain, working as hard as she did.

At fifty-eight, divorced for thirty-three years, there had been men in her life. A few of them had been important to her, for a time, but she had never married again. Marrying the men she'd fallen in love with had never seemed like the right thing for her children. Now they were grown up and gone. There hadn't been a serious man in her life for years. Sometimes she missed the companionship, but she was busy and independent, and didn't think she could make the necessary compromises to share her life with anyone now. She had gotten comfortable as she was, doing what she wanted, traveling as she wished, making all the decisions herself. She had no desire to give that up or even modify it. She knew she had been more accommodating when she was younger. Now it seemed like too high a price to pay for love, which might be fleeting anyway. Her own freedom appealed to her more.

Deanna had never liked the men in her mother's life and openly said so, often to her mother's consternation. She had always been difficult with the men Maddie loved. Deanna was deeply embarrassed by what she knew about her profligate, philandering father, and was relieved he hadn't stuck around, although it was clear that her mother had loved him. But Deanna was suspicious of men as a result. Milagra always said that their father sounded romantic, which even Maddie didn't agree with. He'd been selfish and narcissistic and let them all down when he abandoned them.

Ben was sorry he had never known his father, whatever his flaws were. He had suffered from not having a father when he was young, although Maddie had been a responsible, caring single parent. But with two sisters and a single mother, he longed to have a man around as he was growing up. He was always sorry when Maddie's romances ended, and usually blamed his outspoken, ornery sister for it, which wasn't entirely wrong. Deanna astutely said that if their mother had loved the men enough, she would have married them, but she hadn't, of her own accord.

There was only one man that Maddie really regretted losing, but she knew it would never have worked. Their lives were just too different, and marrying him would have made too much of an impact on her children and changed their lives too radically. She thought of him sometimes and wondered what had happened to him. They had stopped communicating years before, and he was only a tender memory now. She was too busy and fulfilled by her work to spend her time mourning the past. Maddie was always engaged in the present and looking forward to the next project or assignment, and she didn't look back. She had few regrets in her life and was satisfied with the way things had worked out. As adults, all three of her children seemed relatively happy, which was enough for her. Once they grew up, not having to worry about them left her completely free to pursue her work. She was busier than ever and flew around the world photographing subjects that interested her. She could pick and choose now, and had for years. She was always excited when she took an assignment in California, which gave her an excuse to see her son and daughter there, if they were willing, without having to wait for them to suggest an opportune time, since there never was one for either of her children on the West Coast.

It often struck her as unfortunate and the irony of fate that the two children who liked her the most lived so far away. And the one who disapproved of her and didn't enjoy her company was the only one in New York. It was the luck of the draw but she made the best of it, and she loved living in New York. She wouldn't have liked living in San Francisco, and even less the wild, dreary isolation of Mendocino. She loved the people and the pace in New York, the wide variety of cultural options, and having her studio in the city.

She would have felt like a poacher encroaching on Ben's life, or Milagra's, and she knew her daughter-in-law wouldn't have liked it either. Laura's mother was the perfect suburban, country club wife, and Laura had always been ill at ease with her famous mother-in-law. Ben never thought of his mother in that light. She was just his mother. But he knew Laura was fully aware of how important Maddie was and it made her feel as though, by comparison, she fell short in some way. Laura's greatest accomplishment had been marrying Ben, with his very considerable success, and she was content to share in his glory, rather than create her own.

Maddie had never planned her own success. She had discovered her talent, and developed it, through need and force of circumstance, trying to support her children. It had turned out well for her and developed into a life of freedom and creativity that she thoroughly enjoyed. She had earned every ounce of her success. It was precisely that freedom and individuality that irked her oldest daughter so much. Even Deanna's disapproval and criticism didn't daunt her. Maddie was always unabashedly herself.

There was still a remarkable natural beauty to her, and an unstudied sexiness she was totally unaware of, with her hair piled on her head to get it out of her way, and a pen or pencil stuck through it, until she removed it to write something down and her long blond hair tumbled down her back. The men who had loved her had been drawn to her modesty and simplicity. Deanna's strict, uptight, meticulous, and measured style was chic, but much less attractive than her mother's ease and warmth. One of Maddie's men had said about Deanna even as a teenager, "I always feel like she's going to spank me," which had made Maddie laugh. Her daughter made her feel that way sometimes too. Deanna set the bar high for herself and everyone else. Maddie was much more likely to be their partner in crime, and was always nurturing.

It had drawn men to her like bees to honey for a long time, although she had never taken undue advantage of it. There was an innate femininity to her, no matter what she did or wore. She had been beautiful at every age, with a luminous softness, and she was still very striking, although she insisted that she was past all that now. Fifty-eight was far from old, particularly the way she looked, although Deanna wouldn't have agreed.

Deanna only called her mother when she wanted something, when she had a mission of some kind, never just to chat for the pleasure of it. Ben didn't call her often either, but he enjoyed their conversations when he did. He meant to call her more often, but something always distracted him and got in the way. No one made him laugh like his mother, and she was genuinely interested in his life, and proud of what he had accomplished. She consoled him in his losses and celebrated his victories. Deanna felt that Maddie had been an inadequate mother, but Ben never agreed with her. Although Deanna had done well as a designer, she had resented her mother's career, while Ben admired it. Deanna was far less attentive to her own children than Maddie had been to hers. Maddie could do no right in Deanna's eyes, no wrong in Ben's, and Milagra had distanced herself from all of them to live in the fantasy world she created in her books.

There was no man in Maddie's life now. She said it gave her more time to concentrate on her assignments, and she didn't seem to miss having a partner. She insisted to her assistant, Penny, that it was too late for love, and she was good-humored about it. Penny was sure she would meet someone if she was more open to it, but clearly she wasn't. Maddie insisted she was too old to find a man now.

It upset Penny too, on Maddie's behalf, that her children paid so little attention to her. Penny thought they should call her more often just to see how she was. It never seemed to occur to them, judging by how infrequently they called. She was fine now, but what if one day, she wasn't? Then what would they do? Maddie never let herself think about it. There was plenty of time for that.

Penny was all she needed, to help her with her work. She set up all Maddie's appointments, kept her life in order, and organized her travel plans. Maddie had freelance photography assistants who came in to assist her during the shoots. They all considered it an honor to work for her. They learned so much from watching her, and from her clear, precise instructions and explanations. She had taught a photography class at NYU for two semesters, and loved it, but said she no longer had time to do that and her own work. She had loved being with the young people and teaching them what she knew, and was generous with her advice and encouragement, helping them grow, not crushing them with an inflated ego as so many professors in the arts did. She had nothing to prove. She had done it all and had a string of awards to her credit.

Penny had started working for her six months after Maddie had bought the firehouse, and had helped Maddie keep things on track when she renovated it. She loved everything about her job and Maddie, except having to deal with Deanna when she called. Deanna always wanted something from her mother, and was rude and dismissive to anyone in her path. Penny could easily guess that she must be a monster to work for, and hated the hostile, condescending way Deanna treated her mother. Penny was impressed by how little Maddie complained about her, only when she was excessively exasperated or upset by something cutting Deanna had just said to her, which happened often. Most of the time, Maddie said nothing and told Penny it was just Deanna's style, which didn't mitigate it for Penny. She thought Deanna would have benefitted from a good slap in her life at some point, which, knowing Maddie, had never happened.

Penny was forty-two, had never married, was crazy about her white Persian cat, and after a string of bad boyfriends, she had given up on men for the last few years. She worked hard for Maddie and loved her job. She hated leaving on Friday nights to go home to her own dull weekends, puttering around her apartment and doing laundry, waiting to come back to work on Mondays. Maddie was the excitement and inspiration in her life. Penny had a big, noisy Irish family in Boston and kept in close touch with her siblings and nephews and nieces. But on most weekends she stayed home in case Maddie needed her, even though Maddie almost never called on weekends and respected Penny's time off. She loved living in Maddie's shadow and enjoyed making life better for her.

Maddie kept encouraging Penny to try to meet a new man, even on the internet if she had to, but Penny was terrified of internet dating, and had had bad luck with it the few times she'd tried. She was one of those diamonds in the rough that few people had seen the value of, except Maddie, who recognized her for the gem she was. She was unfailingly loyal to Maddie as a result.

"Anything I can do for you before I go?" Penny asked her on a rainy Friday night before she left to take the subway to an unchic part of Brooklyn. She had lived there since she'd come to New York. Penny had red hair and green eyes and a nice face. She was about twenty-five pounds overweight, which she kept meaning to do something about, and said she would, but never did. She had no motivation to do so, and sitting at home in front of the TV all weekend, watching her favorite reality shows and eating ice cream, didn't help. As hard as she was willing to work for Maddie, she did very little for herself.

"I'm fine," Maddie assured her with a smile. She'd been going over contact sheets all day from her last shoot and marking what she wanted to send to the retoucher. She had a keen eye and did just enough, but never too much. She didn't want her subjects to look like they'd had a face-lift for the shoot, or to show them at their most unflattering either. She liked them to look real but beautiful, and she balanced it perfectly. Her subjects were always pleased with the final result. She was very undemanding of Penny about anything other than work. She never called her at home, except in a real emergency. Otherwise she waited until business hours to ask for what she needed. She did all her own personal errands. She never sent Penny to the dry cleaner, the drug store, or out to do menial tasks. She did those herself, and never felt too important to do so.

"What are you doing this weekend?" Penny asked her, handing Maddie a cup of tea that she hadn't requested but appreciated. Maddie thanked her with a smile.

"I'm going to reorganize some closets. I promised myself I would. I'm running out of room, and I've got so much tucked away that I can't fit anything else in. Time to do some weeding out and spring cleaning, and the weather is so lousy, I'm not going out tonight. It's supposed to rain again tomorrow and Sunday too." Maddie loved puttering around the house. It was early May, but they'd had the wettest spring in New York history, and rain had been predicted for the weekend.

"Don't do any heavy lifting," Penny warned her. "I can help you with it on Monday." Although during the week, they were both usually so buried in work, there was no time for closets. Maddie loved doing projects on the weekends. She was always busy with something.

"It's just a lot of small junk in there. I'm not even sure what there is, which is why I want to go through it. I'm turning into a pack rat," she said with an embarrassed grin, and Penny laughed.

"You don't need to tell me that," Penny answered, smiling. Maddie saved every shred of correspondence, no matter how far back, and almost every photograph she'd ever taken. They had extensive archives in storage.

"I'm going to try to throw some of it out this time," Maddie said firmly. "I promise."

"I'll believe it when I see it," Penny said as she

29

put her coat on and left with a wave a few minutes later. She walked through the studio and let herself out through the side door. She wondered if Maddie got lonely on the weekends. She had her work to keep her occupied, but Penny thought she should be seeing her grandchildren, and knew she hardly ever did. Penny's own mother saw her grandchildren constantly. They were in and out of her house, and she was always cooking for them.

Maddie's life was entirely different and Penny felt sorry for her, although Maddie would have been shocked to know that. She had long since learned how to keep engaged on her own, and in many ways, she enjoyed it. She didn't expect to see her children and grandchildren more often than she did.

Maddie made scrambled eggs and a salad for dinner that night. She'd had half a turkey sandwich for lunch while she was working. She wasn't a big eater and hated to cook for herself. Sometimes she just ate an apple or banana for lunch, and Penny scolded her. Maddie thought food was boring and cooking it even more so. She said it was the beauty of being alone. She didn't have to prepare meals for anyone, not even herself if she didn't want to. She'd rather skip a meal and spend the time doing something else.

After she ate, she got a ladder from the studio and dragged it carefully up the stairs to her bedroom closet. She liked doing chores for herself and had a sense of victory when she got the ladder to the third floor, with a firm grip on it. She set it up, climbed high enough to see the first level of shelves, pulled out a bunch of boxes and dropped them on the floor of her bedroom, and then she sat down next to them and started to go through them. As she suspected, a lot of what she found was junk, and she felt virtuous as she made a big pile of papers and old clothes to get rid of. She was going to have Penny send the clothes to Goodwill on Monday. It was several hours before she climbed to the next level on the ladder and pulled out the boxes on the second shelf. She hadn't unearthed any treasures so far, just a box of letters from her kids when they were younger, which made her smile as she glanced through them. Some of them were letters from camp.

She put what was left neatly back on the shelves, looked at her watch, and wrestled with a decision. It was one in the morning. Should she tackle the highest shelf or go to bed and do it in the morning? She wasn't tired, and often stayed up late either reading or working, which was another pleasure of living alone. She didn't have to apologize to anyone for how late she stayed up or the noise she made, with the lights on at two or three A.M. And she wanted to get that one closet done. She had some things she wanted to add to the shelves, and there hadn't been a spare inch to accommodate anything until she started weeding out. She was curious about what was on the top shelf. Whatever was there had been there for a long time and she'd forgotten what it was.

She decided to stay up and do it. She had the time, was in the mood, and she could sleep late on Saturday morning if it took her too long. She assumed it was probably more junk and she could get rid of it quickly anyway. She had a good-sized pile on her bedroom floor already, to donate or throw away. She pulled out several boxes and tossed them to the floor, climbed back down the ladder, and opened them. The tape was dried and brittle. She didn't remember seeing them before, which meant they had been up there for years. The first box she opened was full of photographs of the children when they were younger. She recognized several images that she already had framed around the house, and guessed that they were duplicates.

The second box she opened took her breath away for a minute. It was full of letters in various handwriting, and the photographs mixed in with them made her smile. She remembered the box now. They were old love letters and photographs of

three of the men in her life, the three most important ones since her marriage. She had thrown
away other letters and photographs a long time
ago. But she had saved everything from these three
men. She hadn't thought about them in years, nor
heard from them. She stared at the familiar faces in
the pictures. Jacques Masson was an ambitious
young French chef who was working at a restaurant
in New York and dreamed of opening his own
when she met him. Bob Holland was a brilliant
young venture capitalist, working with high-tech
investments and just starting out in his first big
job with high hopes for his career. And Andy Wyatt
was a cowboy from Wyoming. She had met him
when she'd taken the kids to a ranch there one
summer. She had been madly in love with Andy
and they had continued their affair discreetly for
over a year, until she called a halt to it. She knew it
could go nowhere. They both did. It was getting
too intense to be safe for either of them. They knew
they had to stop but couldn't. Ending it with him
had been one of the most painful things she'd ever
done, but it wasn't the right fit for her, or her kids,
or him.

She had loved all three of them, but leaving
Andy had broken her heart. She sat staring at his
photograph for a long time, wondering where he
was now. He was eight years older than she was, so

he'd be sixty-six now, still probably somewhere in Wyoming. Their affair was eighteen years ago, she was forty then, and he was forty-eight. Ben and Milagra were in high school, and Deanna had just left for college. It seemed as though a thousand years had passed since then. There hadn't been anyone serious since Andy. He had been the love of her life. But she couldn't see herself on a ranch in Wyoming, and he would never have survived in New York. He would have been as miserable as he had been when he visited her, so she had freed him, for both their sakes. She'd never cared as much about any man after him.

She put the photographs back in the box then, set the box on the floor, climbed back up the ladder, and tried to pull down another box. It was bigger and heavier than the first two. She finally tugged it toward her and was juggling it awkwardly when she leaned too far over and lost her balance. The ladder came crashing down with her on it, spilling her across the floor of her bedroom, past the rug and onto the hardwood floor she was so proud of and had refinished when she moved in. She fell with a heavy thud at an awkward angle, pushed the ladder off her, and tried to get up, when an agonizing pain shot through her left leg. She could see that her foot was in a weird position, and when she stood up, she felt like throwing up, and almost fainted. She had to sit down on the floor again and put her head between her knees until she felt less dizzy. She could put no weight on her left foot at all, and she had the sinking feeling that her ankle might be broken or very badly sprained. She hoped the latter, but couldn't tell. She hopped to her bed on one foot, feeling dizzy again, and lay down, telling herself that this was ridiculous. She'd never fallen off a ladder before, or even gotten injured. She was on and off ladders all the time for her work, checking lights and angles for a shot.

She felt worse as she lay on her bed, feeling like a prisoner, knowing she should put ice on her foot, but there was no way she could hop down the narrow metal spiral staircase on one foot to get to the kitchen on the floor below, and then back up to her bedroom again. She had never put in an elevator, which would have been expensive, seemed unnecessary, and would have eaten up space she needed for her studio. Now she regretted it, if this was a harbinger of things to come, if she was going to fall off another ladder or get hurt in the future.

She had no one to call to come and help her. She could have called Penny in Brooklyn, but there was nothing she could do, and Maddie wasn't going to call her at that hour. It was two in the morning by then. She would never have called

Deanna, and she would be in the Berkshires anyway. She felt foolish calling a friend to come and
help her down the stairs in the middle of the night.
And there was no one she was close enough to
reach out to except Penny. She hadn't spoken
to any of her friends in months, she'd been too
busy, and felt awkward calling them now. She
wasn't bleeding to death, and an injured ankle
didn't seem serious enough to warrant calling 911.
All she could do was hope she felt better in the
morning and could make it down the stairs to
ice it, or go to the emergency room if it hadn't
improved.

In the meantime, she lay on her bed, looking
at the overturned ladder stretched across the floor
from the closet, the box she'd dropped with its
contents spilling over the rug, and the one where
she'd found the photographs and letters from her
old lovers. She lay there for a long time, wide
awake, thinking of the photograph of Andy Wyatt,
looking so handsome, smiling at her in the image.
She wanted to go through that box over the weekend, but instead of making things neater, she'd
made a mess. All she could think of was Andy,
while trying not to focus on the excruciating pain
in her ankle and feeling scared, and she burst into
tears as she lay there alone.

Chapter 2

When Maddie woke up in the morning, the pain in her left ankle was worse, and her whole body felt battered. She hadn't really slept all night, she had drifted in a kind of haze, aware of the pain but feeling woozy and in another dimension. She wondered if she was in shock, and had dozed periodically but never slept deeply, always aware of the pain.

She still had the same dilemma about how to get downstairs to the kitchen, and she was also desperate to get to the bathroom. Not knowing what else to do, she crawled to the bathroom, using her arms to pull herself along and her right leg to help propel her, and wincing every time her left leg moved. The pain was more localized in her ankle. When she pulled herself to a standing position on her right foot and saw herself in the bathroom mirror, she was shocked by how terrible she looked. She was deathly pale with circles under her eyes, still wearing her clothes from the day before, since she hadn't dared to take off her jeans and make the pain worse. She was embarrassed to call 911 and hated to disturb Penny on the weekend. She was determined to work it out herself, which was what she always did. Maddie was never dependent on anyone. She thought of sliding down the fireman's pole to her studio, but if she landed hard or bumped her left foot, she was sure that she would faint. No matter how painful it was, she knew she had to take the stairs.

She washed her face with cold water, brushed her teeth, started to brush her hair and decided not to bother. She hopped back to where she had kicked off her right shoe when she went to bed and put it on. The left one had flown off when she fell. She didn't bother with it since her foot was too swollen to get the shoe on anyway. She made her way to the stairs and went down two flights on the circular metal staircase, inching her way along, on her bottom. It was a painful process. She hopped from there to her office on the main floor, ordered an Uber, grabbed her bag and a jacket, and slowly hopped to the front door, stopping every few feet when she felt dizzy. It seemed to take forever, and she was almost ready to faint by the time she got to the front door, slammed it behind her, and waved to the Uber driver waiting for her at the curb. He lowered the window and she called out and asked him to help her. He got out of the car and came over to her, and she gratefully grabbed his arm as he helped her to the car. She cried out in pain as she got in.

"Why didn't you call 911?" he asked as he slid behind the wheel to take her to NYU Hospital.

"I'm sure it's nothing serious. I didn't have a heart attack or anything," she said through gritted teeth.

"It looks serious enough to me," he said sympathetically. "What did you do?"

"I fell off a ladder," she said, feeling stupid again and fighting back tears.

"Maybe you broke your leg," he said, glancing at her in the rearview mirror.

"I hope not. I think I just twisted my ankle and sprained it," she said hopefully.

"It must have been some twist. You look kind of green to me." She was praying she wouldn't throw up in his car at that moment.

"It just hurts a lot. They say a sprain hurts more than a break." He didn't comment but went to get an attendant in the ER when they got to the hospital. A nurse came out with a wheelchair and got

Maddie into it with some difficulty. She gave the Uber driver a big tip, and thanked him. He wished her luck and got back in the car and drove away.

A woman from admissions came to hand her forms to fill out, and a nurse examined her in a cubicle and called the orthopedist on duty. Maddie had to wait another hour for X-rays, and the X-ray technician told her that her ankle was broken before the doctor even saw her. There were tears rolling down her cheeks as he walked into the room. It had been a long, painful night and she felt totally worn out. She was afraid she'd have to have surgery for the break, and maybe even have pins put in.

The doctor checked the X-ray and looked at her. "The good news is it's a clean break, you don't need surgery. We'll put a cast on, which will give you some relief, and send you home with pain medication. You need to keep your weight off it for a week, then you'll get a walking cast, and six weeks from now, you'll be as good as new." He could see how shaken up she was, and obviously in a lot of pain. He called a nurse in to help him, and half an hour later Maddie was in a cast. They adjusted a pair of crutches for her, filled the prescription at the hospital pharmacy, and two hours after that she was ready to go home and ordered another Uber.

"Do you have an elevator where you live?" the nurse asked her and Maddie shook her head.

She was trying to figure out how to manage, and how she'd get back up the two flights of stairs to her bedroom, which was going to be a nearly impossible feat without help. She was still determined not to bother Penny, but she was in too much pain and too exhausted to bump her way up the stairs on her bottom again.

"I'll manage," Maddie assured her as they pushed her to the Uber in a wheelchair. With the cast on, she already felt a little better than she had when she came in. She didn't want to take the pain pills until she got home, in case they knocked her out or made her woozy. She thanked the nurse, and confirmed the address with the driver. She realized then that she could sleep on the couch in the studio. There was a bathroom there, and a fridge. She could send out for food and get to the door on her crutches. It wasn't ideal, but she could make it until Monday when Penny came in. There was even a shower in the bathroom, and there were garbage bags she could use to cover the cast. They had cut off her jeans, and she went home in hospital pajama bottoms. She knew she looked a sight as the driver carried her purse for her and helped her unlock her front door.

"Is there anything I can do for you before I go?" the driver asked her kindly. It was a woman, and Maddie thanked her gratefully.

"I'll be fine," she assured her. She went into the little studio kitchenette after she left, and took her pain pill. She got to the couch in the studio and lay down, remembering that she had a shoot that week and would have to do it on crutches, but she would have two freelance studio assistants working with her. Twenty minutes later, when the pill took effect, she fell sound asleep.

It was dark when she woke up, her ankle was throbbing, and she felt like she'd been on a two-week drunk. She was nauseous from taking the pain pill on an empty stomach. She looked at her watch and was startled to see that it was seven o'clock at night. It had been a hell of a weekend so far.

She was going to call for food, but didn't want any, and found half a turkey sandwich left over from her lunch the day before in the studio fridge. She ate it so she could take another pill if she needed to, and she felt better after she ate. She was dying to get to her bed, but didn't want to tackle the stairs alone again. And she didn't want to bump her ankle while she did it. She lay back on the couch for a few minutes and fell asleep until morning, without even taking another pill. When she woke up, she went back up the stairs on her bottom, dragging her crutches. All she wanted was to take a shower, put on a clean nightgown, and get into her bed.

The whole process of taking a shower took her almost an hour, and she fell into the bed with relief, looked at the mess of boxes on the floor outside her closet, and remembered what was in them. She waited another hour before dragging the box of letters and photographs over to the bed, hopping on her good foot to do it. At least reading the old love letters and looking at the photographs would give her something to do while she lay there. And she had remembered a box of cookies in the sitting room next to the bedroom. She didn't want to go back to the kitchen, and the cookies would be enough to sustain her until Monday morning. She couldn't get back downstairs to open the door if she ordered food. She hated feeling so helpless and hampered, but at least she felt clean now, and the pain in her left ankle was less acute. It had been a hell of an experience and a shock to get hurt and be in so much pain. She'd never broken a bone before.

She settled in against the pillows with the cookies and the box she had brought down from the top of her closet before she fell. She was eager to read the letters and see the familiar faces she hadn't seen in years. It was like a trip back in time, and brought with it floods of memories as she read.

Jacques's letters were the most amusing, in stilted English, and she smiled as she remembered him and flipped through the envelope of photographs that went with them. Bob's letters were the most intelligent, trying to convince her why their relationship made sense and attempting to overcome her reservations. She remembered that he had wanted her to move to California with him, and she wouldn't. It would have been too hard for her children, who were still very young.

Andy's letters tore at her heart the moment she read them. She could see why she had loved him, he was so straightforward and direct, so kind, and so in love with her, as she had been with him. She studied his photographs more carefully and spread them out around her on the bed. Even at nearly fifty, he had been a strikingly handsome man and looked like a cowboy in an ad. There were several photographs of them together looking happy. She stared at the images of him for a long time, and then put it all away neatly in the box, and pushed it to the other side of the bed, since she only occupied half of it.

She turned on the TV so she could hear voices in the room, still thinking about Andy and then the other two men. It had been a long lonely weekend, and she took another pain pill that night. She was just starting to feel the effects of it when the phone rang, and she picked it up, wondering if it was her son, Ben. When he called her it was usually on Sunday nights, if he wasn't busy with Laura or the children. During the week, he was always too tied up at his office.

She almost winced when she heard Deanna's voice. She wasn't in the mood to deal with her, and she was starting to feel drunk from the pill.

"Hi, the weather was awful in Massachusetts. How was it here?" She dove right in without asking how her mother was, or how her weekend had been, just about the weather.

"I'm not sure. I stayed home all weekend." Deanna guessed that her mother had been working, as she often did.

"I've got something to ask you. I didn't want to wait until tomorrow, in case you have a shoot. I need an answer right away." Maddie was already regretting having answered the phone. Whatever it was, she didn't want to hear it. She wasn't up to a power struggle with her daughter. Listening to her, on the first wave of the pain pill, she started to feel sick.

"What is it?" Maddie asked in a tired voice with her eyes closed.

"We're looking for a venue for a cocktail party, as a benefit. Not a big deal. Just about a hundred people. The firehouse would be perfect for it, if that's okay with you." She assumed her mother would agree, but Maddie had done it for her before, and it had turned into a much bigger event, with twice as many people as Deanna said it would be, spilling out onto the sidewalk and going all over the house to explore. Maddie had promised herself she'd never do it again. She remembered it distinctly.

"Actually, it's not okay," Maddie said, feeling weak and dizzy. "The last time I agreed to it it was a mess."

"This will be a much smaller deal," Deanna assured her, sounding sure she could get her mother to consent. "I promise, we'll keep it under better control. We're going to have a gourmet food truck, so we don't need to use your kitchen at all."

"And if someone falls down the stairs, if they go upstairs even if they're not supposed to, I'm the one they're going to sue. Or if they go down the fireman's pole and get hurt if they're drunk." Some people could never resist the temptation, particularly men, although some women had done it too. Maddie didn't want the liability.

"We'll rope it off. And no one is going to sue you, Mother," Deanna said, sounding supercilious and annoyed. She hated the word "no."

"I really don't want to do it," Maddie said, trying to sound firm, although she was feeling sick and woozy from the pill.

"It's for a good cause. You don't sound good, by the way. Are you sick?" Maddie sounded like she'd been drinking. She could hear it herself. Her words were slurring.

"Sort of. Not really," Maddie said, suddenly feeling vulnerable. She needed to be in top form and have all her wits about her when she talked to Deanna. "I had a stupid accident on Friday night, but I'm fine."

"What kind of accident?"

"I fell off a ladder and broke my ankle. It's a clean break, I'm in a cast but it'll be off in six weeks. And I'll get a walking cast in a week or two."

"For God's sake, Mother, how stupid is that? You were on a **ladder** on Friday **night**? When you're by **yourself**? What were you thinking?" The milk of human kindness, and compassion, did not run in Deanna's veins.

"I was reorganizing a closet, trying to get some boxes down from a high shelf," Maddie said simply, but feeling seriously stupid while faced with her daughter's reaction and tone of voice.

"That's exactly what I was afraid of when you bought the place. What if you fell down those stairs? They're treacherous. You can't use a ladder when you're alone there, Mother. You're lucky it was only your ankle, it could have been your hip." It was hardly a cheering thought. "At your age, you

47

shouldn't be living there alone. You should hire someone to sleep in."

"I'm not that far gone yet," Maddie said, pushing back. She didn't like the mention of a broken hip. She had thought of that too. It had a connotation of age.

"You should sell the place and get an apartment," Deanna said firmly, as though Maddie had committed a crime and lost her right to live in a house alone.

"I don't need someone sleeping here. I'm fine on my own. I was here all weekend with a broken ankle, and I'm managing."

"You're too old to live in a house like that. The place is a death trap, you could fall down the stairs or into the hole for the fire pole."

"I haven't done that yet. Anyone can break an ankle, at any age. Accidents happen. I shouldn't have been on the ladder," she conceded. "I won't do it again."

"I hope not. But I think you should start thinking of selling the place. You should have put in an elevator when you moved in."

"I was forty-three years old when I bought the house. I didn't need an elevator, and I don't need one now. I'm not in a wheelchair, for God's sake." Deanna was annoying her, her tone was insulting, and so was what she said.

"You will be eventually," she said nastily.

"I'll figure it out then."

"If you still can, Mother. A fall like this is the first sign that you're not up to living there alone anymore. You should face that now, before something else happens. This is a warning to you. Either hire someone to live in or sell the house. That's what people your age do."

She had it all worked out in her own mind. And then she added insult to injury. "We'll have to get you one of those alarms to wear around your neck in case you fall, if you insist on staying there. And no one is going to be able to carry you up and down those stairs if you get hurt. How did you manage this weekend?"

"I managed," Maddie said succinctly. She wasn't going to tell Deanna that she had slept on the studio couch on Saturday night, had gotten to her bedroom by going up the stairs backwards on her bottom, had been eating cookies all day because she couldn't get to the kitchen, and had only had half a sandwich in the last thirty-six hours. It would have proven Deanna's point. Maddie hoped she wasn't right that this was the beginning of the end. "I'm not even sixty yet, for Heaven's sake."

"You're not far from it. And that's when some people start to fall apart, or get Alzheimer's," Deanna said ominously.

"I know people in their eighties who live alone and don't have Alzheimer's. I was on a ladder. Admittedly, that was stupid of me, but I'm not in a full body cast or on a respirator. I broke my ankle, **not** my hip."

"No, but you will if you do dumb things like that." She had no sympathy for her mother, and listening to her was driving Maddie's spirits into the ground.

"I have a headache," Maddie said quietly. "I'll talk to you tomorrow."

"What about the benefit?" Deanna pressed her, and Maddie dug her heels in after the conversation they'd just had.

"You can't do it here. Besides, given what you think, I'm too old to have a hundred strangers in my house. Good night," she said and hung up quickly before Deanna could come up with another round of arguments in favor of it. Maddie was not going to lend the firehouse to her, particularly if she was going to try to convince her to sell it, or hire live-in help she didn't want, like some old woman who couldn't take care of herself at fifty-eight. Maddie felt worse when she hung up, and she was seething. Deanna made her sound as though she were a hundred years old and losing her mind. And the prospect of no longer living alone was profoundly depressing, even if it didn't happen for another ten years or longer.

Maddie lay in bed that night thinking about it, and everything Deanna had said, and didn't fall asleep until four in the morning. The effect of the earlier pain pill was lost, and her mind was racing. The ankle hurt like hell. She used her crutches to get to the bathroom several times, and was wide awake until she finally drifted off. She slept until she heard the front door close when Penny came to work the next morning.

Maddie called Penny in her office and asked her to come upstairs to the bedroom. Penny looked shocked when she saw the crutches and noticed Maddie's pale face.

"What happened?" She pointed to the mess outside the closet, and the fallen ladder still lying on its side, which told the story. The crutches leaning against Maddie's bed told the rest, and the result of the fall from the ladder.

"I was on my closet-reorganizing mission and fell off the ladder on Friday night." Penny's eyes were instantly ablaze with concern. "And don't lecture me about it. I've already heard it from the doctor, and Deanna says I should hire someone to live with me or sell the house."

"She would," Penny said with a stern look of

disapproval. She hadn't liked Maddie's oldest daughter since the day she started.

"I know it wasn't smart to be on the ladder. I won't do it again," Maddie said, looking subdued. "Deanna thinks this is the beginning of Alzheimer's. Christ, I hope not."

"Don't be ridiculous. You're sharper than I am. Although, I'll grant you, being at the top of a ladder at night when you're alone wasn't smart."

"I know." Maddie was contrite and felt foolish.

"You have a shoot on Thursday. Do you want me to cancel it?"

"No," Maddie said, "I can manage, I'll have two freelance studio assistants. What I need now is help getting to the bathroom so I don't fall, and help with the shower. And after that, I'm starving. I lived on cookies all day yesterday."

"Why didn't you call me? I can't believe you called Deanna instead. Did she come to help you out?"

"Of course not, and I didn't call her. She called me because she wants to use the house for another benefit. I told her she can't."

"Thank God, I remember what the place looked like after the last one. They can rent a place somewhere."

"She'll have to. I won't let her do it here," Maddie said firmly. But she knew she hadn't heard the last of it. Deanna didn't give up that easily. She was hell on wheels when she wanted something.

Maddie took a hot shower, with a garbage bag over her cast, which made her feel better, and Penny helped her down the stairs on her bottom, to the kitchen, and then made her scrambled eggs and bacon with toast. Maddie was ravenous, and happy to see Penny. Her ankle was feeling better too. She had felt depressed and lonely all weekend, and considerably worse after talking to Deanna the night before.

"Did you have time to go through any of those boxes?" Penny asked her, as she sat down beside her, with a mug of coffee.

"I got an idea of what was in them. I made a pile of things to give away, and another pile to throw out."

"Any forgotten treasures?"

Maddie smiled at her in answer. "Not really. Just letters and some photographs of old boy-friends."

"Anyone interesting?" They were all from before Penny's time with her, so she didn't know about them and had never met them.

"Used to be," Maddie said mysteriously, think-ing of the cowboy, Andy Wyatt, again. "God knows where they are now. That was all a long time ago."

"You can google them, if you want, and get in

touch with them, if they still seem interesting," Penny said.

"I'm not sure they'd want to hear from me. Ex-girlfriends are a dime a dozen."

"Not ex-girlfriends like you." Penny smiled at her. "You should definitely google them if you want to get in touch with them," Penny said and Maddie nodded. She wasn't sure which was worse, Deanna telling her she needed someone to live with her and that she would break a hip next time, or falling in love with Andy again. It was hard to decide. Both scenarios had their risks, particularly Andy. They had been so hopelessly in love with each other eighteen years before, and ever since she'd seen his photograph and read his letters, she felt like she was falling for him all over again. It had taken her two years to get over him at the time. If she saw him in person, it could only be worse. She had never been able to resist him. And suddenly she wanted to reach out to him, which she knew was tempting fate. Her life was so simple and uncomplicated now, except for a broken ankle. The last thing she needed was a cowboy from Wyoming, no matter how handsome he was or how much they had loved each other.

The broken ankle had made her feel vulnerable, and Deanna's words had frightened her. Suddenly she wanted someone to protect her. It seemed foolish even to her, she had taken care of herself and everyone else all her life. But what if Deanna was right and this was the beginning of the end? She was staring time, age, and her own frailty in the face. It was terrifying. And even Andy couldn't protect her from it. No one could, which was the worst part. Her own mortality had become real overnight.

Chapter 3

Maddie felt as though she'd had a thousand-pound weight on her all weekend when she finally got to her desk on Monday morning. The broken ankle was an inconvenience, but more than that, it was upsetting. It had brought up issues she'd never even thought of before, and she felt hungover and depressed from the pain pills she'd taken. Deanna's dire predictions for the future loomed over her like a cloud, with the forecast of an impending storm, a hurricane that would hit her life, a tornado she couldn't avoid. She had no intention of hiring someone to live at the firehouse with her. But what if ultimately she lost her independence and was dependent on others? And worse yet, Ben and Milagra, her more benevolent children, lived far away. What if Deanna controlled her life one day, hiring nurses and forcing them on her? What if she was obliged by circumstance, physical necessity, or her children to sell the house she loved and that suited her so well? She felt suddenly at their mercy. She had never felt that way before. Deanna had been an annoyance for years. What if it became a power struggle with her now and Deanna won?

Maddie wondered if she should put in an elevator now, in anticipation of the future. The whole prospect was depressing. She could see a bleak future rolling out ahead of her with the loss of all the freedoms she held dear, and that were essential to her sense of well-being. It had never occurred to her before that she could lose them.

Penny could see how gloomy Maddie felt when she brought her a cup of tea and put a new stack of contact sheets on her desk for her to look over. "How are you feeling?"

Maddie's face told its own story. Breaking her ankle had been a shock, and very painful, but what it implied was even worse. The picture Deanna had painted for her made her want to cry, or run away. But she couldn't run away from time, or the future. Just as Deanna said, it would catch up with her sooner or later, and maybe it already had.

"I'm okay," Maddie said, and convinced neither of them. "I think I'm hungover from the pills I took." She normally hated medication, rarely took any, and didn't need to. "I'm wondering if Deanna is right, and I should put in an elevator, before I actually need to. It might be useful later."

"A lot later," Penny said, frowning. She hated what Maddie's oldest daughter did to her. She always found some way to upset her. Her other two children weren't attentive, but at least they didn't rattle her the way Deanna did, and take pleasure in doing so. "It'll eat up a lot of the studio," she said sensibly. And then more gently she looked at her employer and friend. "Don't let Deanna get to you." It was good advice.

"She thinks I'm losing it, and falling off the ladder is the first sign. Maybe she's right. Old people fall all the time." Maddie was near tears as she said it.

"You're not old. That's bullshit. She's been jealous of you for all the years I've known you, and she probably has been all her life. She's just waiting for you to get really old and start failing so she can finally feel superior to you. Don't let her do that. When you're ninety, or ninety-five, you'll still have more style, grace, and probably energy than she will. You wear me out. I don't love the idea of you on a ladder in the middle of the night either. It was a dumb thing to do, at any age, but you're not falling apart. You had a common household accident, it can happen to anyone. Things like that remind us of our mortality, and that we can hurt ourselves if we're not careful. It's not a sign of senility or imminent old age. And I'm sure you won't do it again. You'll probably be running up and down those damn stairs I hate long after I will." Penny was sixteen years younger than Maddie. "Deanna just likes scaring you and making you feel insecure." Maddie nodded, she knew it was true, but Penny made Deanna sound Machiavellian, and Maddie didn't believe she was quite as bad as that. She was just tactless and unkind, and outspoken. And she probably was right. Maddie would have to give up the firehouse one day, just not yet, and hopefully not for a long time. She loved living there.

Maddie was working on the contact sheets, and not thinking about Deanna or her ankle, an hour later when Penny told her Ben was on the line for her. Maddie was instantly worried. He never called her during business hours. He was usually much too busy for that. Something must be wrong. She answered the phone quickly.

"Are you okay?" she asked him.

"I'm okay. What about you? That seems to be the more relevant question. What happened this weekend?" It was obvious that he knew and wanted to hear her account of the story.

"Did Deanna call you?" The jungle drums were beating. She felt as though Deanna had squealed on her. Maybe she had told him that their mother needed a caretaker too.

"She sent me a text this morning," he said about his sister. "She said you had a bad fall and broke your ankle." He sounded very concerned.

"I'm all right. I did a stupid thing. I was cleaning out a closet and fell off a ladder. Lesson learned. I guess I fell at a bad angle. I didn't need surgery, they put on a cast at the ER and sent me home. It's a nuisance, but not fatal."

He sounded somewhat relieved, but not entirely, at her explanation. "Why didn't you call me?"

"I didn't want to worry you, and there's nothing you could do at this distance. I could have called Penny if I needed to." He felt bad, realizing how alone she was at times. He didn't think about it often, and had no need to until something like this, an accident or an injury or potentially an illness, happened. On the weekends, she was all alone, and Deanna was in Massachusetts. She could have driven down, if it was warranted, but his mother made it sound like a much smaller deal than Deanna had in her text. He hadn't called her back, he had called his mother instead to hear it from her directly.

"You shouldn't be on a ladder when you're alone,

Mom," he said gently. But he also knew that she was on and off ladders all the time in her studio. She'd been doing it all his life.

"I know. I won't do that again. I leaned too far and the ladder fell, and I didn't have time to jump clear. Deanna got all wound up about it. She wants me to hire someone to live in. This house isn't made for that. It would be crazy. I don't want someone sitting here, waiting for me to fall on my face. It won't happen again." But they both knew it might. Accidents happened. She could cut herself badly or slip on the stairs. He'd almost fallen on her stairs several times himself. His feet were too big for the shallow steps, and they were slippery. Laura was terrified of them, and everything in the firehouse, for their kids, and never wanted them to go there. Their whole house in Belvedere was childproofed, but there was no way to make the firehouse entirely safe, even for adults.

"Are you feeling okay otherwise?" he asked her. There had been a tone of panic to his sister's text, as though there was something wrong with their mother and she was somehow slipping. He had picked up on it immediately.

"I'm fine. You don't need to worry about me. How are Laura and the kids?" She changed the subject to get the focus off her, but she was touched that he had called her. His call was of filial love, and didn't have the ring of accusation like Deanna's.

"Everyone's fine here, busy, as usual. I was just worried about you when I got Dee's text."

"She got very wound up about it last night, when she called me about something else and I told her. I'll admit, it was stupid of me. I'm not going to hire a live-in person, though. It would drive me nuts. She's always hated this house. She thinks I should be living uptown in an apartment. This suits me better." Ben knew it was true, it expressed her individuality, and he knew how independent she was.

"Just be careful, Mom. Don't go sliding down the fire pole every day," he teased her.

"I'll try not to, at least till I'm off crutches."

"I'll call you in a few days and see how you're doing. I'm late for a meeting. I've got to go. I love you."

"I love you too, sweetheart. Thank you for call-ing. Give my love to Laura and the kids." It meant a lot to her whenever her children called her, more than they knew.

She spent the rest of the day getting ready for the shoot on Thursday. It was a **Vogue** cover of a famous movie star. She was older and a beautiful woman. Maddie had a knack for photographing mature women and making them look terrific. She hadn't shot for **Vogue** in a while, and she had always wanted to meet the actress. It was going to be a fun day, and she was looking forward to it. She was smiling when she checked the studio, with everything set up the way she liked it. It was a good distraction from her ankle and the cast. She felt back in control again, which was a relief after the weekend. She had just sat down at her desk, and propped her crutches against the wall behind her, when she heard the doorbell, and Deanna walked in two minutes later, unannounced as usual. She never called to ask if it was convenient. Her mother's schedule was irrelevant to her.

"You look terrible" were the first words out of her mouth as she stared at her mother and sat down across the desk from her without being invited to.

"Thank you. You, on the other hand, look great." Deanna was casually dressed in one of her own designs, and meticulously put together as usual, with her dark hair tightly pulled back in a knot, a chic trench coat, and high heels. She was the epitome of fashion. Maddie was wearing baggy jeans and an old black sweater, with one running shoe on, and her crutches close at hand in case she needed them, since she couldn't put any weight on her left foot.

"You look tired, Mother," she said, studying Maddie's face, as though looking for signs of an illness.

"I had a lousy weekend. I feel better today." She had felt brighter as the day wore on, and was pleased that she had gotten a lot done for the **Vogue** shoot that week, despite her cast. She had even picked the music they would listen to during the session, which set the mood for the subject and the crew. "Did you come down here to check on me?" She smiled at her daughter and gave her the benefit of the doubt. Or maybe she had come to harass her about putting the firehouse on the market or hiring a live-in aide. Deanna always had an agenda. It was the way she worked.

"Actually, I came to talk to you about the benefit we need to give here. No other venue will work as well for us." For the moment, selling the firehouse and hiring a caretaker for her mother were on the back burner. The benefit was the hot item of the day, and she had come to convince her mother in person. Deanna was on half a dozen boards and committees, and she was good at getting her way. She was fearless about asking for donations, expensive items for charity auctions, or, in this case, her mother's house as the location for their cocktail party. "Everyone loved coming here last time."

"The problem was, I didn't love having them here. They were invasive, disrespectful, and you had twice as many people as you told me you would," Maddie reminded her.

"We sold more tickets than we expected," she said without apology. "We'll put a limit on it this time."

"I don't want food dragged all over my house. I just don't want the intrusion, Deanna. Or curiosity seekers turning up in my bedroom. I saw photos on Instagram afterwards of all the rooms where they weren't allowed. If they can't follow the rules, which they've already demonstrated, you can't use the house. End of story." She had to be firm with Deanna or she'd run right over her, as she did with everyone, at work and at home. It made her tough in business and got her results with sewers and patternmakers and textile mills. But Maddie didn't like having her daughter's powers of persuasion turned on her.

"I assumed you'd let us use the house again," Deanna said, narrowing her eyes at her mother, "so I told them we could have it. We have to send the invitations out in a week. They're already at the printer. We don't have time to find another venue." It was extremely presumptuous of her.

"Well, you'll have to. I told you last time I wouldn't do it again. It wasn't a good experience for me. This is my place of business and my home, and I can't have people screwing it up. I have delicate equipment here."

"I didn't think you meant it," Deanna said

plaintively, trying another tack, which wasn't going to work for her either. As always, Maddie was gentle but firm, and could be as stubborn as her daughter.

"Well, I did. So you'd better get busy finding another location." Deanna looked furious as she stood up. The gloves were off.

"I think that's incredibly inconsiderate of you. Aren't you afraid of how that will look? The great Madison Allen refuses to help a shelter for homeless children. It won't do you any good in the press, if someone leaks that you refused." And who would leak it? Deanna? She was capable of it.

"That's blackmail," Maddie said smoothly. "If that's how you want to play it, I can't stop you. But the answer is still no. This is my home, I have a right to protect it."

"It's a ridiculous place to live anyway. I hope you're giving some serious thought to selling it now, after your disaster this weekend."

"My 'disaster' had nothing to do with the firehouse. I could have fallen off a ladder just as easily on Park Avenue."

"One of these days, you'll fall down those stairs and break a hip or a leg," Deanna said ominously.

"I hope not. I'm very careful."

"You should at least put in an elevator if you want to stay for a few more years."

"What about a wheelchair ramp?" Maddie said sarcastically. "I'm not incapacitated yet," she pointed out again.

"No, but you will be before you know it. This is how it starts, with accidents at home, then you fall on the street and break a hip. You need to be sensible about this, Mother. You're not as young as you think." They were all low blows, and Maddie tried not to react. It was hurtful listening to her. "You should sell the place before you have another accident here." Listening to her reminded Maddie of the alarm Deanna had suggested the day before, with a button to press for help if she fell. The thought of it made her want to cry. She hoped Deanna was wrong, and this wasn't the first of many future accidents she had in store. It was a grim prospect. "David agrees with me, he thinks you should move out too. You could even invest in a unit in one of those apartment complexes with assisted living facilities you can move into later."

"Do you suppose I could set up a studio there?" Maddie said wryly.

"You can't work forever, Mother." She was the only one of Maddie's children who called her "Mother," and made it sound like an insult. With one fell swoop, Deanna was suggesting that she retire, hire a caretaker, sell her house, move into assisted living, and wear an alarm. She was catapulting her mother into old age at fifty-eight. Maybe sooner or later it would happen. It probably would, but hopefully not for a long time. And some people stayed active, alert, and youthful, and even working, until they were very old. Maddie planned to be one of those.

Maddie was nowhere near wanting to give up the way she lived, and there was no need to. But Deanna saw it all happening on fast forward. Maddie hoped she wasn't right. She felt as though she had her nose pressed against the glass, looking through a window at her worst nightmare, being old and infirm and dependent, no longer productive, and waiting for the end. What she envisioned for herself was working far into the future, at a great age, still expressing her talent, and leading a full life in her own home, not a retirement facility where she would end her days, however luxurious or genteelly disguised. Deanna was pulling back the curtain and showing her what it could really look like, in the worst case. It made Maddie feel as though her days were numbered. It seemed absurd at the age she was now, but maybe it wasn't and Deanna was right. It was Maddie's greatest fear.

Deanna only lingered for a few minutes, her mission not having been accomplished. And Maddie was sure Deanna would try again about the benefit at the firehouse before she gave up. She hobbled around her desk, keeping the weight off her left foot, to kiss Deanna goodbye. Deanna didn't waste time on a hug, kissed the air near her mother's face, and left a minute later. Penny walked in as soon as she heard the front door close behind Deanna.

"What did the Ice Queen want today?" Penny asked, and sat down across from Maddie's desk.

"The firehouse for her charity event, as the first matter of business. After that, she thinks I should invest in a facility with assisted living."

"Now?" Penny looked horrified. "Is she crazy?"

"Maybe not now but soon. She thinks it makes perfect sense, since I'll need it someday. That's not how I see my future," Maddie said bleakly. Nor did anyone else who knew her.

"That's ridiculous, you seem and act younger than I do."

"No, I don't, and even if I appear young, you **are** young. There's a difference. And who knows, maybe she's right. If my health fails, it will all go down the tubes, my work, the firehouse, my free-dom. No one can predict that."

"There's some woman in Florida who's a hun-dred and twelve and still going strong," Penny said stubbornly, wanting to keep Deanna's demons away from Maddie. She was so toxic.

"More power to her. I'm not sure I want to live that long. God knows what she looks like. But I'll settle for ninety-something, and still working. Deanna is predicting a rapid decline in the near future, with my ankle as the first sign. She's trying to convince me of it."

"Don't believe it," Penny said, wishing she could strangle Deanna for the things she said to her mother. She was hateful.

"I'm trying not to. I think my worst nightmare would be if my children ganged up on me and forced me to live in a way I don't want to. That's the kind of thing that breaks people's spirits. What if they take control of my life one day?" It was one of her greatest fears, although she didn't think of it often, but it gave her shivers when she did.

"I won't let them," Penny said staunchly.

"You won't be able to stop them, if it comes to that," Maddie said sadly, "and neither will I. I hope I get run over by a bus before that. It's the kind of thing you think will never happen to you, but sometimes it does. I would hate that, sitting in a chair, staring out a window, remembering the past, with nothing to look forward to. I'd rather be dead."

"Don't say that."

Maddie nodded, but thinking about it made her feel like she wanted to run away, seize life by

71

the horns again, and not just sit there. She didn't want to be helpless, waiting for what Deanna said was inevitable.

She wanted to live her life to the fullest, and she knew she hadn't for a while. She was wrapped up in her work, always running to the next assignment. She wasn't taking much time to smell the roses anymore. With no partner to share it with, she hardly ever took time off now. She just worked, day and night, and now and then she saw her kids. But not often. She hadn't seen Ben in six months and Milagra in almost nine. But Milagra had been working on two books for months, and Ben and Laura just hadn't been able to figure out a good time for her to visit. She hadn't seen her New York granddaughters, Kendra and Lily, in more than two months, almost three. Heads of state of some nations weren't as busy as all of them, and Maddie had a heavy schedule too.

She had a shoot coming up in Shanghai in six weeks, and she had two important shoots in New York in the next week. One on Thursday, and another one the following Monday. She had five weeks free before Shanghai after that, but Maddie knew that other bookings would come in on short notice. They always did. Art directors and editors called her all the time. There was no particular world event she wanted to shoot at the moment.

She'd been working for months on projects back to back. And now, she suspected her ankle would slow her down. She was amazed by how tired she was after her first day at work with a cast and on crutches. She had to go back to the hospital on Friday, to get a walking cast. She hoped she would be less tired with that. Using only one foot and the crutches was exhausting.

Penny didn't leave until after she had seen Maddie get up to her room, on her bottom on the stairs. And then she waited until Maddie's dinner had been delivered by a nearby restaurant and brought it to her in her bedroom on a tray. Maddie had her laptop set up on the bed and was reading emails. She had work to do that night. Her ankle was hurting, but she didn't want to take a pain pill and blitz herself. She needed to focus and concentrate on her work.

After Penny left, she nibbled at her dinner on a tray between emails, and when she finished responding to all of them, which took well over an hour, she thought of the box of letters again. On a whim, she decided to follow Penny's suggestion to look the three men up on the internet. Why not? It couldn't do any harm. Curiosity had been gnawing at her since she had opened Pandora's box, once she got it out of the closet.

She started with Jacques Masson, and typed in

his name for a Google search. It came up immediately as the owner of a string of restaurants in the Chicago area, one in Palm Beach, and another in Las Vegas. He had seven restaurants in all. She studied his website carefully, and his CV, which had lengthened considerably since she'd last seen him. He was only a simple chef then, fresh from France. Their affair had been twenty years before, when he first arrived from Paris with a green card he'd won in the lottery. She went out with him for six months. She was thirty-eight and Jacques had been thirty-five.

They had had a great time together. She fell prey to his French charm and took him seriously for a brief time. He was one of the most entertaining men she'd ever gone out with. She was crazy about him, until she discovered he was a cheater like Stephane. He kept promising her he'd stop, but he never did. Because they only went out for six months, she'd often wondered if she had given up on him too soon, and what would have happened if she'd stuck it out for longer and given him a chance. But he had slept with everyone: sous chefs he worked with, waitresses in the restaurants where he cooked, and two of Maddie's friends, which had destroyed the friendships. It was untenable, and she knew she'd never trust him. She knew it was Stephane all over again, once she had discovered his affairs. Jacques was a much nicer human being than her ex-husband, and he had insisted that he genuinely loved her, but some woman always came along and provided a distraction and a lure he couldn't resist. He was a man who loved women, every size, every color, every type, every age. He tried to tell her that he was a "collector of beautiful women," like men who loved art or fine wine. But his passion for women made it impossible to take him seriously for the long haul. At the time, she had still wanted to remarry eventually. He wasn't a viable option, and she had ended the relationship without bitterness. Eventually he drifted away and they lost touch. He had been thinking about moving to Chicago already by then. He had a job opportunity there, and she didn't want to uproot her kids to move with him.

She saw that his five high-end restaurants in Chicago and in Palm Beach were called Masson, and the one in Las Vegas was called Chez Jacques. There was a photograph of him with a very young girl on his website, and she wondered if it was his daughter. He could have married and had a family in the last twenty years. He was handsome, slightly overweight, and looked like a teddy bear. Despite some gray in his thick mane of hair and the beard he still wore, he hadn't changed much and had aged well. He was fifty-five now, and from the reviews on his website, his restaurants were a major success. He had done well.

She found Bob Holland on Google just as easily. The website said he was the founder of Holland, Hampstead, and Ahern, a venture capital firm in Boston specializing in high-tech investments. They'd both been very young when she went out with him. She was thirty and he was thirty-one, and had just graduated from Harvard Business School with his MBA. She was almost exclusively in fashion then, working furiously and taking care of her kids. They were barely old enough to remember him, and she doubted that they would, although she had gone out with him for two years. He had been a serious contender. He was originally from Boston, although he was working at Lehman Brothers in New York when she knew him. He was responsible and ambitious, and not as much fun as Jacques was when she met him later, but Bob was also steadier, and he wanted to make his mark in the world of high-tech investments. He'd had an offer from a firm in Silicon Valley, when everything was booming and starting to take off out there. He wanted her to move to California with him, but there was little fashion photography happening on the West Coast, and her career would have taken a major hit if she went. She had three children to support and didn't want to be dependent on him. All of it had added up to staying in New York seeming like the right decision.

She remembered that he'd had a chip on his shoulder about not having enough money of his own to invest. He had gone to school with some heavy hitters, and wanted to be one of them. She'd always felt a little out of her league with him. She had no money then either, except what she made, and she spent all of it supporting three kids.

He hadn't liked the people in her fashion world. The photograph on his website showed him looking a lot older at fifty-nine, and the list of companies his firm had funded was impressive. He had clearly made it to the big leagues and fulfilled his dreams. And as much as she loved him for a time, she could never see herself with him long term. She always had the feeling that he would clip her wings. Giving up New York and her career for him had been too much to ask. She couldn't do it.

In the twenty-six years since, he had made his way back to Boston, and apparently started his own venture capital firm, so he'd obviously done well on the West Coast, before heading east again. She hadn't had any regrets about him, although she had missed him at first, but Jacques had been a good distraction six years later, and different from Bob in every possible way. Jacques had seemed much less serious about his career at the time, but had done well anyway, probably not in the same league as Bob, but seven restaurants for a French chef from the provinces was a major coup for him. Both men appeared to have lived up to their dreams, and so had she.

It took her a little longer to locate Andy Wyatt, and there were several options that turned up in her search, and then she found him. He was still in Wyoming, listed as the founder of the Wyatt Ranch, and Sean Wyatt, his son, was listed as manager of the ranch. Sean was a year younger than Milagra, and had been a nice boy. Andy was widowed. He'd lost his wife to cancer not long after Sean was born. He'd been a good father and a good man. Maddie had met him at a ranch she took the children to one summer, and they fell head over heels in love. They were the perfect match, in a way she had never expected to find. Their values were so similar. She had waited until she was forty to find the love of her life. Everything about their time together was perfect, but geography was the one problem they couldn't solve. She had a major career in New York by then, couldn't afford to give it up and didn't want to. It was part of her identity. She had two kids in college, and Milagra to get through high school and into college, and Andy couldn't exist anywhere but on a ranch, close to his roots and in the world he had always known.

At forty-nine, there was no way he could transition into city life in New York, far from horses and mountains and wide-open spaces. He had come to visit her in New York once, and no matter how much he loved her, he couldn't wait to leave. He had said that he felt like the air was being sucked out of his lungs. He was a cowboy to the very bottom of his soul, the way some men are sailors and can't live far from the sea. She understood that about him, but she couldn't give up her identity for him either. Her work was an integral part of her. She wasn't sure she'd make the same decision now, but she thought she would. In the end, they had made the decision together, and knew they had to. The tension was beginning to poison their relationship, which was the last thing she wanted. They agreed that they had to end it, which had been the most painful choice she'd ever made.

They spoke a few times right after the breakup. She'd hoped that they could be friends, but neither of them were capable of it. They loved each other too passionately, and had to stop talking. She cried over him for two years afterwards, and she hadn't had a serious relationship since then. They had ended it seventeen years ago, and it still felt like yesterday. She wondered if they'd be able to see each other now.

Having found the box of photographs and love letters had jogged her memories and her heart, and she suddenly had a longing to reach back into her past and see the people who had been important to her. She didn't want anything from them, but she wanted to remind herself of what they had meant to her, and to see if she'd made the right decisions. She had always wondered about Andy. She could see that he had his own ranch now, and she was happy for him. She was at peace now too. Her children were each in a good place for them, and her work was satisfying, but she wanted to see the men she had loved, and reassure herself that she had made the right choices. She needed to contact them one more time, to validate the past, and who she had been then, with each one of them. She wondered if doing so was a sign of age, or a reminder that she was still alive and had been capable of great love, at least once. It was something she was beginning to feel she needed now in order to move forward in her life.

She didn't think she wanted a man in her life again. It seemed too complicated to her now. But all the men she had looked up on Google had been more than just passing relationships for her, and she wanted to see where they were now. It seemed an important rite of passage to her. Especially with Deanna convincing her that her life was over. She was mildly afraid of seeing Andy again. He had meant so much to her, but maybe they were capable of friendship now, even if they hadn't been then. The sting had gone out of it for her, and hopefully for him too. She wondered if he had married again. He wanted to marry her, and she would have if it hadn't meant spending the rest of her life on a ranch in Wyoming. She couldn't do that any more than he could have moved to New York for her. She wanted nothing from him now, except to know that he was all right, and confirm that they had loved each other. That seemed important, and perhaps it would be to him too. Maybe then, they could both go on in peace.

She wasn't sure when she was going to do it, but it was a pilgrimage she wanted to make. Her broken ankle and moment of feeling vulnerable and frail had opened a window in her soul somewhere. Maybe destiny had led her to the box with their love letters and photographs. It was time. And just knowing that made her feel as though she had grown wings.

Chapter 4

The shoot on Thursday went surprisingly well, in spite of Maddie's being on crutches and less able to move around than she usually was. The studio assistants she always hired for shoots helped her, and she was in full control of the session by the end of the day. The actress she had been assigned to shoot for the cover of **Vogue** had never felt as glamorous or as beautiful, and she and Maddie hit it off brilliantly. The famous movie star was sixty-nine years old, full of life and energy, and she felt like a girl again in the eye of Maddie's lens. The shoot was a great success, and Maddie was certain the editors would be thrilled with the results.

She had a great feeling of satisfaction when she went to bed that night. She was still on top of her game, despite her unfortunate accident.

As soon as she got her walking cast, she could put weight on her left leg again, gingerly at first, but by the day after, she was moving around with ease. She kept the crutches at hand to ensure her balance, but didn't need them as much as she had a week before.

The shoot on Monday went equally well, and at the end of the day, Maddie sat in her office looking pensive. She had a plan. She'd been thinking about it for days, and the more certain she became, the stronger she felt. She hadn't been sure when she wanted to do it at first, but she realized that the time was now. Remarkably, she had no firm bookings for the next few weeks, only several tentative things in the works, which was rare for her. In five weeks she'd be shooting in Shanghai. She had the time now and the desire, and everything about it felt right.

She did everything she needed to do the next day, without telling anyone. She was going to disappear for a few weeks. She was planning to check in with Penny occasionally so she wouldn't worry, and Penny could reach her on her cellphone if anything important happened. But she was going on a trip back in history to quietly close doors to the past, and open the windows to the future. She was excited about it.

On Wednesday evening before she went upstairs

to pack, Penny found her at her desk with a peaceful look on her face, and a bright light in her eyes. She observed her suspiciously. She knew her well.

"You're up to something. I know you are. I can tell." Maddie didn't deny it, and only smiled.

"Maybe so," she admitted cautiously. "I don't want you to worry about me. I'm fine. I'm going away for a while."

"How long a while? Months? Years?" Penny was panicked.

"As long as I need. Don't book anything for the next month. I'll be back in time to do Shanghai."

"You're going away for a **month**?" She almost shrieked it. Maddie hardly ever took a day off, even on weekends. In fourteen years, Penny couldn't remember any time when Maddie had taken two weeks off, let alone a month. "Are you going alone?" She wondered suddenly if there was a man in Maddie's life she didn't know about. Anything was possible. Maddie often kept her most private thoughts to herself.

"I'm going to visit some old friends. I'll see how far I get. I'll check in with you when I can. I don't want to take calls, unless there's an emergency with the kids. I need some time to myself."

"Is Deanna threatening you again? Did you have a fight?"

"No. She's still harassing me about the benefit.

The answer is still no. She can't use the firehouse. You can deal with her after I leave." She stood up then and came around her desk to hug Penny. "Take care of yourself. Thank you for holding the fort."

"Thank you for telling me, I would have had a heart attack if I came in tomorrow and you were gone."

"I know, that's why I said something tonight. And thank you for taking such good care of me. Please take care of yourself while I'm gone." Maddie looked at Penny affectionately. It was the first time she had ever taken time for herself. Finding the box of love letters had started it, but everything Deanna had said to her had pushed her to it, and she had to do it now. She needed to face the past and the future.

"What do you want me to tell clients?"

"That I'm on a long project for a month, and after that I'll be in Shanghai for a week. You can book me after that. I may only stay in Shanghai for a few days, but that gives me some leeway."

"Have you told the kids?"

"Not a word. Ben and Milagra won't know the difference. And after Deanna gives up on browbeating me into letting her use the house, we won't hear from her for a while. I can always call them if they really need me. They'll call you if it's important." Penny nodded and gave Maddie a hug. She left after that, and Maddie went upstairs to pack. She could hardly wait to get started.

She had rented an SUV, which was parked on the street, and was planning to check in to hotels along the way. For the first time in her life, she didn't want to be tied to dates or set plans. She was open to whatever destiny chose to put on her path. She was taking her crutches with her, but didn't really need them now. The walking cast was doing its job, and she wasn't in pain anymore. She didn't need her left leg to drive, so the cast wasn't a problem.

She looked around her bedroom as she fell asleep that night. She had printed out the information on all three men she wanted to visit, and knew how to contact them when she reached their cities, and Andy on the ranch. She hadn't given any of them warning and liked the element of surprise. If she missed them, and they were out of town, it was meant to be that way. She was leaving the whole trip in the hands of the fates, to show her what she needed to see and understand. She wanted to go backward in time, just long enough to touch the past, and go forward with a lighter heart.

She was up at six, showered, dressed, had tea and a slice of toast, and was on the road at seven, heading north toward Boston. She figured she'd be there by noon. She didn't know Boston well, but had liked it when she'd been there, and would be content to walk around if she couldn't reach Bob immediately. He might not even want to talk to her after all these years. She recognized that as a possibility too. The men she wanted to see now, for the first time in years, might not be nearly as excited at the prospect of seeing her.

She had been on the highway for two hours when Deanna called the office and asked to speak to her mother. Penny told her she was out.

"Out? At nine o'clock? Where? Is she shooting on location today?"

"I don't know where she is," Penny said, smiling to herself, thoroughly enjoying foiling Deanna's plan to harass her mother again. It was time someone stopped her, and Maddie had escaped.

"That's ridiculous. You're lying to me. You know perfectly well where she is. She doesn't move an inch without telling you first."

"Well, she did this time. She was gone when I got to work."

"Did she get hurt again?" Deanna asked, sounding worried for an instant.

"I don't think so. She told me she'd be out this morning. She didn't tell me where."

"That's very odd. Well, tell her to call me when she gets back. I've got to resolve this thing about the benefit."

"I think she resolved it," Penny said blandly, chuckling inwardly. "She told me it's not going to happen here."

"We haven't finished discussing it," Deanna said firmly.

"I think she has." Deanna made a snorting sound into the phone and didn't comment, and without saying goodbye to Penny she hung up. "Thank you to you too, Miss Charming," Penny said to the receiver after Deanna hung up, and then she got on with her work. There would be plenty to do without Maddie, for the first week or two at least. And she'd find enough to keep her busy after that. Maddie had wrapped up all her own pending projects before she left, and had spent the weekend doing it. It explained the mountain of work Maddie had left for Penny the previous Monday, which made total sense to her now. She was clearing her desk, and her head.

When Maddie got to Boston, she drove around for a few minutes, trying to get her bearings, and consulted the GPS in the rented car. It took her to the Four Seasons Hotel, where she checked in to a junior suite. It was big enough to give her some space, without being overly luxurious. She sat down for a few minutes after she checked in to the room, thought about it, and called Bob at his venture capital firm. It was noon, and a secretary told her he had just left for lunch. Maddie left her name and number, and went out for a walk. She stopped to have a salad at a small restaurant on the way back. There were young people everywhere. Boston was always full of students. There were more colleges per square inch than any city she knew of. It was a haven for college kids from all over the world.

She went back to her room after she returned, and lay down for a while, thinking about Bob. She wondered if he was going to call her. He called her at four o'clock.

"Is that you?" he asked in a shocked voice. He had just gotten her message after an unusually long lunch, celebrating a big deal and going over final details.

"Yes, it is," she said, smiling. "I wasn't sure if you'd want to hear from me or not. It's been a long time."

"Twenty-six years, to be exact," he said a little drily, curious about why she'd called.

"Looking at your website, you've been busy in the meantime. Very impressive," she said generously.

"You're the one who's a big star now. I went to your show at the Museum of Fine Arts about five years ago. I was going to write to you then, but time got away from me, and then I felt stupid writing to you, and I wasn't sure you'd get it. How are your kids?" She was touched that he asked. He'd been somewhat overwhelmed by them when they dated. Three young children was a lot for him to deal with. He was young then, and so were they.

"Fine. Busy. Grown up. Ben and Deanna are both married with kids of their own. Milagra is writing gothic novels in Mendocino with a flock of cats and dogs. Ben lives in San Francisco, and Deanna is in New York. She's a fashion designer, and he's doing his second start-up. I hardly see any of them, but they're happy, and I work a lot."

"You always did," he said, sounding warmer than he had at first.

"What about you? Married? Kids?" she asked.

"Yes, to both questions. A son at Vassar, a daughter at Princeton. Times have changed." They both laughed. "They're good kids. He wants to be an artist, she wants to go to law school. What are you doing in Boston?" She had thought a lot about how she would answer that question, and had decided that honesty was the simplest course.

"It will sound crazy, but I came to see you."

"I'm not sure I believe that," he said, skeptical. "Why didn't you call first?"

"I decided on the trip on fairly short notice. But you're right, I should have let you know." She felt rude for a minute, he had always been very traditional and conservative about things like that. He was not a spontaneous kind of person, and liked to plan, a little too much for Maddie in those days, especially since her plans changed constantly with three young kids, when one of them got an earache or a babysitter didn't show up. Their lives had been incompatible in a number of ways, which was why the relationship hadn't lasted. But two years had been a respectable run, and she wanted to see him anyway, for old times' sake, if nothing else. "I had one of those weird epiphanies a couple of weeks ago. I was cleaning out a closet and came across a box of old letters and photographs, and there you were. I then proceeded to fall off the ladder and break my ankle. And I decided it would be nice to see you and find out how you are. So I looked you up on Google a few days later, rented a car, drove to Boston, and here I am. It's probably inconvenient as hell." He was quiet for a minute before he answered.

"It's not inconvenient. It's just kind of a shock. I never thought I'd see you again. I'd love to see you, Maddie." His voice was suddenly full of emotion. He'd always had a somewhat stiff exterior, but a soft heart.

"Whenever you want." She was free and had no plans.

"Are you free for dinner tonight?"

"Yes, I am. Do you want to bring your wife?" It would be somewhat disappointing, but she was open to anything, that's what this trip was all about. Finding them where they were and discovering who they were now.

"No, I don't. I'll explain all that when I see you. We have a lot to catch up on."

"Maybe less on my side than on yours. My life hasn't changed much. I work harder and my kids are bigger, other than that nothing is different."

"I don't see how you could work harder than you used to," he said admiringly. "You were the workhorse of all time. Superwoman, with kids."

"Thank you for the compliment." He had obviously worked hard too, as he had then. They had that in common.

"Where are you staying?"

"The Four Seasons."

"I'll pick you up at eight. I drive a black Ferrari, in case you don't recognize me."

"I have a cast on my left leg. I'll wave it at you so you know it's me."

"So you really did break your ankle, not just a figure of speech." He sounded surprised again.

"The real deal. Fortunately it's my left leg so I can drive, or I wouldn't have been able to make the trip. Not right now anyway."

"See you at eight." He hung up a minute later and sat staring into space at his desk for several minutes. He wasn't sure if her sudden reappearance was providential, or just a quirk of fate. Her refusal to move to California with him had ended the relationship, but there had been nothing about her he didn't like. They had just come to a fork in the road and gone separate ways. Now suddenly she was back. And he remembered all too clearly everything he'd felt for her then. But twenty-six years was a long time.

Maddie was wearing black slacks and a white silk blouse when he came to pick her up promptly at eight. As soon as she saw the black Ferrari, she smiled, pulled up her pants leg, and waved her cast at him from the distance, and he laughed as she headed toward the car.

"I'd have recognized you anyway, you know. You haven't changed a bit," he said, looking at her warmly.

"Have you had your eyes checked lately?" she said, smiling at him as he gazed at her for a long time, drinking her in, and then kissed her on the cheek. He had changed very little, except for the gray hair, but his face was the same. She knew he was fifty-nine, and he was trim and in good shape, as he always had been in the past.

He drove her to L'Espalier, one of the best restaurants in Boston. The headwaiter knew him and led them to a quiet corner table. She noticed that he was wearing a perfectly tailored suit and a navy blue Hermès tie with a white shirt. He was very elegant, and more polished than he had been at thirty-one when they met. His hair was immaculately trimmed, he had a smooth shave, and he was wearing a gold Patek Philippe watch on his wrist. He had all the trappings of a wealthy, successful man. He had gotten where he wanted to be, but she could see that his eyes were sad as he ordered a martini for himself and a glass of champagne for her.

"So where do we start?" he asked her.

"Anywhere you like."

"Did you ever remarry?" She shook her head. "Why not?"

"Too ornery, I guess." He laughed at her answer as he sipped his martini, after they'd toasted each other, and he'd said, "To old times."

"Too busy, more likely."

"That too. You work hard for a long time, and pass on things you tell yourself you'll do later, and then one day you wake up, and it seems too

95

late to do them. I bought a wonderful old firehouse in the West Village in New York fifteen years ago, and I live there. I'm happy, but I miss my kids."

"I do too now that they're in college."

"When did you get married?" She was curious about that. Right after her, or a few years later? In California or Boston?

"About two years after we broke up. I worked in Palo Alto for about a year and a half, and got a better offer in Boston. I met my wife the week I moved here. She was in law school. She's an environmental lawyer, and loves what she does. We had two kids, a boy and a girl. We did everything by the book. Her father was in biotech venture capital, he was the head of the firm I went to work for. I married the boss's daughter and moved ahead very quickly, and ten years ago I went out on my own. It's worked out pretty well," he said modestly. He had never been one to brag, but she could see the evidence of his success.

"And?" There was a hitch in there somewhere, she could hear it in his voice and see it in his eyes. Even after all these years, she still knew how to read him. He had always been transparent in some ways. He didn't look like a happy man.

"You know me too well. Everything was fine for the first five years, the honeymoon phase, and then it got rocky after the second baby. We reached a crisis point. The crux of it was that neither of us were sure why I married her. Was it because of who her father was, or for her? I was so desperate to get ahead as a VC that I probably would have married her no matter what, and she knew it. She wasn't sure if I was in love with her, and to be honest, neither was I. It never really worked after that. We were thinking about splitting up, and her father called me in. They're an old Boston family and no one has ever gotten divorced. He told me that as long as I stayed with Elizabeth, everything would be fine. If I left her, he would see to it that my career in venture capital would be dead and buried. I believed him. So I stayed. Neither of us is sure why I married her, but we both know for certain why I stayed married to her. The marriage has been dead ever since. We go our separate ways, which is easier now that the kids are away at school. She's always very pleasant, we're extremely polite and considerate of each other. But there's no love there, and maybe there never was. Whatever we had twenty-four years ago when we married has been over for a long time.

"I was seeing someone else for a while, discreetly, but that got complicated. She's married too, my partner's wife. And he and I were good friends." Maddie cringed as he said it. It was a rotten thing to do to his partner and his wife. Bob had made a lot of bad choices and, in essence, he had sold out, and paid a high price for it. He had led a loveless life for a long time, married to a woman he didn't love, staying with her to protect his career, and cheating on his wife and his friend and partner. There was very little honesty about his life, except his unhappiness, which showed in the sorrow in his eyes. Part of him was dead, an important part. His integrity, and his heart.

"I'm sorry to hear all that," she said, and meant it. "You deserve better."

"I made a choice. I wanted to play with the big boys so badly, and I don't regret it. I shouldn't have married Elizabeth, but if I hadn't, I wouldn't have what I do today."

"Is it worth it?" she asked, sad for him.

"Sometimes. You steal a little happiness here and there and it works," which meant he cheated on her all the time. Maddie hated the choices he had made, for his sake, and his wife couldn't have been happy either. She had also paid a high price for a bright, handsome husband whom her father had threatened into staying with her. There couldn't be much joy in that. Maddie's life was a whole lot simpler, maybe lonely at times now without the kids, but it was honest and clean. Bob lived in a world of subterfuge, lies, false pretenses, and expensive trades, his happiness for a big career. The Ferrari and the gold watch didn't seem worth it to Maddie, and she was sure they had an impressive house. He had mentioned a boat and a plane. But his children had grown up in a loveless home. She couldn't help wondering if there was any part of Bob's heart still intact, or if it had been dead for years. It made her glad for the choice she'd made not to follow him to California with her kids. If he was willing to make such dangerous compromises for his career, who knew what he would have done with her, when better opportunities arose, like Elizabeth and her father's firm in Boston. He might have dumped Maddie, and she suspected he would have. Anything was possible with someone as ambitious as he was. He had sold out in a major way, and there was no one left inside him. He was a hollow shell.

They made it through dinner with less loaded subjects, and he drove her back to her hotel. He sat looking at her for a long time when they got there.

"When are you leaving, Maddie?" he asked her.

"Tomorrow morning." She had decided during dinner. She was glad she had come, but didn't want to stay. Any further contact with him would be messy, and she didn't want that. Their old memories were enough for her.

"Could you stay a little longer?" She knew what he had in mind, it was easy to guess. A little comfort for old times' sake before she left.

"I think it would be a mistake, for both of us," she said gently. "You don't need any more complications in your life, and neither do I. I think we had our shot at it a long time ago. And you probably did the right things for you. You would never have been happy without the career you have now. I couldn't have given you that."

"I'm not happy now," he said and she believed him.

"It's tough to be happy if you're living a lie. Maybe you should take the bull by the horns and get divorced."

"And then what? Start all over again with someone else? Give up half of everything I have? Her father would destroy me. He's still powerful, more so than ever. We have a pretty fantastic life, and an incredible house, a yacht, and a jet. That's hard to walk away from."

"I guess it is," she said, feeling sorry for him, not for his bad marriage, but the bad decisions he had made. She wouldn't have wanted his life, even with all the expensive toys, for anything in the world. He was in a prison of his own making. And she felt sorry for his wife.

Bob tried to kiss her then, and she gently turned her head to avoid it, and kissed his cheek. "Take care of yourself. I'm glad I got to see you. Thank you for dinner." She smiled and got out of the car as he watched her.

"I love you as much as I did twenty-six years ago, Maddie, the day we left each other. It never stopped." She wanted to tell him to give it to Elizabeth, but she knew it was way too late for that.

She waved from the sidewalk as he drove away. She hadn't answered when he said he loved her. She didn't know what to say. The poor man didn't know the meaning of the word.

Chapter 5

Maddie had a text from Bob when she woke up the next morning, asking her again to stay. He'd written it the night before when she was sleeping. She answered him quickly and simply. She didn't want to encourage him. "I have plans in Chicago. Have to leave. Thank you for dinner. Take good care. Maddie." His life had turned out so badly, though all his own fault, and all for a lot of fancy toys and a big career. It made her sad to think about, but she was glad she had seen it at close range. It left no doubt in her mind about the wisdom of her decision to move on twenty-six years before. She had sensed even then that they wanted different things in life. She wanted people and real relationships, he wanted money and power, and was fiercely ambitious and materialistic.

She checked out of the hotel very early and, just for the fun of it, she decided to visit the Harvard campus in Cambridge. She got there an hour after the sun came up on a beautiful day. She had seen it before, and it always impressed and moved her, thinking of the great minds that had been educated there. She took a few pictures with her phone, with the sunlight washing over the campus, and put them on Instagram. She walked around for a while, thinking how lucky the students were to go to school at such an extraordinary institution, and then she got in her car and followed the GPS directions to head for Chicago. She had a long trip ahead of her and wanted to drive straight through.

She called Penny once she was on the highway, to check in, as soon as Penny got to work.

"How's everything at home?" She had only left the day before, but it already felt as though she had been gone for longer.

"Quiet, except for Deanna. She called to talk to you yesterday. She didn't believe that I don't know where you are."

"What did she want? Same thing?"

"Of course, to badger you for her benefit."

"She'll get tired of it." Maddie had noticed missed calls from her too, and didn't intend to respond. She knew why she was calling. "Anything else?"

"No. How are you? I just saw your photo of

Harvard on Instagram. How long are you staying in Boston?"

"I've already left. I did what I came here to do. I saw an old friend. Now I'm heading west."

"All the way west?"

"Maybe. I'll see. I haven't decided yet."

"Thanks for checking in. I worry about you," Penny said gently.

"You don't need to. I'm fine. I'll call you in a few days." She was looking forward to Chicago, she had always liked the city, although she didn't know it well. She felt a little strange being on this journey, to see the men she had once loved. She wasn't hoping to start anything with them, she just wanted to spend a little time with each of them to validate her own earlier decisions. In Bob's case, one dinner had been enough to tell her what she needed to know. She had done the right thing. And if she hadn't? She had no idea what she would have done then. This was a form of free fall for her. She felt as though she had leapt out of a plane and was floating slowly toward the earth, blown by the wind. She had no idea where she would land. She just knew she needed to do this.

She hung up after a few minutes on the phone with Penny and enjoyed the driving. It was relaxing, and she didn't mind that she had a long way to go. She needed the time to think.

*   *   *

It was noon in New York when Deanna called her brother, and nine in the morning in California. A busy time of day for him. She'd been with fit models all morning for the new collection, and had a break. Ben took the call immediately, afraid that something had happened to their mother, another fall or something worse. Deanna had put him on edge with her text message about the broken ankle, and he wasn't sure what to expect next.

"Did you see Mom's pic on Instagram this morning?" were her opening words.

"No, I didn't. I was at the gym, and then I came to work. What did she post on it?" He didn't follow it regularly, but he had it in order to keep current when he was in the mood. Laura followed several people diligently, but she hadn't said anything to him. Though she didn't usually follow his mother. She followed movie stars and socialites.

"I've been trying to reach her since yesterday, and Penny is being mysterious. She claims she doesn't know where she is."

"Maybe it's true. Maybe she's away somewhere, shooting an important subject, like a politician or something."

"Bullshit, Penny knows her every move, and Mom's not returning my calls."

"Did you have a fight with her?" He was always suspicious of his sister's side of any story. She usually left out a vital piece of information and played innocent, which wasn't the whole truth.

"Of course not." She sounded miffed. "I needed a favor, and she hasn't been in a good mood." He was checking Instagram as he listened to her. "It looks like she's at some kind of school."

"She is apparently," he said as the images she had posted that morning appeared on his screen. "That's Harvard."

"What would she be doing there? Early in the morning. And why is she being so secretive about it?"

"Maybe she's photographing the chancellor of the university, or a Nobel Prize winner. She has very important subjects." Deanna knew it too. "Why are you so worried about Mom all of a sudden, other than the broken ankle? It could happen to you or me too."

"Not at two or three in the morning, at the top of a ladder."

"Only because we're married and have young kids. She probably has a lot of lonely nights to fill," he said with more sensitivity than his sister.

"I think she's losing it. Something's going on with her. And why didn't she or Penny tell me she was out of town?"

"I have no idea. Maybe the story is a secret, or some kind of breaking news. A new chancellor, a cure for a rare disease they've done the research for. She covers very major stuff and people. Does she usually tell you everything she's doing?" He sounded exasperated, he had no idea why his sister was being so dogged about her. He knew how tactless she could be, especially with their mother.

"No," Deanna said honestly. She rarely spoke to her brother either. She sent him an occasional text, but that was it. "I think something smoky is happening. And she's never fallen before. I told her I thought it was the beginning of the end."

"Christ, Deanna, why would you say something like that? And you wonder why she's dodging your calls?"

"Well, it's true. She's not young anymore. She should sell the firehouse. The broken ankle proves it. She's going to kill herself on those stairs one of these days. A broken hip will be next." She sounded adamant about it, and he closed his eyes as he held the phone.

"Did you tell her that too?"

"Of course. She needs to hear it. We can't sugar-coat everything for her." He could count on his sister not to do that, of that he was sure. "She's getting older. She should have someone staying there at night, some kind of caretaker. She's got room for it, so she has no excuse. Or she should sell that Bohemian death trap she lives in. The stairs alone are dangerous, and once she's injured, there's no elevator. I told her she should consider one of those assisted living co-ops. Some of my friends have been buying them for their parents, and she can afford it."

"She doesn't need assisted living at fifty-eight."

"Not yet, but she will. The broken ankle proves it."

"Oh, for chrissake, Dee. If I break my ankle playing tennis, should I move into assisted living too?"

"Of course not, you're thirty-five years old. Mom is old now, she's nearly sixty. In a few years the firehouse will be seriously dangerous for her. It already is. I told her she should get one of those alarms to hang around her neck in the meantime, until she sells it, in case she has another fall."

"Oh God. Let me give you a clear picture of what you did here. You told our mother, who cherishes her independence, has a booming career, and is respected around the world, that she was an idiot for falling off a ladder and breaking her ankle and that she should wear a geriatric alarm in case she falls again, which she may never do since she's never done it before. You told her that she needs a caretaker living with her, should sell the house she loves, and should consider assisted living. If you said any of that to me, I'd be profoundly depressed, and she probably is now. What you said is unnecessary and inappropriate, especially at her age, and for someone as vital as our mother. She's fifty-eight, not ninety, and she looks fifty on a bad day, forty-five on a good one. What the hell were you thinking?"

"I'm thinking that she's not acting normal," Deanna said, sounding huffy. "And she's not too young for early-onset Alzheimer's. People her age, and younger, get it all the time."

"People get struck by lightning too. Let me tell you, the one thing our mother does **not** have is Alzheimer's. She's smarter than either one of us, and I haven't noticed her slipping."

"Maybe not, but she's behaving strangely."

"How? Because she went to Harvard without your permission? She's probably there to see the chancellor, which is something you and I wouldn't be invited to do." He knew that his sister had issues with their mother, and at times was jealous of her accomplishments, but this was ridiculous. "Do you ever think about what her life is like? How lonely she must be? She has three children, two of them live three thousand miles away, one of whom is practically a recluse and never speaks to anyone, including her." He had wondered at times if Milagra had some form of Asperger's, although there was no firm evidence of it. She was certainly eccentric. "You live in the same city. How often do you see her?"

"David and I are very busy," she said defensively. "We both have very stressful jobs," as though that explained it, but to him it didn't.

"So does she. Do you ever take her to lunch, or do something with her on the weekends?" he asked and there was silence on the other end for an instant.

"We go away every weekend. I can't stay in the city for Mom. I have my family to think of."

"So do I. That's my point. She is our family. We forget that. We all have our families and lives. Millie and I live far away, and you're too busy to spend time with her. And then you go and tell her she has to have a babysitter, should sell her house, consider assisted living, and wear a geriatric alarm. What about diapers? Did you suggest those too? Jesus, how do you expect her to feel with all that?"

"Maybe that's her reality now," Deanna said harshly. "Or it will be."

"Maybe not. There are plenty of people in their eighties and nineties now, in good shape and fully operative. Some are even still working. You want to treat her like she's a hundred years old at fifty-eight, when she's still busy, beautiful, and at the height of her career. I'm not surprised she's not returning your calls. I wouldn't either. And who knows what she's doing at Harvard, probably working. Or maybe she's having an affair with one of the professors. She must be lonely as hell. And I don't think she's 'slipping,' geriatric, or senile because she broke her ankle."

"I hope you're right," Deanna said, sounding bitter. She didn't like getting scolded by her brother or anyone else. In her life, she did the scolding.

"I hope she goes out and has a good time once in a while, she deserves it," he said, feeling sad for her. "She doesn't need a caretaker, she needs a boyfriend."

"Don't be ridiculous. At her age?"

"Are you telling me you don't know people in their late fifties who have boyfriends and girlfriends, or are still married? Hell, I know people who got married in their eighties."

"I still think she should get rid of the firehouse," Deanna said stubbornly. "It's dangerous, it always was."

"She loves it. What if someone forced you to give up your house in the Berkshires?" He had been there and it was beautiful. Deanna loved it. "Or your coop in New York?" She loved that too.

"That's different," she said angrily.

"No, it's not," he insisted.

"It's not dangerous, for heaven's sake. The place in Massachusetts is an eighteenth-century farmhouse."

"Well, hers is a twentieth-century firehouse. I happen to like it, and it suits her. It's charming, and it's totally her."

"Tell me how charming it is when she breaks a hip or kills herself falling down those stairs. I can hardly manage them."

"I think you need to be more compassionate about her. A **lot** more. She asks nothing of us, she's always available when we want her, and she never complains about how little we all see her and do for her. I don't even have time to call her most of the time, and she never says anything about it. As mothers go, she's extremely low maintenance. Maybe you need to appreciate that instead of trying to shove her into assisted living and get rid of her. Think how that must make her feel. For all we know, she's running away from home right now, and I wouldn't blame her." Deanna didn't answer for a moment.

"I'll take her to lunch when she gets back, if she returns my calls."

"She may not for a while. Why should she? You must have scared the life out of her. I'm late for a meeting," he said as he looked at his watch, and after they hung up, he thought about what his sister had said, and the outrageous things she had suggested to their mother. It broke his heart for her. He could only imagine how sad and hurt she must have been. He wasn't wrong. It made him wonder if he was the only one who cared about her. His sisters certainly made no effort, and neither did he very often. It made him want to invite her out to San Francisco in the near future, if Laura didn't come up with a hundred excuses for him not to. They were always too busy. But he was going to change that. He had made that decision while listening to his sister. They owed their mother more than they were giving her.

At her end, Deanna brushed off what Ben had said. As far as she was concerned, he obviously had a mother complex.

And as they argued about her, Maddie was happily in her car, listening to Beyoncé and on her way to Chicago.

She got to Chicago at one A.M., with Friday traffic and a stop for lunch on the road, and drove straight to the Four Seasons Hotel on Michigan Avenue, the city's "Magnificent Mile." She had called the hotel several hours earlier, and told them when she'd be arriving. She asked for a junior suite like the one she had at the Four Seasons in Boston.

And when she got there, they had a beautiful room for her on the fortieth floor with a view of the lake. She could see the boats from her window.

She took off her clothes, showered, and fell into bed. She'd been driving for seventeen hours and she was going to call Jacques in the morning. She had no idea if he was in town, or if he would want to see her. But that was the beauty of this trip. She was leaving it all up to fate, without forcing anything. And if he didn't see her, that was all right too. At least she'd tried. It was all she had to do. She smiled as she thought about it, and even before she turned the lights off from the switch next to her bed, she fell sound asleep. It had been a long drive from Boston and she had enjoyed the trip.

Chapter 6

When Maddie woke up the next morning, it was a beautiful sunny day, and she was surprised to see that it was after ten o'clock in the morning. She stretched and then got up, crossed the room, and opened the curtains. The view from her room on the fortieth floor was spectacular. She took out her phone, took a picture of the view, and posted it on Instagram. Then she ordered her breakfast, coffee and croissants. She wanted to walk around the city.

She called Jacques before she went out. The number she had was for the offices of his restaurant corporation. When she asked for him, they told her he wasn't expected until that afternoon, and she left him a message. She left her hotel room a few minutes later.

Deanna had just sent her brother a text by then. "Take a look at her Instagram. Where is she now?"

His answer came back almost immediately. He recognized the city instantly. He went there often. "Chicago."

"Why?" Deanna wrote back to him.

"None of our business. She's an adult." And then he sent another text a few minutes later and added "with all her marbles." Deanna still wasn't convinced but she didn't write back to him. She called Maddie's cellphone and it went straight to voicemail. She sent her a text then, and asked where she was, and Maddie didn't answer. She obviously didn't want to communicate with them at the moment. Maddie had told herself that this was her time. She had given herself permission not to call them. For the very first time.

As she headed back to the hotel that afternoon, not wanting to go too far on her walking cast, her phone rang, and a voice with a familiar French accent gushed in a mixture of French and English that made her smile.

"What are you doing in Chicago? And why have you call me?" His English was a little better than when she dated him, but not much. Most of the employees in his restaurants were French. He still trusted his fellow countrymen in the kitchen more than Americans, although he had a Chinese cook in one of his restaurants and a Colombian in another. The Colombian had gone to Le Cordon Bleu, and the Chinese chef had worked in one of the best restaurants in Hong Kong. "I am so happy to hear from you, Maddie." He still said it like "Mah-deeee" and made it sound French.

"I'm taking a driving trip." She had learned something from seeing Bob Holland. She didn't want to tell Jacques she was there to see him, it was too intense. A lot of women chased him, and she didn't want to be perceived as one more.

"What are you doing for dinner?"

"Nothing. I came in late last night, and I didn't want to make plans."

"Well, you have plans now. I just opened a new restaurant two weeks ago. You have to try it. Dinner at nine?" He still liked eating late, and then he had another thought. "Please tell me you don't have a husband with you." He sounded hopeful and she laughed.

"I don't have one."

"Wonderful news." She hadn't seen him in twenty years, and he made it seem as though it was yesterday. He had always been an open, breezy, friendly person. He was perfect for the restaurant business, and people loved him, especially women. But he could be a man's man too, when he had to be. She was glad she'd called him. And she had been reminded again that afternoon that Chicago was a small but sophisticated city. She had a feeling his new restaurant was going to be fancy. She stopped at Neiman Marcus on the way back to the hotel to see if she could find something dressier to wear that night than anything she had brought with her. She was traveling light, and everything she had was casual.

She found a perfect, simple, short black silk dress that showed off her legs, still one of her best features, and a pair of Manolo Blahnik black suede pumps with a low heel, the right height to work with her cast. She looked elegant when she tried the dress on and it fit perfectly. And she had a simple black jacket with her that would be perfect with the dress if it was chilly.

She was impeccably put together when Jacques picked her up at the hotel a few minutes before nine. She was wearing her still-blond hair loose, past her shoulders. She had it colored, but whatever gray she had blended in with the blond and you couldn't see it.

Jacques jumped out of the car as soon as he saw her. He was driving a dark blue convertible sports model Bentley. She grinned when she saw it, and he rushed over to give her a big hug and kiss her. He was a little heavier than before, but other than that, looked very much the same.

"What a pleasure to see you, Maddie," he said and sounded as though he meant it. The car was concrete proof of how far he had come and how popular his restaurants were. Unlike Bob Holland, she suspected that Jacques hadn't married it, he had made every penny himself and looked as though he was enjoying it thoroughly. His restaurant was only a few minutes from the hotel, and the valet took the car keys from him immediately and parked the car in front. Everyone greeted him warmly when they walked in. They had one of the best tables in the house reserved for him, and the sommelier appeared with a bottle of Cristal champagne as soon as they sat down.

"I'm so glad you called me," he said happily. "How are your children?"

"Busy, well, and happy." She smiled at him. He still had the same knack of making everything seem festive. They had always had a good time together. And as she glanced around, she saw that the restaurant was beautiful, with important con-temporary art hanging on the walls. There was a Damien Hirst right above their table, which Maddie noticed immediately.

"I have a daughter myself now," he said proudly.

"I think I saw a photograph of her on your website," she said, and he laughed mischievously.

"No, that is just a friend. Beautiful girl. From

Venezuela. My daughter is only eleven. I never married her mother, but we're good friends and I see her whenever I want to. I got them the apartment just below mine, so she can go back and forth between our two homes." It seemed like a sensible arrangement.

"You never married?" Maddie asked him as they sipped the champagne, and he smiled.

"I don't think marriage would suit me." That had been her conclusion too when they dated. Monogamy was definitely not his strong suit, at least not then.

"Are you still collecting women?" She teased him and he laughed in answer.

"They are my drug of choice. And you, Maddie? Did you marry again?" She shook her head.

"I'm not sure it would suit me anymore either. It's been a long time. And I do a lot of traveling for my work now. I'm away a lot, that's hard to do when you're married." He nodded agreement, and the headwaiter handed them the menus. There were no prices on the one he gave Maddie. At Masson, only gentlemen saw the prices of the meals. The food was all very high-level French haute cuisine **gastronomique,** and Maddie was sure it was delicious. He showed her a picture of his daughter, Paloma, then, and she was a beautiful child.

"Fortunately, she looks like her mother, not like

me. We spend a lot of time together, and I take her on trips with me. Her mother is a lingerie model, or she was. Now she stays home with our daughter." He was obviously providing a nice life for both of them. Even when he'd been poor when he first came to America with a green card and nothing else, he was a generous man. "Are you happy, Maddie?" he asked her after they ordered dinner. It was a question Bob Holland had never thought to ask her, because he was so unhappy himself. He had forgotten that some people were. But Jacques spread joy and pleasure around him like gifts.

"Sometimes," she said, looking pensive for a minute as she thought about it. "Sometimes I miss the old days when the kids were small and still at home. I hardly see them now, and Ben and Milagra live in California. I see them a couple of times a year. But my work is very rewarding. I still love what I do, more than ever." He smiled as she said it.

"You have such an enormous talent," he said admiringly.

"So do you. The restaurant is beautiful. You have a talent for great food and creating a wonderful atmosphere around you."

"I stop in all my restaurants every night. It makes a difference. And I'm in Vegas a lot. If you have time, I'll take you there. The restaurant is a lot of fun. It's pretty in Palm Beach too. I have a house there, but it's a little quiet for me. I want to open a Cuban restaurant in Miami next year, with dancing and a salsa band. Miami is hot!" He was always thinking about business, but he took time out to play too, sometimes a little too much so. She could easily guess that there were always women around him, in Miami, Las Vegas, and Chicago. "I became an American citizen last year," he said proudly. "I've been here for twenty years now. You were the first woman I ever went out with when I arrived."

"I remember," she said softly. "You hardly spoke English then." He still spoke with a heavy accent, but his vocabulary had improved immeasurably. He was an excellent businessman and had done extremely well, not as much so as Bob Holland, but she was sure that he hadn't sold out either. Jacques was true to himself.

"Where are you going on this driving trip of yours?" He was curious about it.

"I'm going to stop and see a friend in Wyoming, and maybe after that, I'll head to California to see my children there. I haven't figured it out yet. I have to be in Shanghai in four weeks. I'm relatively free until then."

"You should stay in Chicago for a while. It's a fun city." He reached for her hand and held it as he said it, and she felt the same warm thrill she had felt twenty years ago. He was sexy and warm, and attractive, and as they looked into each other's eyes, a beautiful, young woman in a sexy, half-naked dress walked over to their table and smiled at Jacques. She spoke to him in Spanish, and he answered her quickly. Maddie caught something about seeing her later, and meeting her at his apartment, and Maddie laughed as the young woman walked away.

"Did I screw up your plans for tonight?" He had been so quick to invite her to dinner, but she had dropped out of the sky with no notice, which really wasn't fair.

"Not at all," he said smoothly. "I haven't gone into religious orders since I've last seen you," he said, and they both laughed.

"I never thought you would. She's very pretty," and she seemed no more than twenty-five years old, or maybe less. He definitely had an eye for sexy, attractive women, and they flocked to him as they always had. He was at least thirty years older than this one.

"She's a sweet girl. We've been seeing each other for a few months. It's not serious. She has a boyfriend who works in Costa Rica. She likes to have a little fun when he's gone." Maddie couldn't help laughing as she listened to him. She had almost fallen for him again. One touch of the hand and she was attracted to him and felt like a woman again. Bob Holland had lost his soul and was no longer the man she'd known. And Jacques hadn't changed at all. There was something comforting about it in a way, and at the same time she knew that if she had let herself fall for him, he would do exactly what he had before, and cheat on her constantly. He couldn't help himself, it was just who he was and had remained.

She hadn't come on this trip to rekindle old flames, but she had been curious to see if any of the embers were still burning. And they could have been with Jacques, physically anyway, but he would have been as big a mistake for her now as he had been before. His morality was different from hers. And his needs. He needed a constant variety of women to keep him interested, and she knew that if she ever fell in love again, it would have to be with one man. She had always been that way, and she hadn't changed either. They would have run into all the same problems all over again. He hadn't slowed down, and, if anything, the girls he was attracted to were younger, as though they could share their youth with him.

He still found Maddie attractive too. He had always thought her a very sexy woman, and he still did. He liked her elegance and her style, her honesty and warmth and openness. She had never played games with him, and he knew where he stood with her. He liked that about her. She had been in love with him, but it hadn't been a lasting love for either of them. There hadn't been enough substance to it. They could both feel that again now. It would have been easy and immensely appealing to go to bed with him, but she knew she'd regret it later.

The meal at his new restaurant was excellent, and she let him talk her into going dancing with him afterwards. Maddie wondered if the pretty young girl was still waiting for him, and she couldn't dance much with her foot in a cast. They had fun together, and she felt young again being with him. He was reminding her of a part of her life that she thought she had put away forever. She hadn't been out dancing in years.

"Don't forget what an exciting woman you are, Maddie," he said to her when he drove her back to the hotel and parked off to the side. "You need a man in your life, even if you don't think so. Life isn't just about work and duty, your talent and your career. You have to play too. It used to be all about your children, then your work. It has to be about you now. You deserve that. Promise me you won't forget it." His words to her were a gift, and when he kissed her longingly, she didn't resist.

She floated up to her room afterwards, glad she

hadn't gone to bed with him, but happy he had kissed her. It would have been wrong to kiss Bob in Boston. He would easily cheat on his wife. But Jacques wasn't cheating on anyone. He was just a man who loved women, and they all knew it. Maddie was smiling when she went back to her room. She was sure he was on his way to the other girl by then, but she didn't care. He had given her a playful, tender memory to take with her, and a wise message. He had told her he was going to Las Vegas the next day. And she was heading for Wyoming, to face whatever she found there. It would be harder to see Andy again, knowing what they had shared. But so far, each of her past loves had bestowed a gift on her. Bob had freed her of any regrets or questions she had about her decision about him, and Jacques had made her feel like a woman again. She had no idea what she would find in Wyoming. But she knew she had to go there, if only to see Andy one more time, and then go back to her life in New York again, perhaps free of the past at last, or still in love with Andy. She was eager to get to Wyoming and find out.

Chapter 7

Maddie took her time driving west after she left Chicago. She liked the city, but she had nothing to do there after she saw Jacques, and she sensed that hanging around would only get her into trouble, and possibly back into a relationship or a fling that would go nowhere and shouldn't. Fortunately, he was going to Las Vegas anyway. He had invited her to join him there, but she'd feel ridiculous being part of his harem at her age, and he was more blatant about it now. He no longer hid his indiscretion and the women who were with him knew what to expect. There was always one who thought she would land him, but Maddie knew better. She couldn't imagine Jacques ever settling down, and being with a man who always had another woman stashed somewhere was disappointing and exhausting. She wasn't desperate for a man, but if she had any, she wanted one of her own, not one she had to share.

He had done something nice for her, though. She had become a work machine in the last ten or fifteen years. She was all about duty, giving her all to the latest assignment and pouring herself into it heart and soul, and then moving on to the next one. Sometimes she got off a plane in another city after taking a red-eye and went right to work. She was always proving that she could do it. Her life was a constant challenge and an endurance contest, and she had the stamina she needed to pull it off, even though she was exhausted some-times. But in the process, she had forgotten all about being a woman, intentionally at first. After Andy, she never wanted to love someone that much again. It had taken her years to get over him and not wake up feeling a lead weight on her heart every morning, the constant reminder of loss. By the time she was no longer in acute pain, she was too deep into her work to let herself care about anything else. She told herself she didn't need or want a man, or a tender touch. She saw the world through her camera lens, and nothing else. She had blinders on and kept them there.

Jacques's gentle words when they said goodbye the night before had let the light in, like opening the shutters on a window. She had forgotten how beautiful the sky could be, how thrilling the world was. Her photographs spoke of agony and loss, mothers, children, lovers, the wounds of grief were on their faces and tore at one's heart. She had forgotten about joy and laugher and a lighter touch. She had been serious for so long, steeled against the pain of leaving Andy, and now she was smiling as she drove along.

Jacques had always seemed a little foolish to her, and easily distracted, with his immense charm and roving eye, but he was smarter than she gave him credit for. He knew how to live and enjoy it. She wanted some of that back now. She had been more lighthearted when she'd met him, although even then, she had been focused on her children and trying to be a good parent. Too much so, Jacques always thought. The world seemed suddenly broader now and feeling her emotions was a relief. He had reminded her that she couldn't stay numb forever. She felt suddenly more alone now, not with gritted teeth holding on tightly, but with an open heart.

Once she was well out of Chicago, in open country, the beauty of the wheat fields caught her eye, mile after mile, as the gentle breezes moved them. She stopped in the early afternoon, and pulled over to take some pictures. She used a camera she'd brought along, and took a few with her phone to put on Instagram.

She felt peaceful as she saw the fields stretching to the horizon as far as the eye could see. There was a gentle solitude to it that wasn't painful for once. After she posted some of the photographs on Instagram, she got in the car, turned the music louder, and drove on. There was a message from Deanna on her phone, and she didn't bother to listen to it. She knew it would be about the benefit. It occurred to her that her daughter needed to learn how to let go of things, and so did she. Deanna was so intense. Maddie was just serious, but she didn't bludgeon people the way Deanna did. It wasn't an appealing trait in anyone, and made Deanna unpleasant to be around.

As Maddie got back on the highway, it was late morning in California and Ben saw the beautiful images of the wheat fields. They were different from the photographs she usually took. There were no people in them, no sense of suffering, and he had a feeling that she was at peace when she took them. He couldn't tell where she was now, somewhere in the Midwest in an agricultural area, and he wasn't sure where she was headed. He thought that maybe she was trying to prove something to herself, that she was not the lost soul and rapidly deteriorating elderly person that Deanna had told her she was. His mother was searching for something. What, he didn't know. When he checked her Instagram again late in the day, he saw a field of wildflowers that were a symphony of blue and yellow. Happiness exuded from the pictures, and a kind of unbound joy. It was an explosion of color beneath the bright blue sky, and he felt happy seeing them and sensed that she had been happy when she took them, instead of just wanting to give others pleasure. He hoped she found whatever it was she was looking for, either a person or inner peace, but he had a feeling she was on the right track now. He didn't try to call her, and left her on her journey without intruding. He wanted Deanna to do the same. Maddie had earned it. She had done so much for them. She needed something for herself now.

Maddie stopped at a motel that night, after driving for ten hours. She was tired but relaxed. The room was simple and clean, with no frills and an old TV. They charged her fifty dollars for the night, and she lay on the bed and looked around. She had stayed in a variety of places on her travels, in tents, in cabins, sleeping in the back of supply trucks in war zones, in huts or even barns with farm animals, in India and Pakistan, Tibet and Nepal, in Somalia and the Sudan. She had been in some of the poorest countries in the world and in palaces and here at home in America. The room was small and bare. It reminded her of a monastery she'd stayed in in Spain, where they took in pilgrims. It had what she needed, a bathroom, a shower, a bed, clean sheets, and in this case, the luxury of a TV. She turned it on and saw that there had been a shooting at a university in Mississippi, and she turned it off again. There was nothing she could do about it. She didn't want to see the tearful faces of shocked students mourning their friends, heartbroken parents, or bodies being taken away. She was on a mission of her own, and all she wanted right now was peace, and to heal her own wounded soul.

Deanna had taken away something important from her after she broke her ankle. She had robbed Maddie of her faith in the future, her confidence that everything would be okay. What Deanna had foretold was a descent into hell, the worst that Maddie could imagine, a loss of health and intelligence, purpose and freedom. Maddie couldn't imagine anything worse except the loss of her children. But the prospect of losing herself was frightening too. She needed to get away to find herself again, in a place where Deanna and her dire predictions couldn't reach her. She knew she couldn't let those dark things happen to her. She had run away when she left New York, but in the stark motel room, driving through the heart of America before that, and seeing the men she had once loved and no longer did, she had begun to find herself again. The broken ankle didn't matter to her, and it wasn't bothering her now. What was much more dangerous was that Deanna had tried to break her spirit and had overwhelmed her with fear. Maddie had started the trip longing for someone to protect her, and in the peace surrounding her, she remembered that she could protect herself, and she didn't intend to lose that again.

There was a truck stop near the motel, and she walked there to buy herself a sandwich, brought it back to the room, and ate it. There was no sound except the distant hum of trucks on the freeway, which lulled her to sleep after she finished eating and took a shower.

She woke in the morning, after a sound sleep, as sunlight streaked into the room. She dressed and left the key at the front desk. No one else was up yet, and she went back to the truck stop, had breakfast, then set off again. It was a gorgeous day. She saw that she had a text from Ben when she left the truck stop and opened it with some trepidation. She wondered if he was going to try to track her down. She didn't want them chasing her. She needed this time to herself.

"Beautiful pictures, Mom. I love you" was all he said. He asked no questions and she was relieved.

She didn't want to lie to him, or tell him where she was going and what she was doing.

"Thank you, I love you too," she answered, and drove off with a lighter heart.

She kept up a good speed on the road. She knew she had another ten hours of driving ahead of her if she wanted to get to Jackson Hole, Wyoming, by that night. It was the largest town closest to Andy's ranch. The ranch was forty miles out of town, according to her GPS. It was away from all the tourists and city slickers who came to Wyoming to say that they had been on a ranch, and to admire the magic and grandeur of the Teton mountain range. Maddie had been there with Andy years before. He'd taken her to the rodeo with him, she loved the honky-tonk of it, mixed in with the genuine aspects. The clowns, the steer ropers, the men who rode the bucking broncos hoping to win some money, the teenagers riding their horses, the rodeo queen on her best horse in her fanciest rodeo gear, wearing too much makeup and an earnest expression. She had taken wonderful pictures. And Maddie had cried when they sang "The Star Spangled Banner." It actually meant something there. But no matter how much she loved it, she was still a tourist, even with him, and she couldn't see herself living that life forever, any more than Andy would have survived on the streets of New

York. He would have been a lost soul forever, and she couldn't do that to him. He needed to exist in his natural habitat in order to thrive, and so did she. Wyoming wasn't it for her, no matter how beautiful it was or how much she loved him, and he loved her.

The terrain grew slowly more rugged, and the air cooler as she drove through the day. She had stopped to take pictures again along the way. There were bluffs and red clay hills where she could easily imagine Indians roaming, native villages, and war parties. She sat in the shade of a tree for a while and admired the scenery. There was nothing ominous or aggressive about it. Everywhere she looked, she had a sense of peace and beauty.

Ben could sense it with every photograph he looked at as he followed her journey. He didn't write to her again. Deanna had sent him an irritated text halfway through the day, so typical of her.

"What the hell is she doing?" He didn't bother to answer her, she wouldn't understand it anyway. For all her intelligence and talent in design, his sister was obtuse. She was too intent on herself to be able to relate to what anyone else was doing or feeling, particularly their mother.

As the terrain grew rockier and rougher, Ben suspected he knew where his mother was going. And as the mountains came into view, with their velvety purple sheen at sunset, he figured out who she was going to see. He remembered those mountains so well from his youth, and he had loved them too. He had been excited at the idea that they might live there one day, but he was involved with his student life at Berkeley, and it never happened. He had missed Andy afterwards too, but he'd had other things on his mind by then. He wondered now how long his mother had missed Andy, maybe all seventeen years since he'd gone out of her life. He hoped not, for her, but suddenly thought it might be true. He didn't want to bother her, she was obviously doing something important to her. There was a sacred quality to her pictures now, almost like a religious experience. They were deeply spiritual, and the mood seemed very private and intimate to him, maybe because he knew her so well. To others, they would just be beautiful photographs, and to his sister they were a total mystery.

She got to Jackson Hole at nine o'clock that night, and drove past the shops and restaurants, and tourist traps selling souvenirs. There were a dozen dude ranches in the surrounding area, and she drove ten miles out of town to Moose, where she found a small bed and breakfast, took a room, and then she went out for a walk and looked up at the mountains. She could see their shape against the night sky in all their grandeur. They were as majestic as she remembered, and as she sat on a log, the sky filled with stars. She saw two fall as she sat there, and the Big Dipper was as clear as though a child had drawn it. She saw the Milky Way, and the lesser-known constellations Andy had taught her. She hadn't thought of them in years. But she was here now, in his country, and in her mind, those stars belonged to him and were part of him and the magic he'd brought her. She had loved everything about his life, except the fact that he wanted to stay here, and she knew she couldn't. It had been the only bone of contention between them. Everything else had worked perfectly, for more than a year. And then she walked away from it. She regretted it now, but there had been no other choice then, nor was there now, so there should be nothing to regret, except that she did.

She hadn't realized then that being alone after she left him would mean she would die alone one day, or fall down the stairs and injure herself, as Deanna said she would, or end up in assisted living. She hadn't known or cared that it meant she would live alone for seventeen years after him, and wake up every day, except for rare, occasional nights, with half the bed unused, that no one would ask how her day was, or make her laugh at small stupid things, or make the future seem less frightening, and no one would want to know what her dreams were. Not wanting another serious man in her life meant that she would grow old alone, and already was, with no one to share her life with and make the remaining years as meaningful as the earlier ones had been.

She had thought leaving him meant making her own rules, doing what she wanted without considering someone else, and living in a city that was familiar to her. But it meant so much more. It meant having to be brave all the time, and carrying the full load herself, not having someone to share her burdens with, or her joys. She hadn't fully understood the meaning of the word "alone" or what it would feel like day after day for seventeen years, and for the rest of her life, if she wasn't brave enough to share her life again. Loving him had meant risking pain, and losing him had been so much bigger and worse than she had anticipated. And yet it was the choice she had made, and he had respected it. He had never tried to come back, nor did she. Once she was on her solitary path, whether out of stubbornness or pride, she had stayed on it. And now she wanted to face him again. She wasn't even sure what she'd say when she saw him, or why she had come. But a force stronger than she was had propelled her toward him, across the country and the years, and now she was here.

She wondered what he would say to her and what it had been like for him. They hadn't spoken in seventeen years, since a little while after she left. She had still been young then, although she didn't realize it, and now, after the fall off the ladder, she felt so old, as Deanna said she was. And Jacques said she wasn't. She no longer knew which was true.

She walked back to the bed and breakfast, with the mountains seeming so close. She could almost feel them breathing, they were so alive. They had a soul, just as Andy had said to her. She lay down on the bed with her clothes on when she got back to her room and fell asleep.

It took all the courage she had to get up the next morning, knowing what she was going to do. There was no avoiding it now. She had to face what she'd been running from for all these years, how much she loved him and needed him, or thought she did. She had been afraid of that, that she'd become dependent on him, and lose herself in Andy's shadow. He was a big man, although he never forced her to do anything, and had a deep respect for her, enough to let her go when she wanted him to, no matter what it cost him.

She stood under the shower for a long time, trying to clear her mind. She was too nervous to eat breakfast and dressed carefully. She had found her old cowboy boots in the back of her closet in

New York and put the right one on. The boots were just worn enough not to make her look like a New Yorker trying to be cool on a ranch, which he had teased her about when he first met her and the boots were new. They had aged nicely in her many trips to see him for over a year. And she had brought the kids to the ranch for a second time before their relationship ended. Ben had been disappointed when she told him it was over. The girls didn't care as much, although they liked him too.

She drove thirty miles from Moose, in the direction the GPS told her Andy's ranch was. It was in the foothills of the Tetons, and the area was beautiful. She left the houses and small B and B's behind her after the first few miles, and to buy a little time so she could compose herself, she stopped and took some pictures. There was a deer standing in a clearing and another one in the tall grass, they didn't move when they saw her. She remembered with ease that Andy always knew what she was thinking, and understood her better than she understood herself. She had no idea what she would tell him about why she was there, but he would sense it without words. She didn't know if she had come back to him, she didn't think so, but she needed to see him. It was visceral, more than any decision she had made.

The entrance to the ranch was simple but

impressive, with his brand emblazoned on a wooden archway. Their website said it was one of the biggest horse ranches in Wyoming, which had been his dream. She didn't know how he had done it, but she was proud of him. The website said it had been in existence for a dozen years.

There were neat outbuildings, and a big barn, several corrals, and three stone houses, one with a sign that said "Office." Horses were everywhere, galloping through fields. Her heart was pounding when she parked the car and walked up the steps of the building marked "Office." It looked like a serious operation, and there were ranch hands going about their business, some taking horses to the barn on lead lines, others loading them into trailers to go somewhere. Andy sold horses, and there was an auction on the premises once a month, according to the website. There was a large parking lot, which suggested that the auctions were well attended.

A woman at the desk glanced up at Maddie and smiled.

"I'm here to see Mr. Wyatt. He's not expecting me. I'm an old friend," she said, sounding nervous to her own ears.

"Of course. I'll get him right away," the woman said, stood up, and disappeared before Maddie could say her name. She left Maddie to sit in one of the big comfortable chairs in the waiting room. There was nothing showy about the office, but it seemed efficient and businesslike, and several people walked past her. She walked outside to get some air and admire the horses. The website said he sold Arabians, among others, and she could identify them as she waited for Andy to appear.

She could feel her heart pound, and after a few minutes, she saw a familiar shape loping toward her with his distinctive walk, she would have recognized him anywhere. His battered hat with the wide brim was pulled down low over his face the way he always wore it, and she stood smiling as she watched him. Just seeing him was like coming home, and when he was a few feet from her, he turned his face toward her, and she realized with a shock that it wasn't him. It was a younger face, so similar to Andy's but different. The man looked serious and familiar, and she slowly realized that it was his son, Sean. He was as surprised as she was. She realized that she hadn't specified to the woman which Mr. Wyatt she wanted to see, Sean or his father, and she had called the wrong one.

"Sean?" Maddie smiled at him, and his smile slowly reached his eyes when he recognized her. "You're all grown up." She remembered that he was a year younger than Milagra, which made him thirty-two now. She hadn't seen him since he was fifteen. He looked so much like his father that it was easy to recognize him.

"Maddie?" He was stunned. "What are you doing here?" He knew she was famous now, his father had told him and showed him pictures she'd taken over the years. She hesitated before she answered the question.

"I came to see your father. It's been a long time."

He nodded, and didn't say anything for a minute, and then waved her to a wide porch so they could sit down. She followed him up the steps, and they each took a seat in two big wicker chairs. And then he looked at her, with tears in his eyes.

"It would have meant a lot to him, but he probably wouldn't have wanted to see you at the end. He died two months ago. It went fast, he wasted away pretty quickly. Did you hear he was sick?" She felt as though a wrecking ball had just hit her heart, or a sledgehammer. She had come too late, fate had intervened.

"No, I didn't," she said in a choked voice, too stunned to speak at first. "I just wanted to see him. I know it's been a lot of years, too many. I'm so sorry. I wish I had come sooner. The ranch is beautiful, he must have been so proud of it."

"He was," Sean said. "He saved every penny to buy it. It was in foreclosure, and he got a good deal. He was pretty tight with a buck," Sean went on, grinning. "He had some money put away and we scraped up the rest, and we've been building on it for the last twelve years. We've been doing well," he finished proudly.

"I can see that." She was still in shock, realizing that she had missed Andy by two months. Their meeting wasn't meant to be.

"He never stopped loving you, you know," Sean said gently. "He talked about you a lot. There was a woman he hung out with. She runs a restaurant in town, but she always said the same thing. They were good friends, but he wasn't in love with her. He was in love with you. He said you did the right thing. He would never have had this if he had moved to New York, and he couldn't have lived there. You would have hated our first few years here. We lived in an old bunkhouse in the barn with no heat and no plumbing for the first two years, until we could afford to put in electricity and indoor plumbing into his house. We built my house two years after that. And we built the office five years ago. It's still a work in progress even now. But we've got the best horses in the state. My dad really knew horseflesh. He never thought it would grow to be as big an operation as it is now, our auctions pull in people from half a dozen states. They're a big deal." He looked like a kid again as he said it. "It's going to be hard now, running it without him."

"You can do it," Maddie said gently. "He had a lot of faith in you, even as a kid."

"I know he did." He blushed and pushed his hat far back on his head, the way Andy used to when he talked to her on the ranch where he worked and she first met him. "I hope I can live up to it," Sean said. "I'm married and have two kids now, with two more on the way. We're having twins in a month, if they wait that long." He smiled at Maddie, and she felt tears well up in her eyes. She had cheated them out of the rest of their lives together, or had she? Sean said that Andy thought she had done the right thing. He had the ranch he always wanted and his son working with him, and grandchildren. And what would she have done here? She didn't belong here, no matter how much she loved him, and he knew it too. "We have two boys," Sean added, "the twins are girls. My wife will have her hands full. She helps us out in the office, but she won't be able to for a while. Her mom helps us with the boys, but four will be a lot for her to manage, or us for that matter." He smiled nervously as he said it, still startled that he was soon to be the father of four.

"Ben has three kids, and he lives in San Francisco. Deanna has two girls."

"Milagra?" He had had a huge crush on her, which Andy and Maddie used to chuckle about when they were alone. Milagra had played the femme fatale with him, and liked him too, even though she would never have admitted it. He was a year younger than she was.

"She lives in Mendocino and writes weird gothic books." Maddie smiled at him. "She isn't married." Maddie always had the feeling she never would be, but didn't say it to him. She was too immersed in her gothic world and involved with herself and her menagerie of stray dogs and cats. And by no stretch of the imagination could Maddie imagine her as a mother of four, or even one child, let alone twins. Maybe they had all made the right choices.

She had wanted the best for Andy, and in trying to respect him and be honest with herself, she had stepped away and allowed him to follow his dream. And she had followed her own dreams too. She had wished he could be part of them, but he couldn't. They weren't meant to be together, only to love each other, which was a great deal to both of them. Their love had lasted for eighteen years, more than most people ever got to share. They would have torn each other apart if they had tried to force things and stayed together. She could see that more clearly than ever now, sitting on the porch with Sean and looking out over the ranch Andy had built, some of it with his own hands, and all of it with his perseverance, sacrifices, and ingenuity. It had been a labor of love for him.

"Can I show you around?" Sean asked her shyly, and she nodded. She followed him off the porch, and he took her through their horse barns, past the breeding pens, which were a growing operation. They went through all the buildings, and he got in his truck and drove her to the far reaches of the property, and the entire time the mountains were standing behind them, like a mystical blessing over the whole ranch.

"Your father loved those mountains," Maddie said as she looked at everything with him, and could feel Andy everywhere.

"Yes, he did. He went riding up there the day before he died. I think he was saying goodbye to them. I always feel like he's up there somewhere now," Sean said in a gruff voice and Maddie nodded.

"He's always with you, Sean. He always will be." Andy had breathed life into the ranch.

"With you too, Maddie, he always was. It would have killed him to move to New York. I'm sorry you couldn't be together, but he was meant to be here."

"I knew that then. It was just shit luck that our lives were so different."

"I don't know. Maybe that's a good thing. You brought something special to each other. He always said that he was braver because of you."

She smiled at the thought. "I think I was braver because of him too. I had to make my dreams happen, to justify not staying with him."

He nodded. "My wife, Becky, and I went to high school together. Sometimes that keeps things small. She went to Cheyenne afterwards and got her CPA. She does the books for me. And her brothers work on the ranch here. It's kind of a family operation. That's what you need here. People you can trust. Selling horses can be a risky business."

"So can life," Maddie said quietly. She was still shaken by the idea that Andy had died two months earlier, and she had missed him. It shocked her to realize that a man she had loved so much was dead now. That made her feel old too, although he had been eight years older than she was. He was sixty-six, too young to die.

After the tour, Sean stopped his truck outside one of the two stone houses. "Dad and I rebuilt these houses with our own hands. Some of the other buildings were here, and falling down when we bought the place. We fixed them up, and remodeled them, put in insulation, new roofs, heating, plumbing, all of it. I'm going to have to add on to this one next spring. We're going to turn Dad's into more offices. We need them, to run the auctions. It's a lot to keep track of." He looked slightly overwhelmed, but he had only been running the place on his own for two months, and he was young.

Maddie followed him up the front steps, and into the house as he called out to Becky. She was in the kitchen feeding the boys lunch. Sean's oldest son was five, and had just gotten home from school for lunch, and his little brother was two. Becky stood up, smiling at them, and Maddie had never seen anyone so pregnant. Sean explained to her who Maddie was, and she looked touched immediately.

"I'm sorry, Maddie. I've heard so much about you. Sean's dad talked about you a lot." Maddie nodded, fighting back tears again. "Would you like some lunch?"

"I'll get it," Sean said immediately. "She's supposed to be resting," Sean explained to Maddie. "She never does, but it's okay now if the twins come early. They'll be fine, although the doctor would like them to stay where they are for another two weeks, if possible, for their lungs."

"Both of the boys weighed ten pounds when they were born, and the doctor says the girls weigh eight pounds now, so we'll be good," Becky added. Her arms and legs were slim, and she had a pretty girl-next-door face with big blue eyes. Her long blond hair was in a braid down her back. She was beautiful, and probably had a trim figure when she wasn't carrying sixteen pounds of baby. The thought of it made Maddie wince. "I'm ready," she said, as Sean put two turkey sandwiches on the table with a bowl of potato chips, and Maddie thanked him and helped herself to one of them. They were a sweet family and she could imagine how much Andy must have enjoyed them, and seeing his son happy. It must have been wonderful building the ranch together. It really had been his dream.

Maddie chatted with the two children and Becky and Sean all through lunch. Sean showed her around the house they had built. The boys shared a room and the twins would too until he added on to the house in a year or two, when he had time to do it. Maddie stopped in the living room for a minute and looked intently at a framed photograph of Andy, leaning against one of the corrals, beaming at the camera, with his favorite hat on, and his weathered cowboy boots. The picture was pure Andy, and he seemed like he was smiling at her.

"We had just sold the best horse we'd ever sold at auction, for the highest price anyone's ever gotten around here. It was last year, right before he got sick. I think it was one of the happiest days of his life." Sean reached out and grabbed the photograph then and handed it to her. "You should have it. He would want you to. I've got others." Maddie instinctively hugged it to her as though she were hugging him. Then she leaned over and kissed Sean on the cheek.

"Thank you," she said in a whisper, as Becky went to put the boys down for their naps. She was back five minutes later. They were sweet, well-behaved children and reminded Maddie of Ben's boys, Willie and Charlie. Sean's oldest was named Andrew for his grandfather, and his little brother was Johnny. They hadn't decided on names for the girls yet. They wanted to see them first, Becky said.

Maddie thanked her for lunch, and she and Sean walked outside. He had to get back to work. He had spent three hours with her, and she was grateful for the warm reception. It wasn't the visit she had expected, but it felt right and the way it was intended to happen. She was still holding the photograph in her arms, when he walked her back to the SUV.

"Thank you, for everything, for all the things you said," she said softly.

"You meant so much to my dad, Maddie, along with his family and this ranch. He never stopped loving you," and she hadn't stopped loving him either. She wished she could have seen him again, but she knew he had died happy, and had his dream. Sometimes that was all you got, some dreams weren't meant to come true, and theirs hadn't, but this was close enough. She and Sean hugged tightly for a long time, and then she got into her car and carefully put Andy's photo on the floor of the passenger seat so nothing would happen to it.

"Stay in touch, and come back whenever you want," Sean invited her.

"You too." She had left her numbers with Becky. "Let me know when the twins come."

He nodded. "I'm thinking Madison Wyatt has a nice ring to it." He smiled at her, and she realized instantly that it would have been her name if she'd married Andy. But at least there would be a Madison Wyatt after all, if they used her name.

He waved as she drove away, and her heart caught as she passed through the gates of the ranch. She stopped and looked back at everything he had built and loved so much, with the mountains watching over them. He had had the life he wanted. She got out and took a picture of it, and then she got back in the car and drove away. It was the last stop on her pilgrimage and the most important one. Even though they hadn't been together, she knew that Andy was happy at last. Maybe that was what she had needed to know, that she hadn't ruined his life by leaving him. She had freed him to follow his dreams, while she followed hers. They each had their own paths to follow and destinies to fulfill, and they had.

Chapter 8

After she left the ranch, Maddie went back to the B and B to pack. She had no reason to stay in the area after that. She had done what she came to do. She hadn't seen Andy, but she had seen his family and his ranch, and knew the answers to all that she had wondered about for so long. She had a bittersweet sense of loss that she had missed him only by weeks. But she had learned everything she needed to know. She was exhausted, but at peace. She set his photograph on the night-stand and fell asleep. She felt him watching over her, and it was late afternoon when she woke up.

She could have stayed another night there, but she didn't want to. She didn't want to bother Becky and Sean by inviting them to dinner. They had a ranch to run, two young children, and were expecting twins any minute. She didn't want to be an imposition. It was time to move on. She wasn't sure where to go now. She had left herself plenty of time to stay at the ranch, if things turned out the way she had hoped. She hadn't expected that to happen, but she had given herself and Andy the space to explore the options if they wanted to. She'd never expected Andy would be gone at his age. It was a reminder to her that death was not predictable. According to Sean, a year before, Andy had been vital, active, and healthy, and had gotten sick almost overnight with pancreatic cancer. It had ravaged him in a matter of months. It made every moment seem that much more precious and she realized too that Andy wouldn't have wanted her to see him that way after so long. Maybe she had arrived at the right time after all, if she hadn't come back years earlier, when it might have made a difference. But even then it wouldn't have been possible. It never was, from the moment they met. It was an impossible love for both of them. And finally time had run out.

She remembered a trip they had taken to Big Sur once, and she had loved it. She decided to go there now, in tribute to him. She consulted her phone and saw that it was an eleven-hundred-mile drive, and would take seventeen or eighteen hours. She could make it in one day if she drove hard on a route through Sacramento, but she had time on her hands and didn't need to rush. After a few days, she could visit Ben and his family in San Francisco, if they had time. Big Sur was only a few hours south of San Francisco, and an easy drive.

She loved the surf and the dramatic coastline around Big Sur. It seemed like a fitting place to honor Andy and gather her thoughts. They had stayed at the Post Ranch Inn, a beautiful, secluded place. They had gone on long walks together and talked about their future, which never happened in the end. And now it seemed a suitable place to end her trip to see him. There would be a sense of closure to it that was right, now that she knew he was gone.

She felt more peaceful than she had at the beginning of the trip, when her thoughts were in turmoil after what Deanna had said. It had all begun with finding the box of old photographs and letters that had led her back to all three men, then falling off the ladder and breaking her ankle. She felt steady again now, and sure of herself. She hadn't spoken to Deanna since she left and didn't want to. But she had a sure sense now that Deanna couldn't force her to do anything she didn't want to do. Maddie was the master of her own destiny, and of how she wanted to spend the remaining years of her life.

She remembered Jacques's words not to forget that she was an exciting woman, and that she needed more in her life than she had allowed herself to have in so many years. She would have been tempted to try again with Andy. She admitted to herself now that it had been in the back of her mind, but it would have been no more right for them now than it had been eighteen years ago when they met. His family's life on the ranch was warm and wonderful and rewarding, but it wasn't for her. She and Andy both knew it, or one of them would have reached out long before now, but they never had. She was a free woman again, in a way she hadn't been for the past seventeen years. She felt stronger and less alone than she had in a long time.

She put the photographs of the ranch on Instagram before she left the B and B and she got a text from Ben quickly.

"How's Andy?" He didn't want to intrude but he was curious, and hopeful for her now. He had gotten a sense of how solitary she was, and wanted something good to happen to her, before any of Deanna's predictions for her future could come true. He didn't want her to be alone anymore.

Maddie answered him as gently as she could, not sure if it would upset him or not. "He died two months ago. The ranch is wonderful. Sean sends you his love. He has two little boys and is expecting twins any minute. Sweet wife."

Ben took a few minutes to gather his wits before he answered. He could only imagine how she felt, especially if this entire odyssey had been to see him.

"I'm so sorry, Mom. Are you okay?"

"Sorry I missed him, and very sad," she answered, "but things turned out as they were meant to. The ranch was his dream. It's perfect."

"You were his dream too."

"I'm okay," she reassured him. "Shocked at first."

"Where to now? Staying for a while?"

"No. Big Sur. Any interest in a visit from me, five days or a week from now? No pressure. I understand if you're too busy."

"Not too busy. I'd love it. Let me know when. Can't wait to see you," he said, and he meant it. He felt as though he had gotten to know her better through her photographs in the last week on her Instagram. He suddenly had a deeper insight into her solitude, who she was, and what she wrestled with every day.

He told Laura about the visit when he got home from the office that night and she looked instantly uncomfortable.

"I just don't think that's going to work. We're

out almost every night for the next two weeks. I'm on the host committee of two major benefits only a few days apart. The kids are getting out of school soon, and we're going to Hawaii the day they get out. We have a lot to do before then." He looked at her in a way he never had before.

"Why don't you want my mother here?" he asked bluntly.

"I didn't say that. I love having your mother visit, and so do the kids. We're just so busy in the next few weeks, maybe another time." As he listened to her, he realized how often he had let her convince him to fob his mother off and postpone her trips to San Francisco so that they never happened, and he wasn't going to let it happen once more.

"She's had a tough time for the last few weeks. I'm not postponing a visit from her again. You can take someone else to the benefits, if you need to. My mother needs to visit us more than once or twice a year. We see your parents all the time." It was the first time he had objected to the imbalance between how often they saw her family versus his mother. And Laura didn't like hearing it. She was furious when he told her he might not go to the benefits so he could spend time with his mother.

"I'll try to make it work," she said, visibly annoyed about it, and Ben shook his head as he stared at her. There was a steely determination in his eyes she had never seen before and didn't like.

"No, Laura. Not this time. Don't try to make it work. Just do it." And with that he turned on his heel and walked out of the room.

He called Deanna that night to tell her where their mother was, and that she was okay.

"She's in Wyoming. She went to see Andy Wyatt and found out when she got there that he died two months ago." He sounded somber when he said it.

"Is that what all this mystery has been about? Visiting an old boyfriend? She must be desperate. He was never suitable for her."

"They loved each other," Ben said simply.

"That tells you that she's not all there mentally. Why would she go to see an old boyfriend from twenty years ago? What does she need with that now? Thank God she didn't marry him, she'd have been buried out in Wyoming somewhere. That's not her style." As usual, Deanna was harsh and unsympathetic. Ben was as annoyed with her as he was with his wife. He was Maddie's only ally.

"He was a good guy." He was touched by Andy's death and knew how Maddie must have felt when she heard about it.

"She'd have been miserable there," Deanna said sharply. "She knew it too. She knew what she was doing when she left him."

"Maybe she's not desperate, but she's lonely, Dee. I think that's why she went to see him."

"To exhume the past?"

"Maybe just to touch it again, before you put a geriatric alarm around her neck and kick her out of the house she loves."

"You can't blame it all on me. She's getting old."

"Not that old. Maybe she wants a man in her life. She's not too old for that."

"I was thinking more like a nurse."

"I'm thinking like a boyfriend. Don't be such a hard-ass."

"She'll have to face reality at some point."

"Not yet. And hopefully not for a long time. We need to try harder now. I hardly ever see her. You never do either, or not enough, and you live in the same city. She never sees Milagra. And she never complains about any of it. What good is having three kids if you never see them?" He felt acutely guilty after following her Instagram for the last week. Her solitude shrieked from the images.

"We're busy, and so is she."

"We also have young kids and spouses. **All** she has now is her work. That's not enough."

"Well, thank God she didn't go off with the cowboy again."

"Why? What difference would it make to you?

I'd rather know she's happy. I don't care who she's with. That's her business, not ours."

"Don't be such a romantic. She doesn't need a boyfriend at her age."

"Why not? Maybe she does. I hope she finds whatever she's looking for."

"I still think this trip was crazy, and maybe she's getting senile. This could be the first sign."

"That's the furthest thing she is."

He hung up a few minutes later, even more annoyed with her. Deanna was refusing to see their mother as a human being facing a hard time in life. It shocked him and made him sad for his mother that he was the only one who saw it and cared how she felt. His heart ached for her now.

Maddie wasn't thinking of her daughter, or her son, as she checked out of the B and B. She was thinking of Andy, and Sean and his children. She was glad she had gone to visit them. She had a long drive ahead now to Big Sur, but she was looking forward to it.

She took more photographs of the mountains and the light before she drove out of town and found her way to the freeway. It was sunset by then, and she got some beautiful shots. They seemed to symbolize the end of the story, and Maddie wondered, as Ben had, if the trip to Andy's ranch and beloved mountains had given her closure at last.

She felt quiet and peaceful as she drove south. She didn't put the music on. She just wanted to drive for a while, thinking of him. She had put his photograph in her suitcase, wrapped in a sweater so the glass wouldn't break. It had been the nicest gift Sean could give her.

She had driven three hundred miles when she stopped at one A.M. and checked in to a small motel in Nevada. The countryside around it looked barren, and there was a single slot machine in the lobby. She had another long drive ahead of her, about eleven or twelve hours, and so she left at six A.M. She stopped for coffee an hour later, and drove steadily through the day, only stopping when she had to.

She drove along the coast road once she got to Big Sur. The waves were crashing around the rocks. There was a wisp of fog over the ocean, and the sun was lowering slowly in the sky. She stopped and sat looking at it for a long time. The air was cool, and she loved the sound of the ocean. It had been the right place to come. Her mind was full of memories of Andy, the trip they had made there, other places they'd been, his visit to New York, the things they had said to each other, the promises they'd made.

It all washed over her like the ocean, and then swept away like the tide.

She felt cleansed, and whole again. She wasn't frightened of what lay ahead, no matter what Deanna said. Her threats seemed irrelevant now. She felt brave again, and her solitude didn't scare her. She was used to it. Her life would be no different now than it had been for seventeen years without Andy. The only difference was that in the back of her mind she no longer clung to the thought that she could go back to him one day, if she wanted to. He was truly gone now, but she felt ready to face it. And whatever the future held, she would deal with it, alone, as she had for most of her life. The possibility of sharing a life with Andy in the end had been an illusion. She knew that now. She had her children and her work, and whatever life chose to put in her path. She was strong enough to deal with it, just as she always had been. She had found her strength again.

She started the car and drove to the hotel then. The hotel was as beautiful and peaceful as she had remembered it. She was shown to a room with a view of the Pacific. There was a path leading to other parts of the property and hiking trails in the area. She couldn't hike on uneven terrain in her walking cast, but she could go for walks on terra firma, and sit and watch the ocean for hours.

She ordered dinner in her room that night, but planned to eat in the dining room the next day. It was a romantic spot, a destination for couples, and she suspected she might be the only one there alone, but she was used to it. It was the reality of her life, had been for a long time, and maybe would be forever, but she wasn't going to let that spoil it for her.

She set Andy's photograph on the dresser when she unpacked. She had taken the room for five nights. She would go to San Francisco after that, to see Ben and his family, and maybe on to visit Milagra. But first she wanted to soak in the atmosphere of tranquility around her. There were massages and spa treatments. It was all part of the healing process, which was why she had come here.

She had come a long way since she'd left New York: to Boston, to see Bob Holland, Jacques in Chicago, and she had laid the memory of Andy to rest on his ranch in Wyoming. Now she was in Big Sur, alone and at peace, ready for whatever came next.

Chapter 9

Maddie took full advantage of everything the Post Ranch Inn offered: the less strenuous trails because of the cast on her ankle, the views of the ocean, a massage on her first day there. She felt thoroughly spoiled and pampered. She drove a little way to the next town on the first afternoon. She felt rested and relaxed, although there was still a lingering sadness over Andy's death, as much for him as for herself, but she didn't let it pull her down.

She stopped at a little coffee shop for a cappuccino before going back to the Post Ranch Inn. She took it outside, sat at a small table in the sunshine, and noticed a man a few tables away reading a British newspaper. People came from all over to enjoy the coastline and the ocean. He didn't notice her and was reading avidly as she sipped her coffee and looked out at the Pacific. There were whitecaps and a cool breeze. She was thinking of all the places she had been in the last week. It had been an interesting odyssey, even more so than she'd hoped, and she had laid all her old ghosts to rest. She felt freer than she had in years.

She finished her cappuccino and walked past the man reading the English newspaper. He looked up when she did, and smiled at her. She smiled back and nodded, then went to take more pictures and drove back to the hotel.

She ate in the hotel restaurant, then read in her room and went to bed early. The next day, when she had driven to a spot to take photographs, she found a trail that led down to the beach and she followed it. She walked along the ocean for a while, although it was hard on the sand with her cast. She was surprised when she crossed paths with a man going in the opposite direction. He smiled and looked familiar, and she realized it was the Englishman from the coffee shop. She smiled back. It was a windy day and her hair was flying around her. He had his collar up in the stiff breeze. She eventually decided to go back to her car and return to the hotel. It was harder to negotiate the trail going up than down with her cast. She wasn't making much progress when she heard a voice with a British accent behind her.

"Can I give you a hand?" She turned and saw the same man. He hadn't wanted to frighten her, but had been watching her struggle for a while, not sure whether to offer to help her or not. "You're at a bit of a disadvantage with the cast." He smiled at her. She hesitated and then nodded, and he stepped up to where she was, gave her a strong arm to lean on, and half pulled her up the hill as she laughed and felt awkward.

"It wasn't this hard on the way down," she said to cover her own embarrassment. "It's coming off in a couple of weeks. It's easier to navigate on even ground."

"I would think so. Not a skiing accident, I assume, at this time of year." He was tall and slim and athletic-looking, and appeared to be somewhere in his mid-fifties, with salt-and-pepper hair. He had laugh lines around his eyes, which were a deep blue.

"No, a very stupid household accident. I fell off a ladder." But it had turned out to be providential after all, given everything she had done since then.

"Are you down from San Francisco?" he asked her. They were halfway up the hill by then, and it hadn't been easy so far, but he was strong and pulling her along with a firm hand under one arm. She felt a little silly, but she was grateful for the assistance. She might have been stranded on the beach otherwise.

"No, New York," she answered, slightly out of breath from the effort.

"Did you fly in to San Francisco or L.A.?" he asked, making friendly chitchat to cover the awkwardness of dragging her uphill, while she thanked him for the help.

"Neither one. I drove down from Wyoming yesterday. I started from New York."

"That's adventurous," he said, looking impressed.

"I visited friends along the way."

"That's quite a drive. Are you driving back?"

She shook her head. "I have a son in San Francisco, I'm flying back from there. Are you here from London?"

"No." He smiled at her again. He'd been trying to admire her discreetly. She was a very attractive woman. "I live here. In a small cottage. I'm a writer. Big Sur is a good place to write." It made her think of Milagra in Mendocino, which was similarly foggy and windy with a rugged coastline. Writers seemed to be drawn to moody places of the sort.

"What do you write?" Maddie asked.

"History. Biographies, mostly. Very British," he said with a wry smile. "Nothing so amusing as a novel."

"I have a daughter who's a writer. Gothic novels." He nodded, and they both gave a major effort as they got to the top of the hill and back on the path where she had started. "Thank you!" she said again, out of breath. "They probably would have had to airlift me off the beach if you hadn't come along." She laughed, and he smiled.

"Could I interest you in a glass of wine sometime before you leave?" He didn't usually pick up women, but there was something he liked about her. She had an easy, friendly style and a sense of humor.

"That would be very nice," she said. She didn't want to brush him off after he'd been so helpful, and he looked pleasant and interesting.

"Or a cappuccino if you prefer," he offered.

"Wine would be fine."

"Tomorrow then?" He suggested a little place in town as he walked her to her car and she unlocked it. She didn't normally talk to strangers in circumstances like that, on a lonely road, but she wasn't afraid of him. He seemed respectable and kind. "Five o'clock?"

"That's perfect." She smiled at him again. "See you then. And thank you for the damsel-in-distress rescue."

"Anytime." He watched her get into the car and

she drove away, and then realized they hadn't introduced themselves. She didn't know his name, but it didn't matter, since she was seeing him the next day.

She stuck to flat walking trails after that, and called Penny the next day. Nothing exciting was happening in the office, and Deanna had stopped calling, which was a relief. It was the first time Maddie had ever been relatively unavailable to her children for any length of time. She was always accessible to them. But Deanna had been too harsh with her, to the point of being toxic and certainly not compassionate, and Maddie and Ben had been texting. So she wasn't totally MIA, though she hadn't heard from Milagra in weeks, which wasn't unusual. Maddie was planning to send her an email before she left Big Sur, to see if she wanted a visit after Maddie saw Ben. There was no predicting what Milagra would say. It all depended on where she was with her current book.

Maddie arrived at the wine bar at the appointed hour, right on schedule, and her rescuer was already waiting for her at the entrance.

"I'm terribly sorry," he said, "I forgot to introduce myself yesterday, William Smith. I was so dazzled by you, I forgot my own name."

"So did I. Madison Allen." They shook hands and sat down at a table near a lit fire on an outdoor terrace. "I was hardly dazzling huffing up the hill, while you almost had to carry me."

"You do a very creditable damsel in distress. I was quite impressed," as she had been with him. He seemed easygoing and likable. "So what made you drive across the country from New York?" He was curious and she decided to be honest with him. She had no reason not to be, and she'd probably never see him again after she left Big Sur. She'd only been there twice in eighteen years.

"Ghosts," she answered simply.

"Ghosts? A research project? A book? Are there ghosts in Wyoming?" He was amused and she smiled.

"I was visiting them. Three friends across the country whom I hadn't seen in a long time."

He got the drift and was intrigued by it. "Men, I assume." She nodded. He was beginning to find her a very interesting woman, and certainly a brave, independent one to drive cross-country alone. "Were they good ghosts or bad ghosts?"

She looked amused by the question. "Originally, good ghosts, or at least I thought so. I hadn't seen them in twenty years or more. One of them had turned to the dark side, and I think is quite a bad ghost now. The second one is kind of a silly ghost. Naughty, but harmless. The third one was a very good ghost, but I didn't see him. He died two months before I got there." She was serious when she said it, and he nodded, touched by what she said.

"Oh, I'm so sorry. That must have been a bit of a nasty shock, if you didn't know before."

"I didn't. But I had a very nice visit with his son and daughter-in-law."

"What made you want to look them up after so long?" Ever the historian and researcher. She could tell he was a writer by the questions he asked. The question was very personal but she answered anyway.

"I'm not sure," she said, honest with him again. "I found a box full of their old letters, and I thought it was time to lay old ghosts to rest, as they say, and answer some questions I had myself."

"And did you get the answers?"

"Yes, I did, actually."

"Do you feel better?"

"I do. Sad about my friend in Wyoming, but things happen as they are meant to." She had said the same thing to Ben, and she believed it.

William nodded when she said it. "I believe that too, although sometimes that's hard to swallow, if things don't go the way we want."

"It wasn't a possible situation for either of us. But his life turned out well, so I'm happy for him. He did what he always wanted to do. He built a beautiful horse ranch, which was his dream."

"You have two children?" he asked, changing the subject. "The daughter who's a writer and the son in San Francisco?"

"Three. Another daughter in New York. And you?"

"A ten-year-old son in England, in boarding school. I got a late start. He visits me for three weeks in the summer, and a week at Christmas every year. It's not much, but he's young and in school. And I see him when I make occasional trips to England, though no more than once or twice a year. He's a sweet boy. We usually travel when he comes. It's a bit boring for him here, and the weather is very English. He gets enough of that at home." Maddie smiled as he said it. "What do your other children do?"

"My son is an entrepreneur, he's up to his ears in his second start-up. And my daughter in New York is a fashion designer."

"Very varied," he commented, impressed. "Do you see much of them? They must be busy."

"They are. I don't see them enough, but I'm used to it."

"And you, Madison? What do you do when you're not being rescued from beaches and visiting ghosts?"

She smiled at the description. "I'm a photographer." He frowned for a moment, thinking, and then smiled at her.

"Lord, yes, sorry. I didn't make the connection. I've seen your work. Who hasn't?" She smiled modestly in response.

"I travel a lot for my work. It keeps me busy."

"And you drive cross-country. Very impressive. Did you enjoy it?"

"Immensely. It was very relaxing, I like driving and road trips. I never have time to do that. It was a nice change."

They talked about some of his work then, and their travels. He had lived in Hong Kong and Mumbai, which was called Bombay when he was growing up. His father had done business there. He talked about how odd it had been going back to England after that. He felt like a stranger at home, and was sent to boarding school immediately, which he hated, but not going would have been unthinkable. And he was amazed that his son, Theo, liked his school. William said he had gone to university in England at Oxford, and lived in London while he was married. He said the marriage hadn't lasted long. It had been an unfortunate mismatch, and he'd only been married once. He admitted that he found all the ancient traditions in England stifling, and he felt freer to do what he wanted in the States, although he missed his son. And he confessed that a small inheritance from a generous relative had allowed him to leave England and come to the States to write. He had moved to California. First L.A., where he'd done some movie scripts, and now Big Sur. He said it was a good place to write his books, but fairly boring living there. You could only admire the view for so long. He went to San Francisco and L.A. for occasional cultural events, but he spent most of his time writing and not much else.

"Me too," Maddie admitted about her work habits. "I'm something of a workaholic. That and I'm on planes all the time, to some pretty un-civilized places, but I love it. I couldn't do that when my children were young. It would have been irresponsible."

"You strike me as a very independent, adventur-ous woman, and probably fearless in the bargain."

"Not fearless," she confessed, although she had been in some very dicey situations that would have terrified most people. "But independent and adventurous, yes. My older daughter has been complaining about it and thinks I should slow down."

"I don't believe in that. I think you'll stay young forever if you keep doing what you love. There's plenty of time to slow down later, much later, when you have no other choice. But until your arms drop off and your legs fall off, there's no valid reason to slow down." She beamed as he said it. He was a year older than she was, at fifty-nine, and was an only child like her.

"That's what I think. My fall off the ladder was the excuse she's been waiting for to try and get me to sell the house I love."

"Nonsense, that's a terrible idea. I think you should go right on, at full speed, trying to get up the hill on a narrow rocky path with a cast on. It's quite the right attitude about life," he said, and she laughed at him. He was nice to talk to and very knowledgeable on a number of subjects that interested her.

"I'll tell her you said so."

"Excellent. I'll send it to her in writing, if you like. Think of all the famous people who went on at full tilt into their eighties and nineties. You have decades ahead of you before you think of slowing down. Keep the house!"

"That's my theory," Maddie said happily.

"Stick with it. By the way, would you want to have dinner with me tonight? There's a very nice little restaurant quite nearby, if you have no other plans." She liked the idea, and she followed him in her car to a small French restaurant. They had a delicious meal and a lively conversation, and then he drove behind her back to the hotel to make sure she got there safely. He suggested a walk the next morning, and she accepted. It was more fun being with him than taking nature hikes on her own.

He picked her up the next day at eleven, and they walked for two hours, and then had lunch at her hotel. They talked nonstop, laughed a lot, and covered everything from literature to history and art.

She was going to San Francisco the following day, and she agreed to have lunch with William before she left. He took her to a funny hippie place that had been popular in the sixties, and there were a lot of aging surfers there in tie-dyed shirts.

William said he was sorry she was leaving and hoped to see her again sometime, which seemed unlikely.

"I've really enjoyed talking to you, Maddie. I get a bit rusty here with nothing but my work."

"Do you ever come to New York?" she asked hopefully. He had made her stay in Big Sur infinitely more pleasant, and less mournful, after learning of Andy's death.

"There's an American publishing house that reprints my work, but my agent and main publisher are in London," he said in answer to her question about New York. "But I hope our paths will cross somewhere." She had told him that she was going to Shanghai soon. And now she had a shoot booked in Madrid too, and possibly one in London.

181

She was all packed when she met him for lunch, her bags were in the car and she planned to leave immediately after. She was having dinner with Ben that night. Laura was going to a benefit with a friend and had agreed to let Ben spend time with his mother, although she wasn't happy about his not going to the black-tie event with her. The press never paid attention to her when Ben wasn't there, although she didn't tell him that.

Maddie had also sent an email to Milagra, telling her that she was going to spend three or four days visiting Ben and his family, and asking if Milagra had time for her mother to visit after that. But she hadn't heard back from her yet. Maddie knew that if she was writing, she didn't check her emails, and in that case Maddie would go back to New York without seeing her, but at least she had tried to connect with her.

"Where are you staying in San Francisco?" William asked her as he walked her to her car after lunch.

"The Fairmont. It's big and kind of fun. I've really enjoyed spending time with you, William," she said, smiling up at him. He looked as though he wanted to kiss her, but didn't dare, which seemed just as well to her since she'd probably never see him again. It had been a pleasant interlude and he was good company, interesting and intelligent and

low-key, with a good sense of humor and the abil-
ity to laugh at himself. He was very English, despite
how much he liked living in the States.

"I've enjoyed it too," he said. "One doesn't meet
a woman like you very often. In fact, never. I feel
like a bit of a recluse here." She could see why.
Spending too much time there would have depressed her, between the weather and the isolation.

"Well, if you come to New York, call me," she
said brightly. She was in good spirits after spending
four days with him, and he was easy to talk to. She
had given him her numbers in New York, and her
cellphone number and email address. He had what
he needed if he wanted to reach her, although she
didn't expect it. There was no future in it geo-
graphically. It was obvious to both of them. And
they were too old to fool themselves about that.

"Take care of yourself, Maddie." He kissed her
on the cheek, and she got in her car. She waved as
she drove away, and she could see him in the
rearview mirror watching her, then he got in his
own car.

She was excited about seeing Ben when she
got to San Francisco. They were going to have
dinner alone, just the two of them, and she could
hardly wait.

There was a message from him when she
checked in to the hotel. "Pick you up at eight."

Minutes after she got to her room at The Fairmont, the doorbell rang and a bellman staggered in with an enormous vase with three dozen long-stemmed pale pink roses. She gave him a tip after he set it down, and she opened the card and smiled.

"To my favorite damsel in distress. Stay off the steep trails until you get the cast off. Call if you need help. And **never** slow down!—William"

No one had sent her flowers like that in years, and she was delighted as she went to run a bath and dress for dinner with her son. William Smith had style, and even if she never saw him again, the four days she had spent with him had been fun. The roses were gorgeous. It was nice having a man take her to dinner and send her flowers. Jacques was right! It made her feel young, whether she ever saw William again or not.

Chapter 10

Maddie was waiting on the front steps of The Fairmont when Ben drove up in the Range Rover Laura usually used to drive the children. She had taken his Mercedes to the benefit with her friend. She had been chilly with him when she left for the evening. She didn't like being preempted by his mother, and it had never happened before. But Maddie had never jumped ship for two weeks before either, driving cross-country alone, and avoiding communication with her children. Ben had gotten the point that he needed to pay more attention to her, after his older sister had handled the situation so badly that their mother had literally run away from all of them. He needed to take matters in hand and he had. He wanted Maddie to know now that they cared about her, she wasn't just the forgotten mom, even if she felt that way. And he wanted to see if any of Deanna's outrageous claims about her had any truth to them. If so, he wanted to discover it for himself.

When he pulled up, she was wearing a chic black pantsuit, one black shoe, and the infamous cast on the broken ankle that had started Deanna's assault on their mother. Her hair was neatly pulled back, and she was wearing makeup. She had a tan, and she beamed the moment she saw him. What struck him was how youthful and beautiful she still was, and looked nowhere near her age. He hadn't seen her in almost seven months, and was ashamed to admit it when he flipped back through his appointment book and figured it out. She hopped into the Range Rover with ease, agile despite the cast.

"You look terrific, Mom," Ben said warmly after he hugged her. There was a sparkle in her eye, and despite the sad news about Andy, she was in better spirits than he expected. He hadn't had an evening alone with her in eight years, since he'd married Laura, and she was very touched.

He drove down the hill to an excellent Italian restaurant and had asked for a quiet table where they could talk. He had expected her to be tired from the trip, and instead she was full of energy,

and was proud to be with him when the maître d'
seated them. Ben asked for champagne for them
before they ordered dinner.

"That's quite an adventure you just had," he said
quietly. He had followed her the entire way on
Instagram, and she still hadn't called Deanna, or
even texted her. She'd had no contact with her
since she left New York.

"I needed to get away," she said seriously. "After
I broke my ankle, things got out of hand. I had a
few run-ins with Deanna, and I needed time
to think." He didn't admit that he'd heard all about
them from his sister, and he could easily understand why she had dropped everything and run for
a while. With threats like Deanna's, he might have
done the same. Ben was a quiet, thoughtful man,
and he was assessing his mother as they spoke.

"What made you decide to look up Andy after
all this time?"

"I found a box of old letters in the closet the
night I fell. Not just from him. There were some
from a man you probably don't remember, Bob
Holland. You were about seven when I started dating him."

"I vaguely remember him," Ben said as the
waiter came and set the menus on the table
and left.

"We dated for two years, and I was fairly serious

about him. He moved to California for a venture capital job in Silicon Valley. We lost touch after that. I googled him and he has his own firm in Boston now. I wanted to catch up and see what had become of him."

"And did you?" Ben was intrigued by what she was saying.

"I did. I always wondered if I'd made a mistake turning him down. I didn't. He totally sold out. He married a woman from a prominent family in Boston, realized he'd made a mistake, and stayed married to her to protect his career because her father owned the firm he worked for. Somewhere along the way, I think he sold his soul to the devil for a major career and everything that goes with it. He's been having affairs for years, would have been happy to do the same with me, and he's not a nice guy. I definitely dodged a bullet there," she said with a smile at her son, and he laughed.

"Sounds like it, although the trappings might be amusing."

"Not in exchange for being married to the wrong woman. He's had a loveless life, and he has no soul. Then I went to Chicago and had dinner with Jacques Masson, whom you probably do remember." Ben grinned as soon as she said the name.

"I was in high school when you dated him. I

had a lot of fun with him." He smiled at the memories Jacques's name conjured up.

"So did I, and he hasn't changed a bit, except that he owns seven restaurants now, drives a Bentley, and the girls in his life have gotten younger. He's having a ball. He has an eleven-year-old daughter he seems to be crazy about, but he didn't marry her mother. He's going to be a player forever. I guessed that one right. He cheated on me all the time," she told Ben, now that he was old enough to hear it. "I got tired of it when we were dating. He's still a nice person though. He said to send you his love."

"Were you thinking of going back to either of them, Mom?" He wondered if she was looking for a husband now, before she got any older. He thought maybe Deanna had driven her to that, but Maddie shook her head.

"No, but I made strong decisions in my life, particularly after Andy. I never fell in love again, and I like my independent life, but when I read the letters, when I was laid up for a few days with my ankle, I wondered if I was right. I just wanted to see for myself who the men in my life were twenty or thirty years later. I knew my decision with Andy was right. I didn't want to live in Wyoming, and I didn't think he could survive in New York. It would have killed his soul." Ben didn't disagree with her from what he remembered of him.

They stopped talking and looked at the menus then, and the waiter took their order. "I never second-guessed the decision with Andy, and we only spoke a few times after we broke up. At some point, when the right situation hasn't presented itself, you make a decision. Either to settle for something that's not right and make your peace with it, or get bitter at the way your life turned out, or put your energies in another direction. I put mine into the three of you, and whatever was left over went into my career. And once you all grew up, and had less time to spend with me, understandably," she said gently, "I poured everything into my work. It became the whole reason for my life. If it hadn't, I wouldn't have been able to let go and let you have your own lives. I had to find something else to dedicate myself to, body and soul. For the last fifteen years, it's been my job. I lost interest in dating after Andy. I didn't think I'd ever find a man I loved as much, so I developed my own life to justify what I'd done, and I've always assumed I would just keep plugging away forever and that would be my life until the end.

"None of you really need me anymore, you have your own families and partners, and Milagra has a life that seems to suit her, so I've had my career. I figured I would keep at it and come back to the firehouse and curl up between assignments, and then get back on the road again. It's been good for me until now, and it fills the void you all inevitably left when you grew up. I never questioned it until now. I just stayed on my path. I figured I'd go on forever the way things are. It never occurred to me that could change.

"But when I broke my ankle, Deanna gave me a clear picture of what could happen, and what the future could look like. She wants me to sell my house. She thinks I should buy a co-op in an assisted living facility, in anticipation of when I can't take care of myself. She wanted me to wear one of those geriatric falling alarms. All of a sudden I could envision everything I care about, and everything I've built my life on, being taken away from me: my work, my home, my freedom, my independence. I guess it could happen, but it had never occurred to me. I never thought I needed anyone to take care of me, not a husband or a man, and suddenly I could see where those choices could lead me, and maybe already have.

"After Andy, I decided it was okay to be alone, but that could land me in assisted living, no longer working, and wearing a falling alarm. It made me suddenly question everything I've done, and where I'm heading. It's premature, but she seems to think

I belong there now. I need to take control of my life again, and I just wanted to double back and make sure I had made the right decisions. I've been fine with being alone for all these years because I assumed that I could work forever, do what I wanted, live where I wanted, and take care of myself. Deanna is sure I can't. It was a pretty horrifying realization. I needed to be alone to think about it and decide what I believe and what I want to do about it."

"And what are you thinking now?" His heart ached while he listened to her, and he felt sick at what his sister had done, and how she'd handled it. Maddie hadn't had a stroke, she had broken her ankle. She wasn't dying, and she certainly wasn't senile or feeble and failing in any way, but Deanna had made their mother feel that way, and doubt herself and fear for her future. It was almost abusive, and his sister had the delicacy of a bull elephant.

"I calmed down while I was driving," Maddie said, "and I realized that I'm still me and she can't make me do what I don't want to. I'm still of sound mind and body. I'm fifty-eight years old, not a hundred. There are plenty of photographers who have worked into their nineties, and I want to be one of them. I love my house and I'm not moving. If I need assisted living one day, I'll figure it out then, but I hope I won't. I know lots of old people who still live in their homes. And I'm not old yet, or not as old and helpless as Dee thinks, or wants to believe. I'm not falling apart because I broke my ankle. She had me running scared for a while, but I'm not scared anymore. Yes, I'll get old one day, but I'm not there yet. And I'm not afraid to be alone. I made the right decisions for me.

"When I saw the men I had cared about, I realized I'd been right all along. I don't need a man with no soul or integrity who'd sell himself for a plane, or a guy who can't keep his hands off every woman who walks past him. And as much as I loved Andy, he was never the right man for me. Even if he'd been alive when I got to the ranch, he doesn't belong in New York any more than I belong in Wyoming, and neither of us ever did. If I get old alone, it's okay. It's a choice I made because the right situation never came along, and the one I have works well for me.

"I'm not moving into assisted living just because I'm not married, or selling my house because Deanna doesn't like my stairs and her high heels get caught in them. It's my life and my house, I've made my own decisions. I'm not going to give up my work, or sit around waiting to die wearing an alarm now, because I'm going to get old one day. When I do, I'll deal with it, but I hope it's a long time off. And I'm not going to grab the nearest man so I don't end my life alone. If I am alone, then that's okay. It took me a while to figure it all out again. She had me panicked, but now I'm fine."

She had come full circle back to where she'd been at the beginning, only her resolve had been strengthened. "I haven't spoken to Deanna since I left New York two weeks ago, and I didn't want to. She had me on the run. And none of these decisions are hers to make, they're mine, until I truly can't make them anymore. She even suggested I had Alzheimer's. Your sister is not the most tactful person I know." She still looked upset about her older daughter, and Ben agreed with her. His mother's thinking processes and the conclusions she'd come to were entirely reasonable. The one who wasn't was Deanna, and Ben intended to point that out to her again, after listening to his mother work her way through it. The trip had done her a world of good, and he was glad for her, and sorry that Deanna had upset her.

"I'm sorry you had to go through all that, Mom. Deanna should be horsewhipped."

"Sometimes it's good to take stock and make sure you're on the path you want to be on. I am. And it was kind of fun seeing Bob and Jacques again." She almost giggled as she said it, and Ben laughed. "I'm so damn glad I didn't marry either of them. It would have been a huge mistake. I was right the first time, and about Andy too. If I'd seen him, I'm sure I would have felt the same way about him. I really loved him, and I'm sad he's gone now. I'd have loved to see him again, for old times' sake, but I wasn't confused when I made the decision to leave him. I did it for the right reasons. Not everyone you love is the right person to marry. He wasn't for me. I do get lonely sometimes, but I'm better off alone, enjoying my life and work, and all of you when you have time to see me, than married to the wrong person. I don't need a man to protect me, or to keep me from feeling old."

"I want to see more of you, Mom. I've been remiss about it. I promise I'm going to do better in the future. That really is my fault." It was even more his wife's, Maddie realized, but she didn't want to say it to him.

"I know how busy you are. You all are," she said, gently touching his hand. "That's how it should be. It's up to me to keep myself busy and engaged."

"You shouldn't have to fill every minute of your life with work, you have a family." He was going to talk to Deanna about that too. And Milagra, no matter how weird she was, could make an effort too. Because one day they truly would no longer have their mother, and she had been good to them for all their lives, much better than they were to her. Instead of pushing her into assisted living with a geriatric alarm, Deanna should go to lunch with her sometime, or invite her to dinner or for a weekend. Assisted living was the right solution for some people, but not for a woman Maddie's age, at the height of her career, in good health, and with all her faculties as clear as a bell. And the idea that she had Alzheimer's was ridiculous.

"In a way, maybe it's lucky I broke my ankle. It started such an avalanche that I reevaluated my whole life, and that's never a bad thing."

"It was unnecessary," he said bleakly.

"I would never have seen my past loves again, and that was a good thing too. When I get back to New York, I'm going to be so happy to be in my house, on my own, and doing whatever I damn please." She grinned at him. "And if Deanna shows up uninvited again, I'm locking the door in her face. She's welcome when I say she is, and for the moment that's not the case."

"I don't blame you, Mom. She says whatever she wants to all of us. She needs to watch her mouth in the future, and I'm going to tell her that myself. She can't run roughshod over you. She needs to respect you and where and how you choose to live. You're perfectly capable of deciding that for yourself." He suspected it was why Milagra communicated so little with them. Deanna had always been tough on her, and Milagra didn't want to deal with it. So she had closed the door on all of them and become a recluse. And if that was who she was, it was okay for her to be different, and even weird. It worked for her. She had done well for herself, to the degree she could. Ben's assistant was addicted to her books.

"I think things have turned out fine," Maddie said, looking relaxed as they started eating dinner. "And I had a nice time driving across the country."

"You took some beautiful photographs, Mom." And after realizing how solitary and lonely she was at times, he was never going to let seven months go by again without seeing her. She deserved so much more than that from them.

"Thank you, darling. I'm going to Mendocino, by the way. I wrote to Millie that I was here to see you, and she's letting me come up for a few days." Maddie had heard from her and Milagra had agreed to a visit. The word "let" irked him. They had all shut Maddie out of their lives in some way, for their own convenience and selfish reasons.

"I'm sorry I'm leaving for Hawaii so soon. We planned it months ago, or I'd change it," he said quietly.

"You don't have to. I can come out again if Laura doesn't mind."

"She won't," he said with his lips set in a thin

line. "She'll be happy to see you too." He wasn't going to leave it in Laura's hands anymore. Maddie was his mother and it was his responsibility. He had allowed Laura to manhandle his mother too. He wanted his mother to spend more time with his children, and have the opportunity to know them better, even if they lived in San Francisco. She saw just as little of Deanna's daughters, because Deanna made no effort either. They were all guilty of neglecting their mother, and he wanted that to change. His sisters had been even worse than he was.

They spent the rest of dinner talking about his children, his work, and hers. She almost said something about meeting William Smith in Big Sur, but she felt foolish doing so. Despite the roses, she probably wouldn't have a chance to see him again. But he'd been pleasant company for a few days.

The meal had been delicious, and Ben dropped her off at The Fairmont at eleven, and headed home. She was coming to play with the children the following afternoon, and she would be staying for dinner. Laura said the kids had activities, and she had a committee meeting. Ben told her to cancel the children's plans. Their grandmother was in town, and it was more important for them to see her. Laura didn't argue with him after he'd missed the benefit. They were playing by new rules.

Ben was setting the tone he knew now he should have established years ago, but was too blind to see.

When Maddie came to the house the next day, she had presents for the children, and she handed Laura a gift-wrapped box from Chanel. When Laura opened it, there was a beautiful rhinestone-studded black velvet evening bag inside, since they went out in black tie so frequently, and Laura's face lit up like a child's at Christmas.

"What a nice thing for you to do." She hugged Maddie, who was pleased that she liked it, and then Maddie spent the afternoon on the floor with her grandchildren. Olive was an adorable three-year-old who was fascinated by her grandmother. Maddie played cars and trucks and dinosaurs and soldiers with Willie and Charlie, and all the games she used to play with their father. She hadn't lost her touch, although it had been a long time. Those had been the best years of her life, although she didn't know it then, and how quickly the years would slip by.

She helped the nanny give them baths and looked disheveled when she came down to dinner with Laura and Ben, after she read the children a bedtime story. Her hair was uncombed, Charlie had splashed her in the bath, and the baggy jeans that accommodated her cast were wet. She'd had them sign her cast, and they were thrilled.

"You look like a mess, Mom," Ben teased her, grinning.

"I had a ball." She smiled at her son and daughter-in-law. "And I need a drink." They all laughed and Ben handed her a glass of white wine. The dinner Laura had ordered for them was excellent. Ben had let her hire a full-time chef because she hated to cook.

Maddie left after dinner and went back to the hotel. She'd had a terrific day, and wished she had more of them. She was going to see them briefly the next day, but they all had a lot to do. They were leaving for Hawaii the following morning and she was heading for Mendocino.

Laura looked at Ben sheepishly after Maddie left. "Your mom always scared me. She's really sweet with the kids, and even with me. The Chanel bag is a beautiful gift. I'd forgotten how nice and generous she is."

"She's a sweet person. It's my rotten older sister you need to watch out for, not my mother."

"She's just so famous. I always thought she disapproved of me."

"My mother isn't like that. She's a hardworking woman and she was always a great mom to us, no matter how busy she was. I never realized how tough it is when kids grow up. It left a hell of a hole in her life, especially with two of us out here.

I hate thinking of her all alone in New York, although she's used to it by now."

"We'll have her out more often. I promise," she said and kissed him, and they went upstairs to their bedroom with his arm around her.

Maddie sat with the children while they ate dinner the next day. She told them stories about when their father was a little boy. He came home from the office late, looking harried, and Laura and the nanny had been packing for Hawaii all afternoon. Ben smiled when he saw his mother in the kitchen with the kids. That was how it should be, and he hoped it would stay that way now.

He had called his sister from the office that afternoon and read her the riot act about everything she'd said to their mother about assisted living, and having early Alzheimer's, and all the rest.

"Where did you get off saying that kind of crap to her? She was terrified," he had told her.

"You have to admit, she's been crazy. Driving across the country like that seems pretty insane to me," Deanna said stubbornly.

"I don't think it was crazy at all. She took stock of her life, she went back and saw people she hadn't seen in twenty years, and figured out what she wants to do now **before** she really does get old and falls apart, if she does. But she isn't there yet, by any means. The trouble with you, Deanna, is you have no imagination. And you'd damn well better make an effort to spend some time with her, and be **nice** to her. We all need to do that while we have her. One day we'll be sorry we didn't. And our kids barely even know her. She's terrific with them, just like she was with us."

"She was never that terrific with me," Deanna said, sounding insulted. He just hoped he had gotten through to her. What she had done when their mother broke her ankle was inexcusable.

"Maybe that's because you were a pain in the ass even as a kid. You were hateful as a teenager," he told her. "But we're all grown-ups now, and it's time to give back to her. You owe her an apology."

"For what? Telling her to get rid of that death trap she lives in?"

"That and a whole list of things you had no business saying to her, and you know what they are. She has a right to do what she wants, and live where she wants."

"I'll think about it," Deanna said icily. "Is she coming back to New York now? I assume she's flying, not driving back."

"She's going to see Millie in Mendocino first for a few days."

"I'll see her when she gets back," Deanna said noncommittally.

"Wait until she invites you, or call first. Don't just drop in on her. Have a little common courtesy and respect." He wasn't letting her off the hook.

"Do I need an engraved invitation now?" she said caustically.

"No," he said. "All you need is a heart. It would be a good place to start. She's our mother, Dee. That's a sacred relationship, or it should be."

"Since when did you turn into such a mama's boy? You hardly ever have her out to visit either, and your wife doesn't like her."

"It's going to be different now," he said, and he hung up a few minutes later. It was his last day in the office before their trip to Hawaii, and he was too busy to spar with his bitchy sister. It was just too bad her husband never yanked her chain. Ben thought she needed it.

When Maddie left them that evening, she kissed the children and Laura, and Ben held her tightly in his arms in a hug for a long moment.

"Take care of yourself, Mom," he whispered to her. "I love you."

"I love you too, Ben," she said, looking deep into his eyes, and she smiled at him. "Thank you for everything." There were tears in his eyes when he waved goodbye to her. He was sorry to see her leave. Laura came up and put an arm around his waist.

"We'll have her back soon," she promised. It had been a great visit. Hopefully, the first of many more to come.

Chapter 11

Maddie was just closing her bags, getting ready to check out of the hotel, when William called her. She had sent him a text thanking him for the flowers when she arrived, and she told him on the phone that they were still beautiful.

"How was your visit with your son?" he asked her.

"Wonderful. The best one ever. I spent most of it playing with the kids. Ben and I had a nice dinner alone on the first night. That's never happened before. He sent his wife to a benefit without him, so we got some time together. You just caught me. I'm leaving for Mendocino, to see my daughter. She finished a book, so she's letting me come up."

"How long will you be there?"

"As long as she can stand me, a few days at most.

She likes her own company. She gets nervous if I hang around too long." It intrigued him how she seemed to adjust to each of her children's personalities and needs, and accommodated them. He expected his son to fit into his life, but Theo was very young. Her children were adults and sounded complicated.

"Is that what I have to look forward to? A three-day limit when I see my son, once he grows up?"

"Maybe. Depending on what his wife wants."

"I'd better enjoy him while I can. I had an idea last night and I thought I'd run it past you. I didn't realize you were going to Mendocino."

"I just got the invitation a couple of days ago."

"I'd like to come up and see you. We could spend the day in the Napa Valley, or in the city if you prefer. I'd like to see you before you go back to New York. I'm sure it sounds crazy, but I miss you, Maddie." She was touched to hear it. She had thought of him too, but she'd been busy with her son and grandchildren. She thought about it as he asked her.

"I really need to get back. I've been gone for a long time. My desk must look like a nightmare. I've never played hooky like this." But the idea of a day or two with him appealed to her too. "There's almost no phone service where my daughter lives."

"That must be inconvenient."

"She likes it that way. Why don't I call you when I leave Mendocino? If my assistant isn't screaming for me by then, and if it isn't too short notice for you, you can come up to the city and we can spend a day or two together. I'd enjoy it."

"I'll wait to hear from you. I can be in the city before you get down from Mendocino. I'll book a room for myself just in case."

"Thank you for being flexible."

"It's worth it to see you," he said. She booked a room for herself when she checked out too. She had been planning to stay there for a night before she flew out after Mendocino, but another day wouldn't make too much difference. And she liked the idea of seeing William. There was something very peaceful and soothing about him, and at the same time very masculine. She had enjoyed his company and their intelligent conversations about subjects that interested them both.

She left the city half an hour later and headed north to Mendocino. It was a sunny day when she started her drive, but the weather got foggier and the landscape more austere as she neared her destination. Milagra lived just outside town, and as Maddie drove up to the house, she smiled. It looked like something in one of her daughter's novels. Milagra kept the place neat and tidy, but Maddie always expected a vampire to open the door when she rang the bell. She had stopped at the bakery in town and was carrying a bag of **pains au chocolat** and croissants, and she had bought a bunch of flowers.

It took a long time for Milagra to come to the door, and Maddie wondered if she was out. She finally opened it with a serious expression. She was wearing a ripped sweatshirt with bleach stains on it, and jeans that were torn. It was a fashionable look at the moment, but Milagra's jeans looked as though they had been run through a shredder, not intended by a designer.

"I'm working on an outline," she said, frowning at her mother, who knew the drill. No hello, no hug, no kiss. She had had an idea, and instantly disappeared like a ghost. Maddie always stayed in the same room, and knew where to go. She took her bags upstairs and set them down. The clothes she wore were already damp from a thick mist outside. And she went back downstairs to put the croissants away and the kettle on for a cup of tea.

Milagra reappeared an hour later, looking relieved and pleased to see her mother. "Sorry, Mom. It just came to me right before you got here. I've got to grab the ideas when they come. If I don't, I forget the nuances."

"No worries." Maddie smiled at her, happy to see her. They hadn't seen each other for almost a year. Milagra was waiflike and eccentric and always had been, even as a child. She would hide under the stairs somewhere or in a closet for hours, and not respond when you called her. She had told Maddie when she was five that people were too big and the world was too loud. But she had found her niche, and the people she wrote about were as odd as she was herself. Deanna had complained as a teenager that it was like living with the Addams Family. Milagra was beautiful in an ethereal, translucent, almost transparent way. She hated bright sunlight, and her skin was china white. She had Maddie's blond hair and blue eyes, but everything about her was paler, as though filtered by an invisible film, like a fine white veil. Her three large dogs were asleep in the living room, and the cats were hiding under a chair, eyeing Maddie with suspicion. The dogs had thick curly coats and were a mix of some kind.

"So how are you?" Milagra asked as she sat down at the kitchen table with her mother. Maddie set a cup of tea down in front of her.

"I'm fine. How are you? I thought you just finished a book. You're starting another one?"

"I had the idea in the shower this morning. Sometimes it happens that way, the next idea rolls out right away, or sometimes it takes a lot longer. They want to give me a four-book contract next time."

"That's great. I just drove out from New York," Maddie said by way of conversation. She didn't usually bother Milagra with the details of her life. Milagra didn't want to know.

"Why did you do that?" Milagra looked puzzled.

"I wanted to see some people on the way. I stopped in Boston and Chicago, and I went to Wyoming. I was hoping to see Andy, but he died two months ago. I saw Sean, and he sends you his love. He's married and has two little boys, and they're expecting twin girls." Milagra smiled at the report and nodded. She didn't react to Andy's death at first. She digested it for a while.

"That's sad about Andy. Was he sick?" she finally asked her mother.

"Yes, he was."

"Are you still in love with him?" She always went right to the heart of the matter.

"I loved him, and I was sad when Sean told me he died. But I can't say I was 'in love' with him anymore. I hadn't seen him in seventeen years. That's a long time to carry a torch."

"Some people do," Milagra said dreamily. "I'm a vegan now." She had been a vegetarian before, and her mother could see she'd lost weight. She was rail thin. It also ruled out the croissants Maddie had bought, which were made with butter.

"What do you eat?"

"Mostly greens and beans. I eat a lot of lentils, broccoli, brussels sprouts, kale. Bert always tries to get me to eat fish, but I won't."

"Who's Bert?" Catching up with Milagra was always a challenge. It was like coming in at the middle of a movie. Maddie was never sure who the players were from year to year, although for the most part Milagra led a very solitary life. She needed time to write her books. Maddie worried at times that she lived in an imaginary world, and not a very healthy one at that.

"He's a friend," she said in answer to her mother's question, and offered no further explanation. "Do you want to go for a walk?"

"It's wet out. There was a heavy mist when I came in."

"I'll give you a slicker. I love it like this." Maddie always did whatever Milagra wanted. She was grateful to see her. She was like a mirage that appeared from time to time and then vanished again. They took the dogs with them and walked to the beach. The dogs loped along and didn't seem to mind the damp weather. They dug for shells in the sand once in a while, or ran off with a stick, and Milagra ran with them. She was long and sleek and graceful, and smiled at her mother as they strolled along slowly.

They went back to the house an hour later. Maddie was chilled to the bone. Milagra shook out her damp hair and took off her slicker, just as Maddie noticed a big plastic bag on the porch. She picked it up, and it smelled of seafood. She peeked inside and it was full of fresh crab.

"Bert dropped it off for you," Milagra explained, then took it and made a face at the smell. "Do you like crab?" She knew very little about her mother. She only paid attention to herself.

"I love it." It was fresh and local.

"Who is this Bert? It's the second time you've mentioned him since I got here." Milagra didn't answer, took out a big pot and filled it with water to cook the crab.

"He's just a friend," she finally answered, same response as before, with no further explanation.

"It was nice of him to bring crab for me."

"I told him I thought you'd like it." The way she spoke of him, and refused to answer questions about him, made him sound like an imaginary friend. Milagra had had several when she was growing up. One of them had lasted for several years, a little girl named Jennifer that Milagra said she played with. She outgrew them eventually, but it took a while. All the doctors had ever been able to tell Maddie about Milagra was that she was different. There was nothing wrong with her that they could tell, and she tested normally. She wasn't learning delayed, in fact she was very bright, but she was socially awkward and had an overactive imagination, and now she was making a living from it with her novels. She had had crushes in school, but she'd never really dated, and high school boys didn't want to deal with girls like Milagra. They wanted bold, social ones who wore short skirts, had big breasts, and were willing to make out in parked cars. They didn't want to deal with girls as fey as Milagra. She had won a poetry prize in college, and published her first novel at nineteen. She'd been writing them ever since.

Milagra towel-dried the dogs, and when the water boiled, Maddie dropped the crab in. It was going to make a delicious dinner and it was a shame Milagra wouldn't eat it. "You're sure you won't try some?" Maddie tried to tempt her, but she made a face and shook her head. Maddie had an odd feeling that there was something Milagra wasn't telling her, but she had no idea what it was.

A little while later, Maddie was startled when she heard a phone ring. She wasn't even sure Milagra had one, but she pulled it out of a cupboard and answered. Maddie could only hear Milagra's side of the conversation.

"Mom says she loves it. She's cooking it for dinner. . . . I'll call you later."

"I'm never sure if you still have a phone," Maddie said casually.

"I do. I don't answer it most of the time, and sometimes I forget to pay the bill, so it lapses for a while until I pay. Bert says I need one, it's safer. So I have one." At least he was an imaginary friend who knew how to use a phone. "I don't use it most of the time, except when he calls me."

"Is he like a boyfriend, or just a friend?" Maddie asked bravely, and Milagra shrugged.

"I don't know. I don't see him when I'm writing," she said, which was almost all the time.

"Does he live around here?" She was curious now. She couldn't remember the last time Milagra had a man in her life. And if she did now, it was a major change since Maddie had last seen her. Maddie hated knowing so little about her daughter's life. But Milagra preferred it that way, and Maddie tried to respect it.

"He lives in Fort Bragg." It was the port several miles away. "He checks on me to make sure I'm okay. He's a good person." The crab was cooked by then and Maddie drained it, and put it on a platter to cool off. There was far more than she could eat alone.

"Can I meet him?"

"Sure. I guess so."

"Maybe he'd like to have dinner with us, that's a lot of crab. I can't eat all of it myself."

"I'll ask him," she said, and went to the cupboard where she kept the phone. She told him to come by at six, and Maddie couldn't wait to meet him.

When he rang the doorbell at six o'clock, Maddie was setting the table, and she looked up to see an enormous man filling the doorway. He had a healthy face, red from the cold, and a thick crop of dark hair. He was as brightly colorful as Milagra was pale and almost invisible. He seemed to fill the room when he walked in, and smiled shyly at Maddie. Everything about him was unexpected. He walked over to shake Maddie's hand. He was wearing a lumberjack shirt, blue jeans, and rubber boots, which he left at the door. He was strikingly tall, about six-foot-six, and his hand grasping Maddie's was huge.

"Hi, I'm Bert English."

"Thank you for the crab." She smiled at him warmly after they shook hands. "It looks fantastic."

"I'm glad you like it. I can't get Milagra to eat it. She hates fish."

"Did you get it in town?"

He laughed at the question. "No, I got it on my boat, from my traps. I'm a fisherman. We're fishing crab late this year because we got a late start to the season in December. It took us a month this year to set the prices." Maddie was faintly surprised to hear it, but nothing surprised her in Milagra's world. He had brought a bottle of wine and set it down on the table. Along with his size and coloring, Maddie noticed that he was considerably older than her daughter, and closer to her own age. He looked to be in his late forties, a good fifteen years older than her daughter. But he looked like a gentle person. He sat down on the couch and chatted with Maddie about her trip. He was intrigued to hear that she had driven out from New York. He was intelligent and well-spoken and had read all of Milagra's books. She sat quietly on the floor at his feet stroking one of the dogs while he and Maddie talked, and Maddie tried to figure out his role in her daughter's life. With anyone else, she would have assumed he was a boyfriend, but with Milagra one never knew. Maddie asked him about fishing in the local waters, and he mentioned that his son was a fisherman in Alaska. By the time they sat down to dinner, Maddie liked him. And halfway through the bottle of wine, they were friends. And by then she had no doubt that he was in love with her daughter. But Milagra said and did nothing to clarify his role in her life. As always she was mysterious and impossible to read, and one couldn't assume anything with her.

"I'd be happy to take you out on my boat some-time," he offered as they shared the delicious crab dinner, and Milagra ate lentils and kale.

"I'd love that," Maddie said in response to his invitation. "Could I take pictures?"

"Sure. It would be fun. What about tomorrow?"

"Would you come?" Maddie asked Milagra, but she shook her head vigorously.

"I still get seasick, and the water is rough around here."

"What about you?" Bert asked with a look of concern as he glanced at Maddie.

"I never get seasick. What time do you go out?"

"Five o'clock in the morning."

"Tell me where to go and I'll be there." She smiled at him.

They talked for a while after dinner, and Maddie really liked him. Before he left, he told her where to meet him on the dock in Fort Bragg the next day. Maddie looked at her daughter in amazement when he was gone.

"What a terrific man," she said, and meant it. "And he's crazy about you. How long have you known him?" Milagra was silent for a long time and looked at her mother with wide eyes.

"Do you really like him, Mom?"

"Yes, I do."

217

"I was afraid you'd hate him. We've been together for eight years." Maddie looked stunned by her daughter's confession.

"Does he live with you?"

She shook her head.

"He stays here when I'm not writing. I can't have anyone in the house when I write."

"I think he's a terrific guy."

"I was afraid he wasn't fancy enough for you. That's why I never let you come out." There were tears in her eyes as she said it, and she put her arms around her mother, and Maddie held her tight.

"He doesn't have to be fancy for me, Millie. He just has to be real, and good to you. How old is he, by the way?"

"That's the other thing I was worried about. He's forty-eight. He's been really upset that he's never met you. He wanted to meet you this time. I wasn't sure. He's very smart."

"I can tell," Maddie said comfortably, feeling close to her younger daughter for the first time in years. She had finally let her in and shared something about her life. It was a first.

"Are you really going to go out on the boat?"

"Yes, I am. It sounds like fun." And she could get some great pictures.

Milagra seemed happier than Maddie had ever seen her, and as though a thousand-pound weight had been lifted from her shoulders. "I'm so happy you like him. He's such a good person."

"I can see that," Maddie said as she continued to hold Milagra in her arms. "Do you think you'll marry him?"

"He wants to. I don't think we need to. He makes a good living with his boat. I don't want kids. I don't think I could handle marriage. Too much pressure. Too many expectations. I just want to write, he says that's fine with him. And he has a son. He's twenty-five." He was only eight years younger than Milagra. "He got divorced when his son was two. His wife hated being married to a fisherman."

"You might change your mind about having kids one day," or maybe not. "And now I have an important question to ask you." Milagra looked instantly worried. "Do you have an alarm clock?"

Milagra laughed at the question. "Yes, I do." They went upstairs together to find it. Maddie had already cleaned up the kitchen, and they met again in their nightgowns when Milagra came to sit on Maddie's bed. She had already put two of her cameras in a waterproof case, ready to grab in the morning. "Thank you for liking him, Mom."

"He's not hard to like, and if he makes you happy, that's all I want for you." They had already stood the test of time, after eight years, and

Milagra looked peaceful as she kissed her mother good night.

The alarm went off at four-fifteen the next morning. Maddie got up and dressed quietly. She had sneakers with her, and she could wear one on the boat with her cast. Milagra had told her to take a warm jacket out of the closet, which she did. Bert had rain gear on the boat. And at five o'clock sharp she was on the dock facing Noyo Harbor, and he walked down to greet her and gave her a bear hug. He was impressed that she'd made it, and he escorted her to the boat.

She was startled by how modern and sophisticated it was. He had state-of-the-art equipment and a crew of four experienced fishermen. It was a serious operation, not some slapdash local deal. There was nothing amateurish or old-fashioned about it.

"I take the boat up to Alaska once every year, just to keep my hand in and fish with my son. The fishing's pretty tame around here." She could see that his boat was up to more challenging waters. She took her camera out when two of the deckhands slipped the ropes from the pilings that held them and Bert turned on the engines, and a few minutes later they took off. Maddie quietly tucked herself into corners and disappeared into the woodwork as she shot almost continuously. Her cast didn't hamper her at all, she didn't let it. She got fantastic photographs of Bert and his crew doing their job and working hard all day. The crab season was going to end in a month, but Bert said the catch was still plentiful every day.

They stopped and ate at lunchtime. Bert prepared a delicious meal for Maddie and his crew. The sea got rough after that, with waves that came over the bow. They worked harder then, and had a good catch that day and a fresh load of crab from their traps that would go to the city and bring high prices. He ran a very lucrative business, and as they rode the waves into port at the end of the day, Bert sat down next to Maddie with a smile.

"Well, Maddie, how did you like it?"

"I loved it."

"You work hard with that camera. You didn't stop shooting all day." He had noticed her out of the corner of his eye even when he was busy.

"You work hard with your crew." She was vastly impressed by what she'd seen, and by him. He was a man, and a pro, and she liked everything about him. They truly were friends now.

"Are you all right about my being with Milagra?" he asked, worried.

"Very much so," she said, and he looked pleased.

"You don't mind that I'm older?" Maddie shook her head. "I don't know why she was afraid to tell you for so long. She should give you more credit than that."

"Kids never do that," she said with a wry smile. "They think they know their parents, but they don't."

"I'm glad you're okay about us." He was as relieved as Milagra had been the night before. "I hope we can be friends."

"We already are," she said quietly as they docked and his crew tied up the boat. And then they went home to Milagra, who had worked on her outline all day and was pleased with it.

"Erghhh, you both smell like fish." She wrinkled her nose at them.

"I'll go home and take a shower," Bert said with a grin. He usually went home and cleaned up before he saw her after a day's work. "And then I'm taking you both out to dinner to celebrate."

"What are we celebrating?" Milagra looked puzzled.

"Us, your mom visiting. Everything. And we had a good catch today. Your mom brought us luck. She took about a thousand pictures of me today." He looked pleased and embarrassed all at once.

"I'll send them to you," Maddie promised him,

and went upstairs to bathe. It had been a fantastic day, and she knew she didn't have to worry about her daughter anymore. She was in good hands. Bert English was a fine man. The best. He reminded her of Andy in a way. It hadn't worked for her, but it did for Milagra, and that was all that mattered now. They were perfect for each other, in every way. He was just what she needed to ground her and protect her. Maddie couldn't wait to go through the pictures she'd taken of him. And as unusual as she might be, Milagra had found just the right man for her. It warmed Maddie's heart.

Chapter 12

Maddie's three days in Mendocino were the best of her trip. She and Milagra spent time together, talked or just sat in the same room while Milagra made notes on her outline. And they walked on the beach with her dogs. Bert joined them at night for dinner. He cooked one night and was a superb cook. They had a good time, laughing and telling stories. Maddie had loved the day she spent on the boat with him, and everything about him for Milagra.

She hated to leave, and Milagra promised to have her back soon. And this time, there were no secrets. Maddie and Milagra hugged each other fiercely the morning she left, and Bert had come to say goodbye and put her bags in the car for her. He put an arm around Milagra as Maddie got in the car and looked at them. They were everything she had wanted to be with Andy, and couldn't. Milagra had done what Maddie wasn't able to do, embrace a simple life where she and the man she loved could build their dreams together, far from the life Milagra had had growing up. There was nothing about her old life that Milagra missed, which wouldn't have been true for Maddie if she'd given up New York for Wyoming. Milagra was much better suited to the life she had now in Mendocino.

Maddie kissed Milagra one last time through the car window and then slowly drove away as they waved, standing next to each other. Maddie headed back to San Francisco thinking of the days they had just shared. She knew she was leaving her daughter in good hands. She wanted to call William when she knew her cellphone would work again, but first she wanted to call Ben. She had driven a good distance by the time she reached him in Hawaii. They were having breakfast when she called.

"Everything okay, Mom?" He sounded worried for a minute.

"I had a fantastic time with Millie."

"Telling ghost stories?" Milagra had no common ground with him or her older sister, but Maddie realized now how little they knew her. So many of their assumptions about her were wrong. She was far more capable than they thought her. Maddie had always hoped Milagra would meet the right man, who would appreciate her, and she had.

"No, I spent the last three days with her and the man she's been in love with for eight years, whom none of us knew about. He's a great guy."

"Wow, there's a news flash. Eight years? What's he like? Another writer?"

"No, he's a commercial fisherman and a good one. He's fifteen years older and just what she needed. He's a real person. I think you'll like him. You should come up to see her sometime. You're her brother, Ben, you should get to know her, for both your sakes. And Bert is terrific. She's been hiding him for all these years."

"You're full of surprises, Mom."

"No, she is. I just wanted you to know how well it went."

"I'm glad." He was happy for her, he knew even better now how much she worried about all of them, especially Milagra, who had seemed like a lost soul for so long. One by one, she was finding her children, and getting to know them better as adults. And in his case, her grandchildren. They had shortchanged Maddie for so many years. He still felt bad about it.

"Well, finish your breakfast and kiss everyone

for me. I just wanted to check in and tell you about the visit with Milagra, it was terrific." And very unexpected.

They hung up and she called William next. He was working in Big Sur and sounded distracted when he answered, then became alert the minute he realized it was Maddie.

"I'm on my way back from Mendocino," she told him.

"How was it?"

"Amazing. My children are full of surprises. My daughter has been hiding a boyfriend for eight years. He's a great guy. He's a fisherman up here, and he's perfect for her, simple but also complex, uncomplicated and loving. He adores her."

"You sound happy, Maddie."

"I am. I just wanted to let you know I'm on the way back to the city. I'll be there in about two hours."

"I'll be there roughly an hour after you get there. Are we still on for a day in Napa tomorrow?"

"Why not? My desk in New York can wait another day." She hadn't called Penny yet, but there were no messages or texts when she turned her phone on, so Penny obviously had things under control.

"I'm glad to hear it." He was relieved when she told him. He had already booked a reservation for dinner that night at a new restaurant he'd heard about, just in case she called him. It was supposed to be elegant but unpretentious, with great food. "I'm staying at The Fairmont too. I'll call you as soon as I get in."

She got a text a few minutes later, thought it would be from Penny, and was surprised when it wasn't. It was from Sean. "They're here! Madison Andrea Wyatt and Julie Nicole Wyatt, 8 lbs, 2 oz and 8 lbs, 9 oz. Everyone doing fine. Love, Sean." They'd had their twins, and used her name as he said they would, and Andy's. She wanted to send them a gift when she got back to New York.

The rest of the drive into the city was easy, and she got there sooner than she expected. She checked in to a room, washed her face, and brushed her hair while she waited for William. She wasn't sure why she was seeing him, except that she liked him. They lived on opposite coasts, and once she started traveling for work again, she wouldn't stop. This was the longest break she'd ever taken, and she probably wouldn't do it again for years. She was spending the last two days of it with him because he'd asked her to. She knew she couldn't let herself get too deeply involved with someone she'd never see. But she was still under the spell of the vacation atmosphere she had indulged in for the past three weeks.

She sent Milagra an email, telling her how much she had enjoyed her visit and loved meeting Bert, and that she had had a terrific time going fishing with him, and being with them both. It had been their best visit ever.

William got there while she was watching the news on TV, and he called her from his room. He was on another floor, but it was fun being at the same hotel. She hung up and they met in the lobby a few minutes later. He gave her a hug as soon as he saw her and noticed that she looked happy and rested. As usual, she was wearing one shoe and the familiar cast, now autographed by her grandchildren. She couldn't wait to get rid of it. She was sure her ankle was fine now.

"Do you want to go for a walk?" he suggested. They went to the Marina and walked along the bay, watching the boats, and she told him about her day on Bert's boat.

"That sounds fantastic," William said enthusiastically.

"It was."

"Did your daughter go?"

Maddie shook her head. "She gets seasick. But it gave me a chance to get to know him. I think you'd like him a lot."

"I'm sure I would," he said, smiling down at Maddie. He had thought of her incessantly for the past three days. He couldn't get her out of his head. "You've bewitched me, Madison Allen," he accused her.

"No one's ever said that to me before." She smiled at him.

"Well, I am. What am I going to do when you go back to New York? I like knowing you're here, nearby, where I can get in my car and drive to see you in a few hours."

"You'll do whatever you did before we met," she said smugly, as they sat on a bench to rest for a while.

"Oh, you mean write, do research, answer emails from my agent and publisher, and despair of ever meeting anyone like you? You're not an ordinary woman, you know. Believe me, I tried. I was single for a long time before I got married, and I've been divorced for eight years. You're unique, Maddie. I can't bear the thought of going back to mediocrity after meeting you." It was very flattering, but she didn't know what to do with it.

"We live three thousand miles apart and I travel all the time, to some pretty awful places, or remote anyway. If we fall in love, we'll never see each other," she said practically.

"I can meet you in your awful places, Maddie. That's not a valid excuse for cowardice," he said and she laughed. She wasn't cowardly about other

231

things, but she had been about romance for a long time.

"I've been divorced for a lot longer than you have. Thirty-three years, and I haven't found the right combination yet."

"I suspect you didn't want to. Maybe that's changed," he said hopefully.

"I'm not going to sleep with you," she said suddenly, and he laughed.

"Well, now that we have that settled, we can discuss the rest. Do you have a preference for chaste relationships?" He sounded very British as he said it and she grinned.

"Only recently. I don't want to get it wrong again."

"I don't think you have. From what you've told me, you walked away from the wrong ones. That sounds very right to me. And you've proved it to yourself, driving all over the country for the last month, checking on your old boyfriends to make sure they were as wrong as you thought. What makes you think I'd be wrong for you?" he said. He was being very bold, and she liked it.

"Because I don't want drama in my life anymore, or a broken heart. I do what I want, when I want, go where I want. I'm not sure I could compromise anymore. I'm pretty spoiled. I don't think you're 'wrong,' but maybe I am, for you."

"But you don't want to be alone either. You don't want to wake up at the end of the show and be sitting there alone. Neither do I. I've been whining about my ex-wife for eight years, which I realize now was a clever way of keeping everyone at bay by boring them to death. The truth is, I don't care about her anymore, and what a disappointment she was. She gave me Theo, my son. I'm grateful for that. The rest doesn't matter. And you wouldn't have to make compromises for me. You could do what you want, come and go. I don't want to interfere with your life. I'd just want to share it with you, when it's convenient for both of us. We both have our work. But at least some of the time, I don't want to wake up alone in the morning, and maybe you don't either. And why won't you sleep with me, by the way?"

"Because it's too soon, and it's too big a commitment. Once we do that, we'll both be hooked, and then it all turns into a mess." It had with Andy. It had been agony letting him go.

"A very nice mess possibly," he said with a gentle smile. "Have you taken a vow of chastity?"

"Yes, years ago." She smiled at him.

"I suggest you rethink that at some point. You're too young to give all that up. And so am I." He was a year older than she was, which seemed about right to both of them. "Don't you want to have a partner again, Maddie? I didn't think that I did, but I realize now that I do. I don't want to do everything alone."

"Neither do I," she said. "I just don't want to make a mistake."

"You won't. You're too smart for that."

"So are you. And we've both made mistakes. We all get carried away and overlook the warning signs. Once I sleep with you, I won't care if you're a mistake or not."

"You can't always play it safe, Maddie. Life doesn't work that way. And love implies risk. You can't live without it forever. Work isn't enough."

"No, it's not," she agreed, although she had convinced herself that it was.

"Let's leave the door open, and see what happens. If you decide to run, I won't stop you. I promise."

"I'm running now," she said softly, and he took her hand.

"No, you're not. You called me on the way back from Mendocino. You wanted to see me as much as I wanted to see you." It was true and she was embarrassed to admit it to him. "Let's be brave together, and see if we can get it right, if you want to." He gave her the choice. She didn't answer him for a few minutes, and sat looking at the boats on the bay and holding his hand. "Think of your daughter and her fisherman. She's a brave girl. She learned it from you."

"She's young."

"So are you. You're as young as you want to be."

"I'm not young, William. And what happens when I fall apart? You'll be stuck with me."

"Oh, I'll get rid of you then. I never said I'd keep you when you fall apart. I'm just talking about sex and irresponsibility. You mean I have to stick around when all the moving parts fall off? I never agreed to that." She was laughing at him, and he had said something she liked about being brave together. It was very tempting, and he actually made it seem possible that they might win the lottery of life this time. Maybe they could do it. She had said to Ben that she didn't want to die alone, or wake up alone forever. Maybe this was her chance not to, with William, if things worked out for them. They didn't even know that yet.

"I'll think about it." It was all she would promise him for now, but he could sense that she was turning it over in her mind. He had met her at the right time. Her trip across the country had made her question past decisions, among them the decision not to get involved with anyone again. She had built her own prison, but the door was open now, and all she had to do was walk through it. He was waiting on the other side, with his arms open wide for her. It made her feel young again.

They took a cab back to the hotel then, and had dinner at the restaurant he'd reserved for that night. He didn't harangue her again to get involved with him, or to sleep with him. He had said what he needed to and planted the seed. Now it was up to both of them to water it until it grew into a flowering plant, or a tree, in time. There was no telling how strong it would grow, or how long it would last. That was the risk she was afraid to take. She didn't want the pain of loss again. And he could break her heart, once she let him in. If she did.

He walked her to her room when they got back to the hotel after dinner, and didn't insist on coming in. He was a gentleman. He wasn't going to force himself on her. He wanted her to come to him willingly. He thought she would in time, and she was afraid she would. She didn't trust her own strength to resist him. Everything he said was so appealing. She liked so many things about him. And he was a very attractive man.

They agreed to meet at ten o'clock the next morning to go to Napa. He was waiting for her in the lobby when she arrived in loose casual pants that fit over her cast and a white cashmere sweater.

"You look very virginal this morning," he teased

her, and she laughed. "You really are remarkable. You're the only virgin I know with three children. Quire miraculous, really."

They drove to Napa in his car, through some of the prettiest parts of the valley, and had lunch at the Auberge du Soleil, a lovely French inn and restaurant overlooking the valley and the vineyards. It had been a good decision to go to Napa. It was very picturesque and looked like Italy and parts of France.

She told him about her assignment in Shanghai in the coming weeks. It was getting closer, which was why she had to get back to New York, so she could get ready to leave, and do all her prep work first.

"I could meet you in Hong Kong if you like," he offered casually. "I have the time at the moment. Chastely, of course, if that's required, with two hotel rooms." She could see that he meant it.

"That might be fun. Let me think about it."

She had a lot to think about when she went back now. And she was trying to ignore the fact that he was very handsome, and sexy. He had a kind of natural grace that appealed to her more than she wanted to admit. She was drawn to him viscerally and intellectually. It was a powerful force.

They drove back to the city at dinnertime, stopped for a hamburger at Perry's on Union Street, and then went back to the hotel. He startled her when he made a suggestion then. "Would you come back to Big Sur with me for a day or two before you leave? I'm not trying to seduce you. I just want to be there with you." She had to get back, but maybe another day or two wouldn't matter. And she liked the idea of seeing his cottage with him.

"Can I sleep on it?" she asked him. He was grateful she hadn't turned him down.

"Of course. We can decide tomorrow." She liked the way the word "we" sounded coming from him. He left her outside her room then, and when she went in, Andy's photograph caught her eye in her suitcase. She looked at it, wondering what Andy would tell her to do. Reach for it and try one more time, or do what she had with him, and not take a chance on something they both knew could never work? But this time, she thought, it could. She and William existed in similar worlds and had much more in common. She sat down on her bed, thinking about it, and reached for the phone. He picked it up immediately.

"Let's go back to Big Sur tomorrow. But I've got to get back to New York this weekend."

"I'll drive you to the airport myself. I promise. And you'll still be a virgin." She laughed when he said it.

238

"Thank you, William, for giving me the time I need to figure it out."

"You'll always have the time you need, Maddie," he said solemnly. "Although I can't promise your virginity will be safe forever." She didn't want it to be, even now, but she didn't want to lose her head over him. The truth was she knew she already had.

Chapter 13

They dropped off her rented car before they left the city. The drive to Big Sur from San Francisco was relaxed and easy. They took the coast road for the last part of it, the scenery was rugged and majestic, and then they watched the fog roll in. It gave everything a cozy, intimate feeling as they chatted on every subject. She found she could talk to him about anything, their marriages, their children, their childhoods, their work. They had both lived self-imposed solitary lives for years. He hadn't dated anyone in a while. He said it was too much work spending the evening with women he never wanted to see again. He'd rather stay home and do research for a book, which he admitted was pure laziness. He had tried internet dating a few times and thought it was ridiculous and potentially dangerous. She had come to similar conclusions years before, and eventually stopped making any effort to meet someone, and avoided it in fact. She had come to think of herself as untouchable, and then undesirable, with the excuse that she was too old, which he scoffed at. They both knew people older than they were who had met and fallen in love, but they had convinced themselves it would never happen to them.

"Why did you come to America when you got divorced instead of staying in England?" She was curious about it. He was still so British in so many ways.

"I was escaping. I didn't want to run into Prudence in London or watch her date all my friends. I got a chance to write the script for a historical documentary in L.A., and I leapt at it, and then I stayed. Los Angeles seemed too artificial and distracting, so I slowly moved north, first to Santa Barbara, and then I came here. It suited me at the time. I became something of a recluse for a while, and it got comfortable. That's not necessarily a good thing. You lock yourself in a room, and after a while you forget where the door is, and eventually you don't care. I've thought of going back to London a few times, but Theo is away at school now, and I like my life here. I don't want to go back to all the people I knew growing up, who want to know why I never married again and can't find a woman I care about. I'm constantly having to explain things there, and justify what I'm doing, when I go back for a visit. It's a clean slate for me here. I never thought I'd stay this long, but now I like it. People do what they want in the States, far more than they do in England. The people I know in London are leading their parents' lives, with less money and less style. I don't have to prove anything here or lead a life I don't want. And if I were there, I'd be fighting with Prudence over Theo all the time. I'd want to see a lot more of him than she'd like or agree to. It's probably easier for him with me here too. He loves coming to visit. We do fun things together in the summer, and I take him skiing over Christmas."

"I've never liked the British system of sending children, boys mostly, to boarding school so early. I've known Englishmen who were sent away at seven, and one at five, although I think that was unusual."

"I don't like it either," William agreed. "They think it makes men of us. It just makes us neurotic and awkward with women, and we cover it up with good manners and tradition. I hated boarding school for ten years, and then I didn't want to leave. My parents were strangers to me. I don't want that to happen with Theo. I think I know him pretty well. I'd love to bring him here to school, to live with me. Prudence will never let that happen. I keep hoping she'll remarry, but no one is as foolish as I was. She's run through all my friends by now, and she goes out with some fairly dreadful people. She was dating the drummer in a punk rock band the last time I saw her. I'm glad Theo is away at school. He doesn't need to see all that, although he's quite insightful about her, and more forgiving than I am. He says she hasn't grown up yet, which is about right. And I doubt she ever will. Her parents spoiled her rotten, and then I finished the job. Theo is more grown up at ten than she is at thirty-five. I married a child. The foolishness of men," he said with a wry look. "She was twenty-three when I married her. I was forty-seven, a damn fool thing to do, but I thought I'd best get married before I got any older. I was an old man to her, and rapidly became an old fool in her eyes. I was an opportunity, not a husband."

It made Maddie think of Jacques and his flock of young girls, but William was very different and a much more serious person. He had substance and a foundation Jacques didn't. Jacques was going to play all his life. Maddie found William sexier and more attractive because he was intelligent too. She wanted to read one of his books, although he warned her it would be slow going. His last book was eight hundred pages long, about the last kings of France before the Revolution, and where they went wrong.

When they got to Big Sur, he told her there was a small quaint bed and breakfast just down the road from him, or he could take her back to the Post Ranch Inn. He didn't try to convince her to stay with him, which she had been afraid he would. He had taken her at her word. She was determined not to get carried away on a wave of passion she'd regret later. She didn't trust herself to stay at his cottage, and he didn't suggest it, although he would have loved her to.

"The bed and breakfast will be fine," she said, and he took her there and paid for the room.

"You're my guest this time," he said simply. "Your virginal reputation is secure."

They drove half a mile to his cottage then, and entered through a white gate under an arch of trees. The house was completely hidden from the road and sat perched on a cliff with a spectacular view of the ocean. The entire living room was windows, with comfortable old leather club chairs and couches that looked very English. There were books everywhere, and the kind of friendly disorder men make when they live alone. The house was full of eclectic objects from his travels and some of the contents of his house in England before he moved.

The term "cottage" was a modest description of it, it was bigger than she had expected. His bedroom was upstairs, and a guest room, which he didn't offer to show her, and there was a big country kitchen with a dining table, similar to hers at the firehouse. They were both hungry and he made an omelet and a salad. They sat down to eat, looking at the view.

"I love this place," he said happily. There was a path down to the beach, which was too steep for her with her cast. "I'd have to pull you up on a rope," he teased her. "Theo loves playing on the beach when he's here. It used to worry me when he was younger, but he's good about it now." There was a big terrace where William said he liked to lie in the sun when it wasn't too windy. The house was very exposed on the ocean side, which gave him the incredible view. And he said he loved watching the fog roll in every day.

After lunch, he made a fire in the fireplace, and they sat down next to it, and he showed her some of his books. They were impressive tomes, and the reviews on the dust jackets were equally so. He was a serious writer, as she was a serious photographer. And they had worked hard to achieve their success.

"I'd love to do a portrait of you," she said, as she pulled a camera out of her purse and walked outside to photograph the view. He joined her, and she shot a few frames of him, then he took the camera carefully out of her hands and set it down on a table, took her in his arms and kissed her. She felt as though she were flying through time to a place she'd never been, safe in the arms of a man who loved her. It felt more right than she wanted to admit to him, and she could feel her resolve melting as she kissed him back.

"You'll have to stop if you don't want me to tear your clothes off," he whispered in a hoarse voice and she laughed. At that precise moment, she wouldn't have minded if he did, but she didn't want to have regrets later. They sat outside for a while, and went back in when it got chilly. He had put a cashmere blanket over her, and they held hands as they watched the sunset before they went back to sit by the fire. He poked it with an iron and put another log on. There was something so masculine about him, which she loved, and so well-mannered. He appeared to be considerate in a thousand little ways, always concerned for her comfort and attentive to her needs, both emotional and physical. He was a gentle, loving man, and she wished she had met him sooner. It would have been wonderful to be married to a man like him, instead of always forging ahead on her own. She could see how one could get lazy and spoiled with a man like him, and happy.

They sat talking in his living room until almost midnight, and they were both getting tired. It would have been easier to just go upstairs to his bedroom, but he didn't suggest it and smiled at her as he stood up.

"I'm afraid you'll get demerits at your boarding school if I don't get you in before midnight, my dear," he said, smiling wistfully. He would have liked to wake up next to her in the morning, but he didn't want to violate their agreement, at least not this soon. "I'll drive you back." She put on her jacket and they walked out to his car, feeling sleepy and peaceful. It had been a perfect afternoon in his cozy nest above the sea.

He kissed her before she got out of the car, and they lingered for a moment, and then he walked her inside and saw her to her room, ever vigilant of her well-being and safety. Everyone else in the house was asleep, and they walked upstairs as quietly as they could, and she giggled when the stairs creaked. He kissed her again before he left, told her to call him when she woke up, and she heard him drive away a minute later. He called her on his cellphone as soon as he got home.

"You've ruined this place for me," he said plaintively in a velvety voice born of desire and fatigue. "It seems empty without you now. I hope you spend the night with me here sometime soon."

"So do I," she said, the words just slipped out. She had created the tension of his wanting her by not sleeping with him. It hadn't been intentional, but the result was that he only wanted her more now, if that was even possible.

"You make me feel very young, Maddie. I feel like a schoolboy. It sounds a bit mad, but I love you. I'm just sorry we didn't meet sooner. We've wasted so much time until now, not knowing each other. I want to make up for lost time and not miss a minute now."

"I hope we will," she said gently.

"I hope so too," he said earnestly. "Sleep well. I'll pick you up in the morning. Do you sleep late?"

"Never."

"Wonderful. I'm an early riser. Don't be afraid to wake me."

They both went to bed then and thought of each other, and she fell asleep before he did. He lay in bed for a long time, remembering every moment of the day he had spent with her and wanting more.

She took him at his word and called him at eight the next morning. He had been up and dressed for two hours by then, hoping she would call soon. She had forced herself to wait until eight to do so. He came to get her ten minutes after she'd called him, and drove her back to his place, where he had coffee and warm biscuits and jam waiting for her, and freshly squeezed orange juice, which was delicious.

"I love the fruit in California," he said as he drank his juice. There was a lot about America he liked, and he said he had no desire to live in England again. He loved the freedom and opportunities life in the States provided, even as a writer. She took more photographs of him over breakfast on the terrace, and got a wonderful one of him laughing when she said something he thought was funny. The fog bank behind him provided a moody backdrop for her shots of him. After breakfast, he drove her to a beach path that was more accessible to her than his own, down the steep cliff where he lived. They walked for a while along the beach, although she was slowed down by her cast. They only passed the occasional local resident walking a dog, and most of the time had the beach to themselves.

"God, I love being with you," he said as he hugged her, while they stood looking out to sea together. They had agreed that she had to leave the next day, he was dreading it and she was worried about it too. She realized how far they had come and that despite all her safeguards and caution, she would miss him.

"When will I see you again?" he asked her over lunch, and reiterated the offer to meet her in Hong Kong.

"I'm not sure where I'm going after Shanghai. I have three options at the moment, and I don't know if I'll have a break or only enough time to get to the next shoot."

"Is that your only hesitation?" he asked, looking straight at her, and she nodded. She wanted to see him again too.

"Right now, the options are Paris, London, and Madrid, and a very, very slim chance I'll have to go to New Delhi."

"That would be fun too. I'm game for wherever you want me. I can do my work on the road. I'm not particular about where I do my writing," he said, unlike her daughter, who had to do it at home with no one in the house. "I bring my computer and I can work on the plane." He was even more flexible than she was.

"I'll know more when I get back to New York." At least all the options were civilized this time, she wasn't shooting in Somalia or Pakistan, although that could change if a disaster happened somewhere in the world and she decided to go there. She called her own shots these days, except for her important clients' complicated schedules, which was the case in Shanghai.

The day sped past them faster than either of them wanted. They cooked dinner together rather than going out. They had to get up early. She was

251

on a nine o'clock flight, had to check in by eight, and had to leave Big Sur at four-thirty in the morning to be sure they made it in time. Since she had returned her rented car in San Francisco before they left, she had offered to hire a car and driver to pick her up, but he wanted to drive her himself.

"I want to see how you behave at that hour of the morning," he teased her.

"I'll probably snore all the way there."

"I wouldn't mind a bit, just to have a few more hours with you," he said gallantly. "They used to wake us up at five o'clock at my boarding school. I haven't been able to sleep past six ever since. It's a great bore really. I'm always creeping around trying to be quiet while everyone else is asleep."

He took her back to her B and B at ten-thirty so they could both get some sleep, but not until after they kissed longingly on the couch in his living room, and not going any further was exquisite torture for him, and agony for her too. She hated to leave him, but they had respected their agreement, and managed not to wind up in bed.

"I'm not sure if it's a sign of extraordinary restraint and a sense of honor, or old age in my case," he said as he drove her back and she laughed.

"Honor, I'm sure," she said, smiling at him.

"Thank you for your faith in me," he said as he kissed her passionately again before he left her. "I hope you don't intend to maintain your virginity for too long. I'll have to start taking cold showers several times a day." She kissed him tenderly and then she left him. She finished packing, put out her traveling clothes for the next day, closed her eyes, and it felt as though the alarm went off as soon as she did.

She showered quickly, brushed her hair and teeth, put on makeup, dressed, and was downstairs with her bag when William drove up promptly at four-thirty.

"I wish we were traveling together," he said as he handed her a warm scone and a thermos of tea.

"So do I," she admitted after she thanked him. He was supremely organized and attentive to her. She had never been so spoiled in her life. She was usually the one who attended to details. If they ever actually got together it would be a contest as to which of them could take the best care of the other.

They were quiet for a while as they drove north. They took the highway this time, instead of the coast road, and it was a foggy morning. It lifted slowly as the sun came up.

"Dammit," he said as he saw the fog lifting. "I was hoping your flight might be delayed." He smiled at her.

"I'm dreading what I'm going to be facing in

my office when I walk in. I've never taken a three-week break from work in my entire life. I'm going to have a mountain of stuff waiting for me to tackle before I leave for Shanghai."

"You'll get through it," he said confidently. He had a strong suspicion of what she was capable of, military precision and maximum efficiency. But she wasn't obnoxious about it. She just got things done.

They talked a lot during the last half hour of the trip to the airport, as though trying to store up memories. She promised to call him when she landed. With the time difference, she wouldn't get home until seven-thirty that night, which was four-thirty for him on the West Coast.

"I hope I get to see your firehouse one day. It sounds delightful, treacherous staircase and all." She had told him all about Deanna's objections to it, which he thought ridiculous. There were plenty of elderly people, which she wasn't, living in old houses in England that had far worse hazards.

They pulled into the airport departures lane at five minutes to eight. She checked her luggage at the curb while William went to park the car, and was back ten minutes later, as she waited for him with her boarding card in her hand. She was all set.

"They're boarding in twenty minutes," she told him as they walked into the terminal. She was in no rush to go through security because she'd have to leave him then. He couldn't go with her to the gate, since he wasn't traveling himself.

There was a sudden feeling of desperation for both of them as everything speeded up, their words became more inane and staccato, and finally he just pulled her into his arms and held her, and was startled to realize she was shaking. He looked at her in surprise and kissed her.

"My God, woman, I love you," he said intensely. "What will I do without you now?"

"Meet me in Hong Kong," she said, sounding breathless, "or wherever I go after Shanghai." He smiled as she said it.

"That's my brave girl," he whispered and kissed her lightly on the lips as they called her flight. It was time. There was no putting it off any longer. She had to leave him. "Take care of yourself," he said gently. "Don't work too hard," but they both knew she would, and thoroughly enjoy it.

"You too. I'll let you know what the plans are," she promised, kissed him one more time, and thanked him.

"For what? Loving you? How could I not?" It was all moving so quickly. It was dizzying.

She lined up for security and passed through the metal detector as he waved at her and then touched his heart, and she touched hers in return.

She put her shoe back on her good foot, grabbed her carry-on bag, and waved a last time, and then she disappeared into the sea of travelers and he stood there, staring at strangers and missing her. She texted him a minute later and he felt his phone vibrate in his pocket and took it out. "Soon. I promise. I love you," was all she said. He texted her back, and then left the airport, torn between over-whelming joy to have met her and sorrow knowing that he would have to live without her now until they met again. It was only the beginning, but felt like the end.

Chapter 14

As she had promised him she would, Maddie called William when she landed at JFK. Texting wasn't enough. She wanted to hear his voice. He answered the moment he heard the phone. He'd been waiting for her call. She was in the cab on her way into the city. It was three-thirty in California, and he was sitting on his deck, thinking about her as he had been all day. What had happened to them seemed so magical as to be almost impossible to believe. What were the odds of finding the love of his life at fifty-nine?

"How was the flight?" he asked her with a tender tone.

"Long. It always seems that way going east. I thought about you the whole way."

"Good thoughts, I hope."

"Very good thoughts," she reassured him. She was beginning to believe what was happening to them, although there was an unreality to it now that she was back in New York, as though she had dreamed it. It felt like a miracle to her too. "I can't wait to see you again."

"I'm supposed to be finishing a book about Winston Churchill, and all I can think of is you, Maddie. And you're so much prettier than he is." She laughed. "I'll call you at home when you've had time to settle in."

"I'll be up late, you can call anytime. And I slept on the plane."

He promised to call her and smiled when they ended the call. She was real. She existed. And he was the luckiest man in the world. For a few hours, while she was on the flight, he felt as though he had imagined her and she was a mirage, a wish he'd had all his life and never believed would come true. And now it had.

She was quiet, thinking about him on the drive from the airport. The city was all lit up, the Empire State Building standing tall to greet her. She wanted to salute it. She had left three weeks before, feeling broken and old. But she had returned feeling whole and strong, and renewed, and just young enough to enjoy it, but not young enough to be foolish. She was in precisely the right space, which proved that you never knew what life had in store. At the darkest moments, the sun could pierce through the clouds.

The driver helped her with her bags when she got to her house and she smiled as she looked up at the firehouse. No matter what Deanna thought of it, it was home, and where she belonged.

She felt like her old self when she walked in. She put her purse down and walked across her studio to her office. There were neat stacks of papers to go through on her desk, thoroughly organized by Penny, according to priority, and then she saw a vase with two dozen long-stemmed red roses that were the tallest she'd ever seen. The card read simply, "I love you, William." She had known they were from him the moment she saw them, and she wondered what Penny must have thought. She hadn't told her about William yet. She needed time to digest it herself and figure out if it was real, or just an interlude on her freedom trip. But it seemed very real now, and so were the roses.

She walked upstairs to her bedroom and remembered the nights she had spent there in pain with her ankle, her deep hurt over Deanna's words, her sudden doubts about the future and about herself. It was all washed away and it felt good to be back. She knew the box of old letters was back in her closet, on the top shelf, but there was a new chapter now. The old letters and the men who wrote them were history, even Andy, who was gone, and had been when she left New York even though she didn't know it. Her trip to see him had been pointless, except to confirm that she'd been right to end it, and to lead her to William, which was how life worked. Each part of the journey led to another. Each door opened to reveal another one. And then finally the view you had been seeking, and hoped was there but were never sure, appeared. She was sure now about getting there. And she loved the feel of her home, and knowing it was hers. She knew it was going to take some adjusting to get used to sharing it with someone, if that was how things turned out.

She worked at her desk until midnight to see what was there and determine what she could take care of quickly. Other things would take longer, but it had all waited for her. And no one had died because she'd been away for three weeks. That was a good lesson for her too. Everything that seemed so dire in the course of every day usually wasn't and could wait.

She went back upstairs then to unpack. She set the photograph of Andy on a table in her small sitting room. She smiled as she looked at him, and felt a twinge of sadness again, for what they had shared, what they'd never had, and what a fine man he was. It made her think of Bert in Mendocino again, and how glad she was that Milagra had him in her life and had shared that with Maddie on her trip. So many good things had happened in the three weeks she'd been away, her time with Ben and his family. Meeting William. The bond she had renewed with her younger daughter. She still had Deanna to contend with but she felt strong enough to deal with her now too. In the end, the men she had gone to see were unimportant. It was everything else that mattered. They had turned out to be brief chapters in the story. The rest was her life, and she hoped William could be part of it now, the real part, not just another chapter. The main event. It was nice to discover that at any age you could have hope, and new faces entered the story to give fresh meaning to life.

William called her right after she got into her nightgown, and she thanked him for the roses. He was very generous with her.

"When are you getting your cast off, by the way?" he asked her, pleased that she loved the roses.

"Day after tomorrow. Tomorrow I have to work. And I'll have to see my daughter one of these days."

"Is she likely to just show up?" Maddie had mentioned that she did that just to annoy her.

"Probably. That's what she usually does. I can handle it." He was sorry for her that one of her children was so difficult and unkind and spoiled things for her. The other two seemed to be headed in the right direction, but were far away, and so was he. He hated not being able to protect her, although she had been fending for herself for a long time and seemed to be good at it.

"I wish I could take you dancing to celebrate your cast coming off."

"I'm just excited not to have to shower wearing a garbage bag on my left leg anymore, and to be able to wear two shoes again." The experience had been humbling, but it had led her to good places in the end, since it had started her odyssey across the country, which led her to him. A true blessing in disguise.

They talked for almost an hour, and he felt guilty for keeping her up and told her she should go to bed. She had to be up early the next morning to work with Penny and find out the status of all her bookings.

William was smiling when he hung up. She was on home turf and sounded good. And she still loved him. It was good news.

Maddie closed her eyes, thinking of him, and the next thing she knew it was morning and the alarm was going off. She showered and dressed in a T-shirt and the baggy jeans she'd worn for over a month, for her cast. She was at her desk with a mug of tea when Penny walked in, gave a scream of glee to see her at her desk, threw her arms around her, and gave her a hug.

"Welcome home, stranger." They chattered for a few minutes, Penny disappeared and came back with a mug of coffee for herself, ready to work, and then gazed at Maddie seriously. "You owe me an explanation," she said as Maddie looked puzzled.

"For what?"

"Who are the roses from?" Penny knew everything about her life, and there was no one she could think of who would send her roses like that. She had been dying to read the card, but hadn't.

"Ah . . . yes . . . the roses . . ." She was grinning like a Cheshire cat.

"That is not an explanation. Who is he?" They were obviously from a man, and she and Maddie were close enough for Penny to ask and want to know. Maddie wasn't sure what to say yet, or how much she wanted to tell. She liked the idea of keeping it quiet for the moment.

"He's a writer. I met him in Big Sur."

"And?"

"A good guy. He's English."

"You're holding out on me."

"I took some pictures. I'll show you."

"I have a feeling a lot's been going on that I don't know about. Who did you see on your trip?"

Maddie had told her very little from the road, which wasn't like her, but she had been moving fast and covered a lot of ground, and hadn't been ready to talk, so Penny hadn't asked until now. She could see that Maddie was in good form.

"I saw my old boyfriend Bob Holland in Boston. I was thirty when I dated him. I broke it off. He turned out to be a bad guy all these years later. Worse than I would have imagined. He wasn't a bad guy then, just ambitious. He took a lot of shortcuts to get what he wanted.

"I saw Jacques Masson in Chicago, also an old boyfriend, and a huge womanizer. He cheated on me all the time, he hasn't changed.

"Then I went to see Andy Wyatt, the love of my life, in Wyoming. He died before I got there, but I was right about him too. His heart and soul were in Wyoming, mine were here. I saw his son and daughter-in-law and their babies.

"I met William, the writer, in Big Sur, when I couldn't get up a steep trail at the beach with my cast. I spent a few wonderful days with Ben and Laura and the kids, and I had dinner alone with Ben for the first time in eight years. My son is a fantastic person!" she said, with eyes full of love for him and gratitude for what they shared. "Then I spent three days in Mendocino with Milagra and her guy."

"Wait. Stop! Missing information. Her **guy?**" Penny looked shocked.

"Bert. He's a commercial fisherman, they've been together for eight years, she's been hiding him the whole time. He's terrific. He may even get her home for a visit one of these days. He's dying to see New York. He has never been here. I approve of him heartily, although Deanna won't, for all the obvious reasons. And I guess that's it. I saw William again after Mendocino. We went back to Big Sur for a couple of days."

"Holy shit, you have been busy, woman. You didn't leave a stone unturned."

"No, I didn't." She looked like the old Maddie again, but an even better version, rock solid, happy, and at peace. Penny was thrilled to see it.

"So are we going to see more of William, or was it a passing fling?"

"We'll see," she said cryptically. "And just for the record, it was not a fling. For now, we have work to do. Where am I going after Shanghai?"

Penny took her cue and switched to work mode, but she was floored by everything Maddie had tackled and where she'd been. "Paris is on. Madrid got canceled. New Delhi is still pending, they're not sure when they can do it. But you have a free week after Shanghai. You could do Delhi then if they confirm, or come home for a week, or go straight to Paris from Shanghai. Tell me what you want."

"What's after Paris?"

"Nothing right now. You come back here. Or you could do New Delhi then, if they drag their feet now. And there's something cooking in Pakistan, but not for a while, I think. The French president wants a portrait to use for official purposes. They want him to look handsome, competent, and powerful. The Spanish royal family wanted a portrait with their daughters, but they had a scheduling problem and had to postpone it. And, we have an inquiry from Japan, but it's nothing definite yet." Listening to her, Maddie realized how fast her life moved once she was back at work. She had substituted everything in her life with work for so long. The void her children had left, her decision not to have a man in her life. It was going to be hard for William to keep up. She was a moving target. The challenge in their relationship would be that. Could he put up with it, and would he want to? Or would he expect her to slow down? She wasn't ready to yet, even for him. But for now, she had a free week after Shanghai, before Paris, unless she had to go to New Delhi or Pakistan. But tentatively, she could meet him in Hong Kong, although that could change at a moment's notice. She wondered how he would react to the constantly shifting sands of her life. That would be key. She wanted to see him. She just wasn't sure when, or where. Her schedule was going to put him to the test, and her too. They might have hard decisions to make, both of them.

She sat down at her desk and began to go through Penny's neat stacks in earnest. There was a tall pile of contact sheets she needed to review. She handed Penny her cameras with the digital images to print. She wanted a set of the Mendocino shots for Milagra and Bert, and the ones she'd taken of William for him, and a set for herself. Penny was the most curious to see those. And Maddie had a few sweet shots of Sean and his family to send them.

"Oh, **Vogue** wants you to do the cover for the December issue. You have to shoot it in September. They want your input on the model or a choice of three major actresses. They're calling you tomorrow. And you have an appointment to get your cast off tomorrow at nine A.M. I bet you'll be happy to get that done, although it certainly didn't seem to slow you down."

Maddie smiled at her. "No, it didn't."

By midafternoon, Maddie had finished the contact sheets, approved the bills that needed to be paid and signed the checks, approved her travel arrangements for Shanghai, and put a semblance of order back in her life. The groundwork had all been laid for her by Penny, but Maddie made all the decisions. Penny appeared in Maddie's office doorway, as she signed the last check.

"Deanna is on the line," she said with an ominous expression, and Maddie sighed and picked up the phone. She had to face the music sooner or later. She wasn't looking forward to talking to her, or seeing her, after their exchanges before she left. But the tables had turned. Maddie was strong again. "Hi, Deanna, how are you?" Maddie sounded curter than she intended, and Deanna sounded cowed when she answered.

"I thought I'd come by later. Does that work for you?"

"I . . . uh . . . yes, of course." It was the first time in years that Deanna hadn't just shown up at whatever time worked for her. "Are you okay?"

"I'm fine. I missed you," she said, and Maddie was struck by how subdued she sounded and wondered if something was wrong.

"I missed you too." She felt dishonest when she said it, because she hadn't. She had been relieved not to have contact with her for three weeks.

"What time is good for you, Mom?"

"Uh . . . actually, five-thirty or six would be great for me. I should have things wrapped up by then."

"That's perfect. I'll come from my office when

I'm finished." Maddie hung up a minute later and stared at Penny in disbelief.

"She must be sick. She asked what time is convenient for me."

"I'll stick around. I can always interrupt if she gets too out of line."

"I think I can manage it." Three weeks before, Deanna had been beating her to a pulp emotionally on a daily basis. "But thank you. I wonder if something's wrong. Maybe she and David are having problems." She couldn't imagine any other reason for Deanna to sound so civil. Something had to be wrong. She sounded almost humble.

She came promptly at five-forty-five, looking very trim and chic as usual in a black linen dress with wide white cuffs and high-heeled sandals, and her dark hair in a tight bun, looking serious. She walked into her mother's office and didn't sit down. Penny was still in her office next door, and hadn't left yet intentionally. She didn't trust Deanna for a minute.

"I just came to see how you are," she said hesitantly as Maddie waved her to a chair.

"Are you okay? Everything all right with you and David?"

"Of course. Why?" She looked shocked.

"You seemed very quiet on the phone," she didn't want to say that Deanna had never had the courtesy to call before dropping by before. It was a first.

"No, we're fine," she said as she slid onto a chair facing her mother's desk. Deanna hadn't hugged her mother when she walked in, which wasn't unusual for her. She was the least affectionate of Maddie's children, and was even that way with her own. "The last few weeks have been kind of a shock. You've never cut me off before. You just left. You didn't say anything. You didn't take my calls. You've never done anything like that." Her eyes filled with tears as she said it, and her lip trembled, and Maddie felt sorry for her. She had brought it on herself, but Deanna didn't understand that. She had no concept of her effect on others. She had been brutal with her mother, and Maddie felt that her lack of communication had been warranted, to protect herself.

"I know I was hard on you when you broke your ankle, but I was worried about you. I didn't want you to get hurt again." In the meantime, Deanna's brother had given her hell and hadn't minced words telling her what he thought of her, and how badly she had upset their mother. "I don't want you falling down the stairs one night and killing yourself."

"I know, my being on the ladder was damn stupid, but I can still manage on my own. I'm not ready for assisted living yet."

"I know. I was wrong to say that. Ben told me. David was pissed at me too. He said I was too harsh, and I guess I was. I didn't mean to drive you across the country on some crazy trip." She obviously felt guilty about it.

"You didn't. I've been wanting to do that for years. I'm glad I went. It was good for me in a lot of ways." Maddie looked confident and in control again and was gracious with Deanna.

"Ben says you're lonely," Deanna said softly, still shocked at the idea if it was true. She never saw that side of her mother or her vulnerability. She only saw her strength, which was what Maddie chose to show her.

"Sometimes I am lonely," she admitted for the first time. "You all have your own lives, as you should. And I've been alone for a long time. Most of the time I like it. Sometimes I don't. But your words hit me hard. No one can hurt you like your kids." She smiled at her daughter, no longer angry at her. She felt strong and centered again.

"Do you want to get married again?" Deanna looked anxious at the idea. "Is that why you went to see Andy Wyatt? . . . I'm sorry about him by the way. Ben told me."

"Thank you. I don't think I'd have married him, even if he'd been alive when I got there. All the same things were still true. He wanted a life in

271

the wilds of Wyoming. I didn't. I roam all over the world, but home is here." Deanna nodded, reassured. It had been a strange feeling being out of touch with her mother for all these weeks, and she didn't like it. "But I'm not ready for an alarm around my neck either. Give me a few years." Maddie smiled and felt better than she had in years, and younger, and Deanna could see it. She had dropped ten years on the trip.

"I missed you," Deanna said softly, and Maddie got up from her desk, came over and hugged her. "When Ben said you had run away, and probably because of me, I felt terrible. David gave me hell for that too. I know you're not ready for any of the things I suggested, I just thought you should be prepared."

"That's a lot more preparation than I'm ready for," Maddie said. It reminded her of what William had said, that you should never prepare for old age, just let it happen and deal with it when it does. "Maybe I'll get lucky and just keel over one day, while I'm still busy and having fun. I'd rather go that way than with an alarm around my neck. I'll just use the fire pole when I can't manage the stairs anymore."

"Ben said you would." Deanna smiled. "I always hated how different you were from other mothers when I was growing up. Now I think maybe I liked it, or I should have."

"That's lucky, because I don't think I'm ever going to learn how to be like everyone else," Maddie said with a smile.

"I wouldn't want you to be," Deanna said, which was possibly the nicest thing she had ever said to her. She left a little while later after they hugged again, and Penny stuck her head in Maddie's office after Deanna was gone.

"How was that?"

"Nice actually. She said she missed me while I was away. I think I scared the hell out of her when I left and cut her off."

"She ripped my head off every time I told her I didn't know where you were," Penny said and they both laughed. But Maddie was proud of Deanna for coming to see her and apologizing. She had never done that before.

Penny left for the night a few minutes later, and Maddie called William and told him about Deanna's visit. Maddie running away from everything had woken her up. She had been meek as a lamb. The one thing that Maddie hadn't done was tell Deanna about William. She wasn't ready to yet. She didn't know where it was going and she didn't want to deal with Deanna's reaction. She hadn't told the others either. Only Penny knew.

She admitted to William that it felt good to be

back but she missed him too. And he sounded pleased to hear it.

They talked about her schedule for the next few weeks, and she told him about the free week after Shanghai, when she could meet him in Hong Kong, with the caveat that either her New Delhi or her Pakistan trips could preempt the free week closer to the time. But if not, they could have a week together in Hong Kong, and then she had to fly to Paris.

"Could I join you there too?" he asked cautiously. "I have the time. Would it be an intrusion?"

"Not at all. I'll be busy in the daytime, but we could go out at night."

"I want to hop over to England for an afternoon. I'd love it if you'd come with me, you could meet Theo."

"That could work," she said pensively. "The trouble with my schedule is that it can change at a moment's notice. As long as you don't mind that, you can come with me for most of what I do," or at least some of the trips. She liked the idea of being in Paris with him, and Hong Kong, if it worked. "The subjects and magazines I work with flush my plans down the toilet regularly, which is why I don't have any personal ones as a rule. I keep myself free for work." But now she wanted to be with him too. It would be a juggling act for sure.

"I'll book a flight to Hong Kong, and if it doesn't happen, that's fine. And I can book Paris too." She gave him the dates and he jotted them down. "That's going to be very soon," he said, sounding pleased, if it happened. It was in a week, which wasn't long at all.

"Where do you stay in Hong Kong?"

"The Peninsula."

"I always stay there too."

"I've agreed to separate rooms, but separate hotels might be a bit much." She laughed at what he said. "Where should I book in Paris?"

"The Ritz." She stayed in the best hotels whenever she could and billed them to the client. It made up for all the times she had to ride on muleback into the mountains, or sleep in a tent or the back of a truck in a war zone with missiles exploding around them. There were two extreme sides to her work. She wasn't going to take William on dangerous missions with her, just the fun ones. Paris was sure to be that. And it would be nice to meet his son. They had a lot of good times in store, and probably some adventures that would be less so, but William was delighted that she was letting him come with her. It really was a dream come true, for both of them.

She thought about Deanna again after they hung up, and how far she had come in only three weeks. With her husband's and brother's help, she had backed down, and Maddie was safe from her for now, until the next time. With Deanna you never knew. Maybe something had really changed. If so, it would be an enormous relief, and she had made great strides today. Maddie sent her a text, thanking her, and saying how much it meant to her. There had been tears when they hugged. Deanna was a child who thought she had lost her mother for three weeks. It had been a frightening feeling, and she hadn't recovered from it yet. She had never thought that her mother would have been capable of cutting her off and ignoring her as she had. But the lesson seemed to have been learned. Penny was still stunned by Deanna's change of attitude when she left that night. She appeared to have been defanged. Maddie and Penny both just hoped the fangs wouldn't grow back.

Chapter 15

Maddie's appointment to get her cast removed went smoothly. She had healed faster than expected. The cast came off, and the skin on her ankle looked white and had the texture of a raisin, all puckered and wrinkled. An X-ray showed that the bone had mended completely. She had full use of her leg now but the ankle was still stiff and they gave her exercises to strengthen it. They told her to be slightly careful with it, so she wouldn't break it again. But the pin should help strengthen it.

Forty-five minutes later, she was back in her office with two shoes on for the first time in six weeks. She had a phone conference with **Vogue** at ten about the December issue. They selected a famous actress for it, and Maddie couldn't wait to shoot her. It was going to be a rare treat and privilege.

After the call, Maddie rushed out and bought matching dresses for Sean and Becky's twins, and two pink teddy bears.

She left for Shanghai the following week to do a sitting with an important businessman. He owned several art galleries and had a significant art collection himself. He was a serious, very conservative subject. He spoke perfect English and Maddie enjoyed the shoot, and talking with him.

She spent the week in Shanghai, and boarded the plane to Hong Kong, wildly nervous, and excited about seeing William. She had only seen him in Big Sur and San Francisco, and now they would be halfway around the world together. She wondered if it would feel different. They had asked for rooms side by side if possible, or at least on the same floor. Traveling together would be an interesting test, to see if they got along. He knew Hong Kong well since he'd lived there for several years as a boy, when his father worked there. Maddie had had shoots in Hong Kong many times and loved it. Going to terrific places was one of the perks of her job, and even more so if she could go with him.

They were planning to stay for five days and then fly to Paris, without stopping in New York. The New Delhi and Pakistan trips had been rescheduled for later. It had all worked out. The gods were smiling on them and had since they'd met.

The Peninsula had sent a Rolls to the airport for her. When she checked in, they told her that William had already arrived. He had checked in two hours before she did. She called his room when she got to her own, and he was out. When she called his cellphone he didn't answer. It gave her a chance to unpack, take a bath, and change. She had just put a red linen dress on with a white linen jacket, when she heard a knock on the door. She opened it, and he stood there smiling at her, looking devastatingly handsome in gray slacks and a blazer, an impeccable blue shirt, and a tie.

"Wow!" she said when she saw him and he swept her into his arms and kissed her. Her room had a spectacular view, and when she saw his, she thought it was even better. He had taken a large suite, right next door to hers, as they'd requested.

"Are you exhausted?" he asked her. She wasn't. She had slept on the flight, and they decided to go exploring. He had the car and driver the hotel had gotten for him, a Bentley, and they drove past the house where he'd lived as a boy on The Peak. His family still had money then, he'd explained to her, and eventually went through most of it. He had preserved the small inheritance he'd gotten from a great-uncle, and he earned his own income as a writer. They both made a healthy living, but weren't frivolous. They were able to do the things they enjoyed, had homes they loved, and could indulge in occasional luxuries. They were fairly evenly matched, which made things easier. Neither of them had to apologize to the other for how they lived.

They did some shopping, and William took her to lunch at T'ang Court in Kowloon. He couldn't take his eyes off her. It seemed like months since he'd left her at the airport in San Francisco. She filled the gaps about what she'd been doing in New York. It felt like a honeymoon to both of them, except for the fact that they were staying in separate rooms. He didn't complain about it, he was just glad that they had five days there together, and then Paris to look forward to. She had never done anything as exotic with any man, even with Stephane. They had a baby at home almost as soon as they were married. He was a hot photographer then, and was already cheating on her. She got pregnant again, with Ben, four months after Deanna was born. They didn't have time for romance or the money to afford a trip like this. The men she dated after him didn't either. Whatever exciting trips Maddie had taken after her divorce, she had taken by herself, between assignments. She had never spent a week like this with any man. And it was exciting just being with him. Whatever they did seemed like fun. And he knew Hong Kong well.

They didn't go back to the hotel until the late afternoon. Maddie was going to lie down before they went out for dinner. William had asked the concierge to make reservations at L'Atelier de Joël Robuchon, which Maddie knew from Paris but had never been to in Hong Kong. He wanted to take her to Macao to go gambling one night. It was an exciting, vibrant, sophisticated city and Maddie had always liked it.

They were walking arm in arm as they went back to the hotel, and when they got to their floor, he kissed her.

"Do you want to come and hang out in my room for a while?" He had a bedroom and a living room, so it didn't sound like a proposition, just an invitation. Everything went so smoothly with them that it seemed odd to be apart at all. She skipped her nap and the honeymoon atmosphere persisted as he poured them a glass of champagne in his suite and toasted her. "Thank you for meeting me here, Maddie." He leaned over and kissed her then, and her resolve slipped away from her like fog in the sun. He couldn't stop kissing her, and she couldn't keep her hands off him. They were both breathless, and his eyes pleaded for what he didn't put into words. He didn't need to, she wanted him just as badly, and suddenly all her fears lifted from her. They wanted each other so desperately, they couldn't stop and didn't want to. Not making love no longer made sense. They had waited a lifetime to find each other and didn't want to wait any longer.

"I love you, Maddie," he said as he scooped her up gently, and she kissed him as he carried her into the bedroom, laid her down on the bed, and carefully peeled her dress away from her and revealed the beauty of her body that time had scarcely touched. They lay naked moments later, making love with all the tenderness and caring they felt for each other. They were like two halves of one whole, and they didn't stop until they came at the same time and lay breathless on his bed afterwards. Neither of them could speak for a moment.

"Good God, Maddie . . . what you do to me . . . you're the most beautiful woman I've ever met."

She looked at him shyly and rolled closer to him again and kissed him. "I don't know who did what to whom, but I've never known anything like that."

He ran a gentle finger down the length of her body and smiled at her. She made him more of a man than he'd ever been before, and she felt like more of a woman with him. All her years of resolve to lead a nunlike existence no longer made any sense at all. Not with him.

"It's a shame we don't want babies," he whispered to her, "it would be such fun trying."

"I've had my share," she said gently. She didn't want to say she was too old. She wondered if he would have had more children if he had fallen in love with a younger woman.

He knew what she was thinking and shook his head. "The answer to that is no. Theo is more than enough for me. And now I have you. That's all I need." She wanted him to meet her children, but they hadn't had time yet. And she didn't want to deprive him of babies, if that was important to him, but she couldn't imagine a life without him now either. They made love again before they got out of bed, and then had to rush for dinner. As she put on one of the robes in his bathroom to go back to her own room, he looked at her with a question and mischief in his eye.

"Would it be too forward or premature to ask if you'd like to move in with me, and sleep in my room while we're here, now that you've lost your virginity?" She laughed when he said it.

"I'll move in after dinner. You don't mind?"

"Terribly, but I'll grit my teeth and bear it. It will save me the embarrassment of pounding on your door all night in the hallway when I want to make love to you again. One suite might be more convenient for that kind of thing." She laughed and kissed him again, and dashed the short distance to her room without anyone seeing her. There was no question, he made her feel young again, and grown up too. They seemed to have the best of both. They knew what they wanted and were smart enough to realize that they had found it at last. Neither of them wanted to let go. They wanted to seize the gift with both hands.

He picked her up in her room on the way to dinner, and she was wearing a sexy black cocktail dress she had pulled out of the back of her closet for the trip. She'd brought several, including the one she'd bought in Chicago. The one she wore seemed particularly appropriate tonight. This was a day and a date they knew they would both remember forever. It had been unforgettable so far.

"We should come back here every year to celebrate our anniversary," he suggested as they left for dinner. It was as glamorous and fun as everything else about the trip. She loved being with him.

"You know, my real life isn't nearly as elegant as this in my funny old firehouse. I run around in blue jeans and tennis shoes all day on my shoots. I don't get to dress like this very often. Maybe you won't like me as much when we're not on a trip riding around in a Bentley." She looked faintly worried and didn't want him to be disappointed.

"I'll try to get used to it," he said, smiling at her. "I don't wear a dinner jacket every night in Big Sur either." He hadn't worn one that night either, but he was wearing a very handsome dark suit he'd had made by his tailor in London. She liked being able to dress up with him, but being relaxed when they went home too. She had a feeling he could do both, just as he could be seriously intellectual sometimes and fun at other times. She didn't want to win him unfairly and pretend to be something she wasn't. She was a hardworking woman. Her shoots were very physical, and she didn't care how she looked when she did them. Paris was going to be fun too, though. Their life together was one of contrasts and complexities, which both of them were good at managing.

They went for a walk after dinner, and then back to the hotel. He helped her move her belongings to his suite, and then they notified the desk that they were giving up Maddie's room. The front desk thanked them for the information, and Maddie lay in his arms on the bed, beaming.

"This feels like being married," he said dreamily, and she laughed.

"Not my marriage. I was pregnant three times in three years, worked like a dog, and my husband dumped me after cheating on me for all three years. Maybe your marriage was like this, William, not mine."

"Not mine either." He smiled at her. "Unless we fight all the time and you shag all my friends." They had both been married to cheaters and were sensitive on the subject. "I don't know what I was thinking. Maybe I meant that it feels like being married to you, whatever that feels like. And to think, only yesterday you were a virgin." She laughed and kissed him, and they were both surprised by how easily they adjusted to sharing a room and being together all the time. His bathroom had an enormous bathtub. They took a bath together the next morning, and then went back to bed and made love again. They were having trouble leaving the room.

Maddie sent text messages to all her children about how wonderful Hong Kong was, but what she really meant was how wonderful William was. Only Penny knew she was there with him. Her children didn't need to know yet how fast this was going, although they would soon when they saw Maddie and William together. It was going to come as a surprise to all of them. She had given them no warning that there was a man in her life.

They managed to leave the suite at noon, went out to lunch, did some more shopping and exploring. They had dinner in one of Hong Kong's best restaurants every night. They never got to Macao to gamble. Their five days went by too quickly. They were totally at ease with each other by the time they left, as though they'd been together for years.

They had fun on the flight to Paris and William had reserved a beautiful suite at the Ritz. She had a room booked there too, which she had Penny cancel before they left Hong Kong. She had less time to spend with him in Paris. She had to work and was planning to spend four or five days with the French president at the Élysée and elsewhere, to get the photographs they wanted. And they had one serious portrait sitting. She left the suite early every morning to observe the president at his breakfast meetings. William planned to go to some museums on his own, and do some writing. He had work to do as well. They had advanced from honeymoon mode in Hong Kong to a semblance of real life in Paris. He laughed when she said it.

"If this is your work life, Maddie, sign me up anytime." She left in a smart black pantsuit every day, with an assistant she often used in Paris, half a dozen of her favorite cameras in a bag, and a slew of equipment the assistant had rented and took charge of: lights, filters, tripods, backdrops, and everything she needed.

"I'll have to take you to a war zone with me sometime," she teased him and his face clouded when she said it.

"I don't like to think of you doing assignments like that. I know you have to and you love them, and I've seen the images you capture there. But I don't want anything to happen to you. It took me so damn long to find you, I don't want to lose you."

"You won't. I know what I'm doing. I know how to get out of the way fast." But they both knew that there were times and places and people who didn't play by the normal rules of any war, and bad things could happen. And when they did, they happened fast, and did a lot of damage. But William also knew he couldn't stop her and wouldn't try.

They had several late dinners in Paris when she finished work, some of them with her assistant. They made love whenever she had the time. She felt like she was leading a double life. That of the photographer she had been for more than thirty years, and the woman she had become with William. They were almost two distinct, separate people in her mind.

At night, they walked around Paris, in awe of its beauty, before they went back to the hotel. Maddie had always thought it was the most beautiful city in the world.

They left Paris after five days of intense work for Maddie, flew to London, and checked in to a small hotel. Theo's boarding school was two or three hours out of the city, in Sussex, and he was expecting them. His father had written to him that he was bringing a friend. Theo was excited to see him. They were taking him out for the afternoon, for a high tea at a local restaurant, and then back to school. The school wouldn't allow William to take Theo out for the night, but at least they could see him for several hours. William was excited and impatient as they drove through the lush countryside to the school. It was one of the oldest in England, and the grounds were immaculately kept. There were playing fields and boys of all ages engaging in various sports and walking from one building to another. They had to go to the headmaster's office to collect Theo, and Maddie waited in the car while William went to get him, so as not to intrude on a private moment between father and son.

It was a long wait, and then she saw a tall, thin boy with dark hair walk out of the main building with William. The child was smiling broadly and so was his father. Theo was talking animatedly, and William pointed to the car. They walked over to it a moment later. Theo looked shy for a minute when he saw Maddie in the passenger seat on the left side.

Theo bounded into the back seat then and William introduced them, as Maddie stuck out a hand to shake Theo's.

"Hi, I'm Maddie," she said warmly. "I'm happy to meet you. Your dad has told me so much about you. And this is a beautiful school." Theo shrugged when she said it, and wrinkled his nose.

"They built it in 1459. They cooked the food then too," he said with a disgusted look and Maddie laughed. He had a distinctly British "public school" upper-crust accent, even more so than William. It was an all boys' school. "Are you my dad's girlfriend?" He got right to the point, and William looked shocked.

"Theo! That's very rude."

"Well, is she?" He turned to his father, while Maddie waited to see what William wanted to say on the subject.

"Yes, she is. But could we be a bit more gentlemanly about it?" Maddie was touched that William hadn't disavowed her, and Theo didn't seem upset, which was a relief too.

"Mum has a new boyfriend too. He plays in a band. He's the lead singer." The last one had been a drummer, there had been a lot of them. William didn't look pleased. "What do you do?" he asked Maddie, and she smiled at him as they headed toward a park in the village, to kill time before they went to eat. There was no place to go except the shops on the High Street, which wouldn't interest the boy. It was hard to know what to do for only a few hours.

"I'm a photographer," Maddie answered his question. He was intrigued by that.

"Like the paparazzi?"

She laughed and shook her head. "No, I take portraits of people, like presidents and movie stars and famous people. But they sit for me, so I can take their picture. I don't run up and surprise them. I take pictures of moms and children, or models on magazine covers. Most of it is pretty tame stuff, though sometimes I go to shoot the aftermath of earthquakes, or war zones, but not very often." She had her camera out, to take pictures of William and his son. She had asked William's permission to do it.

"Paparazzi get punched in the nose a lot," Theo informed her.

"Yes, I think they do. They can be pretty rude, and people get angry at them."

"Do you live in California too?" Theo asked her. She could feel him sizing her up.

"No, I live in New York. In an old firehouse."

"Then how can you be boyfriend and girlfriend if you don't live in the same place?"

"That's a good question." She smiled at him. "I think we'll visit each other."

"That sounds complicated," he said, with the wisdom of youth.

"It might be," she admitted, and William smiled at her.

He parked the car then and got a soccer ball that he'd brought with him out of the trunk. He and

Theo kicked the ball around while Maddie watched and took pictures of them. Theo's uniform shirt was hanging out after a few minutes and his tie was askew, he was having fun with his father. Maddie got some great shots as they forgot about her. They played for an hour, and then it was time for tea.

Theo ate as though he'd never seen food before and he asked Maddie if she had children. She said she did but they were grown-ups now.

"That's too bad, that must be sad for you," he said sympathetically, and wise again. "Do they live nearby?"

"One of them does, she lives in New York. The other two live in California, so I don't see them very much." He nodded, taking it all in. William let him eat whatever he wanted, and Theo slumped back at the end of it, having eaten a plate of tea sandwiches, shepherd's pie, and scones with fresh clotted cream and jam. It was classically British, and the food was very good.

"I wish we had food like that at school. Our food is disgusting. All we get all the time are boiled potatoes and stew. I hate the food there." It made Maddie want to visit him more often. He was soaking up his father's attention, and William loved it. She could see how much he loved the boy.

They went back to the school after tea. It was seven o'clock by then, and Theo clung to his father for a moment with tears bright in his eyes when they said goodbye. She could see tears in William's eyes too. She turned and walked away to give them a few private minutes, and then Theo called out to her.

"Bye, Maddie! It was nice to meet you. I hope no one punches you in the nose!" He laughed and ran back into the main building as they looked after him. He was a small figure in a big stone doorway, waving at them, and then he was gone.

William didn't talk for a few minutes as they walked back to the car, and she held his hand. She could feel his pain from saying goodbye to his son, and her heart ached for him.

"He's an adorable boy," she said in a gentle voice when they got back in the car.

"Thank you for being so patient with him. His mother isn't much on manners, and he's aware of every hoodlum she goes out with. He meets them all. She hides nothing from him, she's very indiscreet and forgets he's only ten. That's why I want him in school here. It's more wholesome for him," he said in a voice filled with emotion.

"Thank you for saying I'm your girlfriend."

"You're not?" He sounded shocked.

"Happy and proud to be. I didn't know how you would frame it for Theo."

"At least you're respectable. I hope you can come

out to California when he's with me. Or maybe I could bring him to New York. He might enjoy it. There's lots for a child to do there." Suddenly she not only had a man in her life, she had a ten-year-old boy too. It was a little startling, but she liked it. Theo was a year older than Deanna's older daughter.

"If I'm there, I'd love to see him," she said warmly, and they drove back to London. He had nothing else to do there, and they were on a flight to New York the next morning. William was planning to stay with her for a few days and then go back to Big Sur. She was excited about showing him the firehouse, but a little anxious about having a man stay with her. She hadn't lived with anyone in a long time, and it was one thing being in a suite in Hong Kong on vacation, or even the Ritz in Paris while she was working, but quite another to have a man in her home, where she lived and worked. She was somewhat concerned about how that was going to play out. He could sense her tension on the flight home the next day.

"What's up?" he asked her. She seemed distracted and wasn't talking to him. "Worried about something?" He already knew the signs of her moods, and sometimes seemed to read her mind. He was insightful and astute, and sensitive, and not afraid of any subject with her, which she really liked. There were no taboos between them, even though he was polite. He did it in a gentle way.

"No, I'm fine," she insisted, and then she fell asleep and he watched a movie. When she woke up, she was no chattier. She was worried about what would happen if he hated her house and thought it was ridiculous, or uncomfortable, or too small, or as ugly as Deanna said it was. What if Deanna was rude to him? She wanted to introduce them, but Deanna was unpredictable and could be icy or critical, or flat-out nasty. They weren't on vacation anymore. This was real life, and the firehouse was a dollhouse of sorts. The rooms weren't big. It didn't have sweeping ocean views like his "cottage" in Big Sur. It was funny and cramped and eccentric, and she loved it. But what if he didn't? She closed her eyes, thinking about it, and as they landed, she felt him take her hand. She opened her eyes and looked at him. He was smiling at her.

"Whatever it is you've got your knickers in a twist over, it's going to be fine." There were tears in her eyes when she smiled back at him. He was such a good man.

Chapter 16

JFK was crowded and noisy and their bags took forever to arrive in the luggage area. It had been a long day and Maddie was edging toward cranky as they waited. Then finally they had them. She was eager to get home. They found a taxi at the curb and the driver put their bags in the trunk. They'd been gone for almost two weeks in Hong Kong, Paris, and finally London, and she'd been in Shanghai for a week before that. It had been a fabulous trip and everything had gone smoothly.

They were also lovers now, which raised expectations. This was not a passing fancy or a fling or a vacation romance. And even the peripheral issues were important. If they hated each other's homes, or cities, pets, or children, it mattered. He had told his ten-year-old son she was his girlfriend. That carried responsibility with it. They were wonderful in bed, but what if they failed at everyday life? His staying with her in New York would be their first taste of it. And she wasn't sure how long he was staying or what that would feel like, or if she would feel crowded by his presence while she worked.

He had said he would stay a few days, and then fly back to California, but she wasn't sure how many a "few" was. One? Two? Five? Ten? She didn't want to be rude and ask him. What if he and Penny hated each other? She needed Penny to run her life, and Maddie had an allegiance to her. Everything seemed complicated all of a sudden. It was what she'd been worried about in the beginning. She had lived alone for years now. In fact, she hadn't actually lived with a man since Stephane. She'd had her children, and had never let any man stay with her while they lived at home. Andy had stayed with her for a short time at their old apartment, and that had been a disaster. He had been uncomfortable and the children weren't used to a man in their home. But now at least there were no young children in the mix.

When the cab pulled up at her address, they got out. William paid the driver and he carried the bags to the front door. Once he had deposited them, William took a step back and took a good look at the house while Maddie dug in her purse for the keys and couldn't find them.

William was studying the bell on the outside and was staring at the details.

"It's an amazing building, Maddie," he said as she found the keys and opened the door, which led them directly into the huge open space with twenty-foot ceilings, previously for the fire trucks, which she now used as her studio. He was gazing up, and around, studying everything, and noticed her collection of antique fire hats from everywhere. There were some beauties, and he smiled when he saw them. "The space is fantastic," he said, and everything he laid eyes on was pristine and freshly painted. She kept it in immaculate condition since important clients and magazine editors came there often. Then he spotted the brass fire pole and pointed at it. "Oh my God, it's terrific! Is it still serviceable?" She smiled as she nodded. "I have to try it." He looked like a kid as he said it. It was hard to imagine him sliding down the pole in his suit.

She showed him her office on the same floor, and Penny's next to it. Everything looked orderly and businesslike. There were binders on shelves, floor-to-ceiling file cabinets, printers, the computer Maddie used for work, and just outside their offices the narrow circular metal staircase Deanna objected to so vehemently. He was fascinated by all of it. He followed her up the staircase to the living room and kitchen, and then another floor to her bedroom and sitting room, and finally the three cozy, empty guest rooms on the top floor. It had everything she needed. She had no idea how it would look to him, but she wanted him to love it, and took him to all four floors.

His eyes were shining with delight as he took it all in, and suddenly he understood. "Is this what you were worried about?"

"Part of it," she admitted. "I love this place, and I'd be sad if you hated it."

"How could I hate it? It's magnificent. It's every boy's dream. You're the only woman I've ever known with her own firehouse. Wait until Theo sees it!" And then he glanced around, as though searching for something. "Where does the pole start from?"

"There's an access on every floor." She had had cabinets built to conceal it, so no one would fall down the space around it. They were on the top floor when he asked her, and she pulled open the doors and showed him.

"Thank you, my love," he said, kissed her, reached out with one arm, wrapped his legs around the pole and sped downwards as she watched in amazement, and heard him squeal with glee, and the thump when he landed on the rubber mats in the studio.

"Are you okay?" she shouted down.

"Perfect!" he yelled back, and she met him as she headed down the stairs, and he walked into her bedroom, found the right doors, and did it again, as she laughed at him. He went down six times in all, from every floor, and met her in the kitchen to declare it the coolest house he'd ever been in. Andy had only known her uptown apartment, which had made him acutely uncomfortable and was too serious and conservative for him. She had bought the firehouse two years after they split up. William was like a kid at Christmas when he found her. Penny had left them some chicken and a salad to eat when they got home. He was in love with the fireman's pole and the whole house. And he'd had an idea while she was giving him the tour.

"Would it be possible to use one of the upstairs guest rooms to do some writing?" It was away from everyone and quiet, the kind of space he needed to work in if he was going to spend time with her in New York, and he had some editing to catch up on.

"Of course. No one ever goes up there. They were for my kids, who never used them. I've always lived here alone."

"Not anymore, my darling. Whenever you want

company, just call and I'll come running. And I'd much rather use the pole than the stairs." She laughed as she listened to him. He was like a kid at an amusement park. She set dinner out for them, and they ate while he sang the house's praises to her. "This place is so much fun. No wonder you were panicked about your daughter wanting you to sell it. You can't possibly give up this house if you live to be a hundred."

"She hates it. It's not chic enough for her."

"I think it's incredibly chic. I wanted to try on all the helmets as soon as I saw them. Your clients must love it here."

"They do, and so do I," she said with a sigh of relief. She didn't dare ask him how long he was staying and risk seeming inhospitable. But she had three shoots in the coming week, and she could suddenly envision him sliding down the pole in the middle of them. It was going to be an art sharing the house with him. But at least he loved it. It was a major hurdle overcome, and one less worry, a big one.

He helped her tidy the kitchen after dinner, and they went upstairs and showered together. No more luxurious huge bathtub in the Hong Kong suite at the Peninsula, but her shower was big enough for both of them, and afterwards they climbed into bed and made love with all the passion and thrill they had shared in Paris, Hong Kong, and London. Now they had made the firehouse theirs too. It was a brave new world for both of them.

Maddie started work with Penny at eight the next morning and they were going through files and plans when William made his way down the stairs with a mug of tea and smiled in at them. Penny gave a start and stared at him. He was even better-looking than she had imagined from Maddie's description of him and the pictures she'd taken. He was younger and sexier in real life, with a killer smile. Maddie had mostly said he was nice and extremely intelligent. She had forgotten to say he was a hunk with a fantastic body and great face. He looked like he went to the gym in California and stayed in shape.

"Sorry, I didn't mean to disturb you," he said to both of them, and Maddie introduced him to Penny. He chatted with her for a few minutes and then went upstairs again, to set up his computer in one of the guest bedrooms.

He reappeared at lunchtime, via the fire pole, which shocked Penny, and he asked Maddie if she wanted to go for a walk in the neighborhood and get some lunch. He compared it to Notting

Hill in London, with lots of little shops and small restaurants. They went to a nearby deli and had sandwiches, and Maddie told him she wanted to introduce him to Deanna and David.

"Is that wise?" he asked her. "She won't give you a hard time? Daughters don't always like their mothers having boyfriends." Particularly women like Deanna. He could already tell she was jealous of her mother from what Maddie had told him.

"She might react, but you have to meet her sometime. And she's being careful with me right now. She outdid herself when I broke my ankle, so she's on her best behavior."

"Why don't we take them out to dinner? She might be better in a restaurant. What's her favorite restaurant or food?"

Maddie was touched by the thought he put into it. "Anything French or sushi. David is easy, he doesn't care."

"I'm not worried about him. Blokes usually like me. Your daughter might not."

"She'd have to be very stupid not to." Maddie couldn't think of a single thing about him that Deanna might object to. He was successful, civilized, good-looking, from a good family, well-educated, and nice to her. A home run.

Maddie called her after lunch, and Deanna said they were busy every night for the next week.

"That's too bad. I have a friend here from California, a writer. I thought you and David might like to meet him." There was a pause at the other end while Deanna reconsidered.

"Actually, our plans are soft for tomorrow night. I can switch something," she said hesitantly.

"That's wonderful! Le Bernardin?" It was one of the best French restaurants in New York. It served mostly fish. "How about seven-thirty?" Deanna didn't like late nights. She went to the gym at six every morning, and looked it. She had a beautifully toned body.

Maddie called the restaurant and was able to get a table at the time she wanted. Then she told William, and thanked him for the idea.

"Now we just have to hope she doesn't hate me."

"She won't," she reassured him and kissed him, and then she went back downstairs to her office. It was actually nice having him there, and he wasn't interfering. If anything, he was helping her with Deanna. She wanted them to meet and for it to go well. And if possible, she wanted to introduce them on this trip, so he wouldn't be a secret anymore. Trying to hide him would only blow up in her face later. William's idea to meet over dinner seemed like a good plan. But she was nervous about it.

William could sense how tense she was in the cab on the way to the restaurant the next evening.

She hadn't seen him all day. He'd been upstairs writing. He was a singularly easy guest. He took care of himself, stayed out of her way, and let her work. They got together at night for dinner and passionate lovemaking. It was working well.

Maddie and William were the first to arrive at the restaurant. It was early and the headwaiter gave them one of the best tables. Deanna knew about those things and would like that. She loved going to good restaurants, David just liked going out.

They had just ordered a glass of wine when Deanna and David walked in. He was wearing a suit without a tie, and Deanna was wearing a very chic black dress she had designed herself, with her usual tight hairdo, and a heavy gold bangle and earrings. As always, her outfit was perfect and she looked great.

As they approached the table, Maddie noticed Deanna looking startled when she saw William. By the time they got to the table, her lips were a thin line. Somehow, she had gotten the impression that they were helping to entertain an elderly author, not a handsome man who looked like he was on a date with her mother. All of a sudden, Deanna's antenna was up. David seemed comfortable and relaxed, in anticipation of a good dinner.

William stood up politely, and Maddie introduced them. They all sat down, and the headwaiter asked if they wanted an aperitif. Deanna declined, and David ordered red wine, like William.

"So you're from California," David said conversationally, he hadn't heard the English accent yet. "L.A.?"

"Actually, I live in Big Sur. It's a bit gloomy at times, but it's peaceful."

"What brings you to New York?" The banter continued between the two men, while Deanna glanced questioningly at her mother. Maddie was innocence itself. She could play the game too.

"I'm on my way through from London."

David was staring at him by then as though trying to remember something, and suddenly looked as though he'd been struck by lightning.

"Oh my God, William Smith. The biographer?" William nodded with a warm smile and squeezed Maddie's knee under the table to give her courage. "I've been trying to buy your books for the United States for our publishing house for years. Someone always outbids me. But I haven't given up yet. What a pleasure to meet you. I love your work." Deanna looked slightly less like an ice sculpture when she saw how excited her husband was about William. He turned to Deanna then and explained that William had written some of the best, prize-winning biographies of the last fifty years, some truly important ones.

Things started to relax little by little after that. The wine helped, and the excellent food once they ordered. William told countless funny stories. David was trying desperately to woo him, so Deanna didn't dare be too unpleasant to him, but she was chilly nonetheless.

"How do you two know each other?" Deanna asked suspiciously halfway through dinner, as though her mother were famous for picking up strange men on the street.

"She photographed me recently for my next book," William filled in smoothly, and they both remembered the photographs she'd taken of him at his cottage. "I've wanted her to do my author photo for years." Deanna calmed down then visibly, but she still had an odd feeling about them. They seemed too friendly and too comfortable with each other, which wasn't usually Maddie's style. But William carried it off to perfection. He disappeared discreetly at one point to pay the check, without Maddie knowing he was doing it, and Deanna took the opportunity to hiss across the table at her mother.

"Are you dating him?"

"Why? Don't you like him? Actually, we're friends, he's good company. We're both divorced. He's intelligent and successful. I wouldn't see a problem with it if I were dating him, would you?" she asked directly.

"Of course not," David answered for her immediately, ready to pimp out his mother-in-law if it got him William Smith as one of their authors. Deanna looked daggers at her husband.

"I thought you didn't date anymore. Aren't you too old for that?" Deanna said, more like herself than the recent version.

Her mother gave her a quelling stare to warn her she was on thin ice again, with a bad rap for it historically.

"I don't date. I haven't in a long time. But who knows? Strange things happen in life when you don't expect them," she said cryptically.

"Oh my God, you **are** dating him!" Deanna was shocked. She hated thinking of her mother in that context. She much preferred the image of her in an old-age home, with an alarm around her neck in case she fell out of her wheelchair. She was less of a threat that way.

"What difference would it make, Dee? Really? Wouldn't you rather see me happy than alone and sad?" Maddie said, and Deanna didn't know what to answer. William came back to the table, mission accomplished. He could see something had happened, but he couldn't tell what, and Maddie seemed calm and in control.

The meal came to a friendly close, and David gave William his card and told him to call if he had time for lunch before he left town. William promised he would, although he hadn't been impressed by him. It was obvious that he let his wife run the show. And he saw Deanna studying him intently as they left the restaurant together. Deanna and David both thanked him, and so did Maddie.

"It was supposed to be my treat," she reminded him.

"I can't let you pay for my dinner, can I?" He teased her and Deanna watched them with a stunned look on her face. Maddie kissed her and David, the men shook hands, William kissed Deanna on the cheek, and then David hailed a cab while William and Maddie headed down the street to walk for a while on the warm July night.

"What happened when I went to pay the check?" he asked Maddie.

"She asked if we were dating."

"What did you say?"

"Basically I said, 'Why not,' not no or yes, but I left her all the leeway to figure it out for herself. I didn't deny it. David nearly peed in his pants at the thought, if it helps him get you in his stable of authors."

"It won't. I don't like the house, and they never come up with the big bucks." He laughed. "I could see that something had gone on, but I couldn't figure out what. I thought it might be that. Does she object?"

"Based on what? What could she object to?"

"Women like her can always find something. She's tough, Maddie. I understand her better now that I've seen her. I'm not sure she wants you to be happy."

"Neither am I. My other two kids are much sweeter."

"I wouldn't describe Deanna as sweet. But I enjoyed the evening, and I'm glad I met her. He's a bit of a buffoon." Maddie didn't disagree. But she'd done it. They'd met him, and as things developed between them, Deanna couldn't complain that she hadn't.

"Very smooth delivery about how we met, by the way. Now you'll have to use one of my pictures of you on the next book, so you don't look like a liar."

"I'd like that anyway." He smiled at her and kissed her. They went back to the house, and he slid down the fire pole twice, just for the hell of it, and then raced up the stairs to her bedroom and grabbed her.

"What are you doing?" she asked, startled as he kissed her passionately and pushed her onto the bed.

"I'm having withdrawals! Quick! Save me! You're the only one who can! You haven't made love to me since this morning!"

"You're crazy," she said, laughing at him as he took her dress off and fondled her breasts and she unzipped his pants.

"Crazy about you," he said, as their clothes landed in a heap on the floor, and he made love to her. He was more in love with her than ever, even after meeting Deanna.

Deanna called Ben as soon as she got home. He and Laura were about to leave for a dinner party.

"I think Mom has a boyfriend," she said darkly, as though telling him their mother had been arrested for shoplifting or drunk driving.

"Oh? What makes you think that?" He sounded neutral. Deanna sounded panicked. Not furious, but scared.

"We just had dinner with some guy she invited us to dinner with, and they look suspiciously cozy together."

"Is he some kind of derelict or something?" It would have surprised him of their mother.

"He's English, a writer. Some famous biographer."

"And the problem is? Is he a drunk? A drug addict? Recently out of prison?"

"Don't be an ass. I just think it's weird if she's dating again at her age."

"What is your obsession with her age these days? Leave the poor woman alone. I don't think she's had a guy in her life for years. She's a beautiful woman, and if she's found someone, more power to her."

"She doesn't need someone. She has us."

"Really? Me, three thousand miles away who sees her twice a year and calls her twice a month if she's lucky? And you, who never sees her at all, and wants to shove her into assisted living in her fifties? Or Milagra, who hasn't called her since she threw up at school when she was six? What part of that picture do you think is such great company for her? I hope she does have a guy. At least she'd have some fun for a change instead of working her ass off all the time. Is he nice?"

"I don't know . . . yes . . . maybe . . . he paid for dinner."

"At least he's not a deadbeat. So what's your complaint?"

"Nothing. I just think she doesn't need that. It's unnecessary. What if she marries him?"

"What's wrong with that?" Laura was screaming at him by then that they were late. "I think you need to get off Mom's back. For all you know, they're just friends. Did she **say** she was dating him?"

"No, but I could tell."

"Get over it, Dee. She's not just your mommy anymore. She's a grown woman, and she needs a life. Maybe more than she needs children who don't pay attention to her. Maybe next time, she'll run away with this guy. It might be good for her. Where does he live?"

"In Big Sur."

Ben stopped and smiled then. "That's interesting. That was the last stop on her big driving trip. Maybe she met him there. Or maybe he was the last man on her list she was checking out. Either way, he doesn't sound like a bad guy to me. If she introduces me to him, I'll let you know what I think."

"I bet she will," his sister said conspiratorially.

"We'll see. Good night, big sis. Go watch TV and leave Mom in peace." He hung up and hurried out to Laura who was waiting in the car and annoyed with him.

"I like the guy," David said to Deanna when she hung up. He couldn't help overhearing.

"You just want him as an author," she snapped at him.

"True. But I like him anyway. He'd be nice for your mother. It would be good for her to have a man in her life."

"Why?" Deanna said to him coldly.

"Because everyone needs someone to love and be loved by, Deanna. You forget that sometimes."

"She's my mother, not some twenty-five-year-old floozy."

"She's a woman, and she's not as old as you like to think. And you're lucky if she is dating him. He's not some thirty-year-old gigolo. He's a great guy." Deanna didn't answer him. She went upstairs to her bedroom to get undressed, thinking about her mother, and wondering if she knew her at all. It seemed unlikely to her, but maybe Maddie had been as lonely as Ben said when she ran away. But if so, she seemed happy now. Her mother had always been a mystery to her.

Chapter 17

William stayed with Maddie for a week. He did his editing in the bedroom upstairs every day, and they had dinner at night and made love. She was busy planning her next projects, and her trip to Pakistan had taken shape. It was going to be a story about women for **The New York Times Magazine,** and she was leaving for Islamabad in two weeks. He didn't want to crowd her, although they were surprisingly comfortable living together. Deanna hadn't called to inquire further about him, and everything was going well. But he thought he should go back to Big Sur for a while and write another chapter of his current book. It was easier for him to do that at home, with his usual routine and research material, although he could write elsewhere if he had to.

"I thought I'd go back to California on Monday," he said over the weekend.

"Is something wrong?" She looked surprised.

"Quite the contrary. It's very right." He smiled at her and leaned over and kissed her. "I don't want you to get tired of me." It was working out better than either of them had hoped. They had been together for nearly three weeks. "I'll come back after your trip to Pakistan if you want me." It would give him three weeks at home, which seemed like a good balance for now. And Theo was due to arrive soon too. William planned to have time with him in California, and then come to New York for a week to stay with Maddie before Theo went back to England from New York. "Will you be upset if I leave?" He looked worried. He didn't want her to feel abandoned.

"Desperately," she answered and kissed him again. "Actually, I have a lot to do in the next two weeks before I go."

"I just want to say one thing for the record. I know I have no right to interfere in your work, or give you unsolicited advice, but I'm not comfortable with that trip. The piece you want to do is a great opportunity to piss someone off. And Pakistan isn't the safest place these days. I'd feel better if you were going to Paris or Rome or Madrid."

"Nowhere in the world is safe anymore," she said calmly.

"True, but some places are safer than others. That's my two cents for what it's worth, and I know it won't change anything."

"I'll think about it." But he knew she wouldn't.

"You have so many great subjects and clients. People are lining up at your door. You don't need to take on the dicey assignments."

"They're always the best stories. I can't just shoot beautiful people all the time, or presidents and movie stars."

"Why not?"

"Because I want to make a difference in the world, and stories like this one are what do it." It had the weight of **The New York Times** behind it to give it credibility and gravitas. And they had assigned a very well-known, serious journalist to go with her and write the piece.

"People who make a difference get hurt. You're not alone anymore. You have me and I love you. Take care of yourself, please." She nodded, and he didn't mention it again. They had a nice weekend, and on Monday, he left for San Francisco and the drive home.

As soon as he got to Big Sur, he was sorry he'd left New York. He missed her fiercely, her laughter, the feel of her skin, the silk of her hair, the sway of her hips, the smell of her flesh. He loved her fine mind, and everything else about her. She was a lot to miss. But he had work to do too before Theo arrived, and he got down to it the next day, so he'd be ready for his son and to return to New York when she got back. She said she couldn't wait too. And she was excited about the story she was about to do.

She talked to William the night before she left, as she did three times a day. They talked constantly, he reminded her to be careful, and she promised she would. She was packed and ready to go on an early flight. She was only taking a carry-on so she wasn't weighed down with luggage, and she had her heavy camera bag with everything she needed. She planned to wear a chador while she was there since most of the country was Muslim, and she didn't want to offend anyone. Her trip to New Delhi had firmed up too, and she'd be going there in September or October, after she did the **Vogue** shoot for the December cover.

She was only going to the outlying areas of Islamabad for short day trips, and planned to stay in the city the entire time, which was less danger-ous than some of her earlier trips, so she wasn't worried.

She called William from the airport before she

boarded her flight. She checked in to the hotel when she got there and dropped off her bag, and then met with Peter Hamilton, the writer she'd be working with for **The New York Times**. He was in his forties and a prize-winning journalist. It was all very well organized. She didn't try to contact William while she was there, and had warned him she wouldn't. Communications were complicated, and she had told him he wouldn't hear from her, so he wouldn't worry. She was planning to be there for a week or less, and thought she might finish in five days. William was eager for her to wrap up the story and come home. He was uneasy about the trip.

The first three days went well and she got extraordinary photographs of the women she spoke to. She spoke to women in government, a doctor, and many students, women of all ages for their points of view. She and the journalist worked closely together. As he interviewed the women, she took intimate and moving portraits of them. Maddie had the photo credits. They wrapped it up in five days, as she'd hoped, and she was leaving the next day. It had gone like clockwork. Peter was taking a flight out that night.

On her last night at the hotel, she heard a roll of thunder, and then several more, and then an explosion that sounded very near. She'd been asleep, and woke up rapidly as she realized what had happened. A bomb had exploded in the hotel. She looked out her window, and there were flames leaping from windows on other floors. She pulled on her jeans and put on shoes, pulled a shirt over her head, threw on her chador, grabbed her money and passport and one of her cameras, and ran out of her room into the hall. People were screaming and some were on fire. She stopped to help an old woman and a child and guided them toward a staircase where people were fleeing from the hotel. She stumbled down the stairs, shoved from the rear, pressed against those in front of her. People were crying and the heat was overwhelming. They could hear walls collapsing in the building.

She ran out of the building with the others, and fell several times. She saw then that her chador was on fire, took it off, and threw it to the ground, and then ran as far and as fast as she could as another bomb went off. Peter Hamilton had left that night for Mumbai and had taken all the shots from the interviews with him, so she didn't need to look for him. She was alone in Islamabad.

She turned to see the building collapse behind her. A hail of rocks and debris pounded her back, and she kept running until she couldn't breathe anymore. She stopped and randomly took photographs of the scene around her and then continued running away from the hotel. Two soldiers stopped her, saw that she was injured, which she hadn't even noticed, and helped her to an ambulance. One of the soldiers carried her most of the way, and handed her over to Red Cross paramedics on the scene. It was chaos. She passed out then and woke up in a hospital where people were on gurneys and on the floors. Some were bleeding and dying. She tried to stand up, but her left leg wouldn't hold her, and she could see that her right arm was burned. No one around her spoke English. She felt her jeans pockets where her money and passport still were. Her camera was still on the strap around her neck. She lay there for a long time until someone came to talk to her. He was a young doctor and he spoke English.

"I'm okay," she said to him. The others were so much more seriously injured than she was. He left her then and promised to come back later. All anyone knew was that several bombs had gone off in the hotel. No one knew who had done it or why. There were dead and dying everywhere. She was alone in Pakistan, with no way to tell anyone at home that she was alive.

William had been working on a new chapter all day. It had been going well, and he was happy with it. He watched the fog roll in at four o'clock and decided to take a break. He'd been so intent on his work that he hadn't eaten all day. He was starving and foraged in the fridge for something to eat. He needed to go to the store and was too lazy, he didn't want to leave the book for that long. He found a package of sliced chicken and some lettuce, a tomato, and a jar of mayonnaise, made himself a sandwich, and turned on the TV to watch CNN and see what was happening in the world.

There was a building in flames on the screen, and he watched it collapse as people ran screaming through the street, some of them on fire, as soldiers tried to help them and Red Cross ambulances arrived on the scene. It was horrifying but not unfamiliar, and then he saw the banner running below the image "Hotel bombing in Pakistan at this hour." It was four A.M. in Pakistan. His heart pounded as he watched the live feed. He put down his sandwich and stared at the screen. She was there. He knew she was. They said the name of the hotel and it was where she was staying. The reporters covering the story for CNN had to move back to avoid the intense heat and a hail of debris. He sat mesmerized, and all he could do was pray that she was alive and not injured or dead. Not now.

He didn't leave his TV until midnight that night, when they started running the same film clips again. It was noon there by then. He wanted to call Penny but it was 3 A.M. in New York.

He stayed up all night and called Penny at Maddie's house at six in the morning in California, nine A.M. Eastern time.

"Penny, it's William," he said in a gruff voice. All he'd had was coffee since the bombing, and he'd smoked a pack of cigarettes someone had left at his house months before, although he'd quit years ago. "Have you heard anything?"

"No," she said, he could hear that she'd been crying. So had he. "She always lists me as next of kin on her documents, so her kids don't hear bad news first. So if they call anyone, they'll call me," Penny explained. There was no way to reach her. The hotel was gone and her cellphone didn't work there. He had an idea. "Call me if you hear anything," he said.

"You too." They both hung up and he called a friend in the State Department to ask if he would call the U.S. Embassy and see if they had casualty lists of any Americans that had been injured in the blast. He didn't dare say the word "killed."

"It looks pretty chaotic over there right now, Bill. I'll see what I can do. But we may not know anything for a day or two." He could only imagine what Maddie's kids were going through, but the only one he'd met was Deanna and he barely knew her, so he couldn't call to offer comfort or share information he didn't have anyway.

Ben had stayed home from work and was glued to the TV. He didn't call Milagra, since he didn't think she'd know about it. She lived in a bubble. He and Deanna talked all night but knew nothing.

William's friend in the State Department called him at 5 P.M. Eastern time, and said they'd had no casualty list yet.

For three days, William, Deanna, Ben, and Penny sat at their respective television sets with their phones right next to them, waiting for news, and there was none. And then a list of victims was issued, and Maddie wasn't on it. But the injured weren't included, and all four of them realized that she could have been unconscious in a hospital with no papers on her. They might not even know she was American.

William finally couldn't stand it, he booked a seat on a flight to London and from there to Islamabad the next day. He was going over to comb the hospitals himself and see if he could find her. If she was alive and not too badly injured, she would have found a way to contact them by then, and she hadn't. He called and told Penny what he was doing and packed a small bag. He was just leaving his house at six the next morning when his cellphone rang. A raspy voice he didn't recognize said "hello" in a croak. He couldn't understand who it was at first. And then he knew. It was Maddie. She was alive. He burst into tears.

"Oh my God . . . thank God . . . are you okay?"

"Yes . . . I'm okay. They airlifted me to Mumbai. I couldn't call you. I'm fine. I'm at Lilavati Hospital. They're very good. They've been wonderful. I have a bruised leg and a burned arm and a lot of plaster dust in my lungs and that's it. The U.S. Army is flying me to a base in Germany tonight. They'll take a look at me and then I'll come home. Please tell my kids I'm okay. I called you first. I don't want to scare them." He was sure they were already scared by now. They all were.

"Oh God, Maddie . . . I love you so much. I was so afraid you were dead. I saw it on TV right after it happened. I haven't moved for four days. I was flying over this morning to see if I could find you myself." He was sobbing, and so was she.

"I love you too. When it happened I thought of my kids and then I thought of you. I didn't want to do this to you. I'm so sorry." They told her she had to get off then. The military medics had come for her to fly her out. "I'll call you from Germany."

"I love you," he said again. He called Penny as soon as he hung up, and she burst into tears too.

"Shit, I thought we'd lost her this time. She loves doing this stuff. She's gotten hurt before. But she's never been MIA for this long. She always finds a way to call."

"She wants me to tell her kids she's okay. Do you think I should call them, or should you?"

"I don't think they'd care if Donald Duck called them at this point. You should call. You talked to her." She gave him Ben's number and Deanna's. "Don't call Milagra, she probably doesn't know about it. She never reads the papers, she has no TV, and she almost never leaves the house. Maybe Ben should call her if she'll answer, or drive up to see her."

"I'll leave it up to him."

He called Ben first, cut right through the awkwardness, and got straight to the point.

The minute Ben answered, he told him what he needed to know. "Ben, my name is William Smith, I'm a friend of your mother's. She's okay. I just talked to her. They airlifted her to Mumbai, and they're flying her to an American base in Germany now, and after they check her out, they'll send her home. She said she has a bruised leg, some burns on her arm, and a lot of plaster dust in her lungs. She couldn't call until now, but she's fine." He didn't even realize he was crying as he told her son the news, and Ben sobbed into the phone.

"Oh my God ... thank you ... oh, thank God. I thought she was dead when we didn't hear from her. I called **The New York Times** and they hadn't heard anything either. I don't know who you are, but I'm so damn happy to hear from you." He laughed through his tears.

"Do you want to call your sister Milagra?"

"I don't think she knows, but I'll drive up and tell her just in case. I didn't want to scare her till we knew something."

"I was going to call Deanna, would you rather do it?"

"No, that's okay. If you talked to Mom, she'll want to hear it from you. I can't thank you enough. I hope I meet you one day. This is the best call of my life." She was injured, but not severely, and she was alive. They had all thought she was dead.

"Take care, Ben," William said, wishing he could hug him. And then he called Deanna. She knew who he was immediately, and she burst into tears as soon as he told her that her mother wasn't severely injured, and she was alive and on her way to Germany. He told her he had just spoken to Ben.

"Why didn't she call us herself?"

"I don't know. They were rushing her off the phone so they could take her to the plane. I guess she didn't have time. She asked me to call you." He was more careful with Deanna than he had been with Ben, in case she had issues with him. "I'm so grateful she's okay," Deanna said to him. She was still crying, and there was no question in her mind now. Her mother must be in love with him if she called him first. But she didn't care, as long as Maddie was coming home. "Thank you again," she said, and they hung up.

He waited by the phone for the rest of the day, and at midnight in California she called him from Germany. The flight had been delayed. She sounded exhausted and she was coughing. She had just arrived and they hadn't examined her yet.

"Baby, can you get some sleep?" He was so worried about her. But she was in an American military hospital now, and in good hands.

"I slept on the plane, but it was pretty noisy. They airlifted six of us out, all from the hotel." He hadn't slept in days himself, worried sick about her. "We had to wait for the others to be released from the hospital in Mumbai."

"I talked to Ben and Deanna. Ben is going to drive up and tell Milagra in person."

"Good. She'll be scared. She hates it when anyone gets hurt."

"So do I," he said gently. "I'm not letting you out of my sight again." He meant it, but he knew he'd have to if this was part of her job. People got killed that way. And she almost had.

"I'll be home soon. I love you," she said again. "I'll call you tomorrow."

She called him again at three o'clock that afternoon. It was midnight in Germany.

"They said I'm okay and I can go home. I have bronchitis from the plaster, second-degree burns on my arm. And I bruised the leg pretty badly and I think I sprained the ankle I broke a few months ago, but it's not a big deal." It was all a big deal to him. "I fell down the stairs getting out of the hotel. People were pushing, and there were flames everywhere and walls collapsing."

"You're lucky you weren't trampled."

"So many people got hurt. Old people, little kids . . ." Her voice trailed off. "I land at McGuire Air Force Base, near Trenton, New Jersey, at six o'clock tomorrow night. Please ask Penny to send a car for me."

"I'll take care of it," he said, with no intention of sending a car for her. He was going to meet her himself. He called the airline as soon as he hung up and booked a seat on the red-eye to New York that night. Then he packed, called Penny, and told her when Maddie would be arriving.

"I'll pick her up," he told Penny.

"When are you arriving?" she asked him.

"Six tomorrow morning on the red-eye. I'll stay at a hotel."

"No, you won't. Come to the house. I'll sleep here tonight. I can sleep upstairs. I'll be at the house whenever you get here."

"Thanks, Penny."

He left his house two hours after Maddie had called him, drove to San Francisco, and was at the airport in time for his flight. He slept for most of the flight and looked exhausted when Penny opened the door to him at seven in the morning.

"She put us through the wringer this time," Penny said when she let him in. "She's done it before, but she scared us all with this one." It had been a long wait to hear from her in Mumbai.

He took a car and driver to meet her, and he was waiting quietly with the families of the other wounded Americans on the plane. She came off in a wheelchair, holding a pair of crutches. Her hair was tangled, and she was wearing army fatigues they had given her. Her own clothes had been burned, and what she had with her had gone down with the hotel. She still had her one camera on a strap around her neck.

They rolled her toward him, and she spotted him as he stood with tears rolling down his cheeks. She was the most beautiful sight he had ever seen. She thanked the private who had been assigned to her from Germany, and there were medics and a doctor on the flight. Some of the others had been more severely injured. She had been lucky. And as he held her in his arms, William knew he had been too.

Penny was waiting for them at the firehouse when they arrived. Maddie hobbled in on her crutches, and William helped her up the stairs, gently took her clothes off and helped her into the shower, and then carried her to the bed.

"I was so afraid I would never see you again," she admitted to him with tears in her eyes.

"So was I." He settled her against the pillows and she called her children. She had the landline number at Milagra's house. She said Ben had been there with her all day after he heard the news that Maddie was alive. And he had met Bert. Now Maddie had someone for them to meet too. William had earned it.

Deanna cried like a child when she heard her mother's voice.

"Can I come see you tomorrow, Mom?"

"Of course. I'm not going anywhere for a while."

"Is William with you?"

"Yes, he is. He's a good guy, Dee."

"I know he is. He was really nice when he called us. I'm sorry I was a bitch about him." It was always her first reaction, it was stronger than she was and impossible for her to resist. "I think I was just surprised. If he makes you happy, then I'm happy for you."

"He does." He walked back into the room when she said it. He had a tray of food for her. "I'll see you tomorrow. I love you."

She called Ben then, and he cried too. After she hung up, she and William talked for a long time. He didn't tell her what she had to do or couldn't do or what he didn't want her to do. She was a grown woman with a mind of her own. But she realized when she looked at him, and after talking to her children, that her days in war zones, taking dangerous assignments, were over. She had too many reasons to live now. And she had plenty of other work that wasn't dangerous.

"I won't do it again," she said softly, and he heard her.

"I was hoping you'd say that." He lay down next to her and kissed her. She curled up in his arms then. She had thought she would never see him, or her children, or her grandchildren, or her house again. And she realized as she drifted off to sleep and he held her how incredibly lucky she was.

Chapter 18

Maddie was planning to spend a month in New York, recovering from the explosion. Peter Hamilton called her from Mumbai the day after she got home. He'd filed their story with all her photographs, and had included an addendum about the bombing. She told him she had photographs of it and would have Penny send them to the **Times**. The article would be even more powerful now.

Within days, her sprained ankle was healing quickly, her bruised leg felt better. The burns on her arms would take longer, and the bronchitis was already clearing up. She postponed her trip to New Delhi until November, and assured **Vogue** she'd be up to shooting their cover in September, a month after the bombing. William suggested they go to Big Sur for a couple of weeks after the **Vogue** shoot and she liked the idea. It was peaceful and restful there, and she and William could be alone. The week after Maddie arrived from Germany, Theo was due for his holiday with his father. William discussed it with her, and Maddie suggested he come directly to New York. There would be lots for him to do, and William didn't want to leave her, nor miss the time with Theo. He had Prudence put him on a plane to New York. Penny gave them a list of things for Theo to do with his father, and they would have dinner with Maddie at the firehouse at night.

"Are you sure you're up to having a child here?" William was worried about her. She was still shaken by what she'd been through.

"I'd love it. I'm not going anywhere and it will be fun to have him stay with us." She was going to be home anyway for the next few weeks and she didn't want William to miss out. The best plan was to have Theo come to New York, and then they could all be together.

Theo went crazy when he arrived and saw the firehouse. William showed him how to slide down the pole. Maddie liked having them with her while she recovered. Having a child there put life in the house. He and William ran around New York all day and came home to her at night and told her everything they'd done.

By the second week she was home, she was up and around, able to walk on the sprained ankle and bruised leg without crutches. Ben and his family flew in to see her and stayed at a hotel in SoHo, and Milagra and Bert came from Mendocino and stayed with her for the weekend. Penny organized a big family dinner in the studio and had it catered for all eight adults, including William, and the five grandchildren and Theo. Fourteen of them at a dinner, celebrating the fact that Maddie had survived. She introduced William and Theo to everyone. She told them all that she had given up the high-risk assignments and wouldn't be doing them again. The time had come.

"Thank you," Deanna whispered to William after she said it.

"It was her decision." He gave her the credit for it, but he had been part of the reason she had come to that conclusion, and so were they.

Deanna invited Theo to the Berkshires for a weekend to be with Kendra, his new best friend after the dinner.

A new time had come for all of them. Milagra was home for the first time in years, and everyone loved Bert. Milagra took him all over New York, and he was awestruck. Ben and Laura promised to come to Big Sur when William and Maddie were there. Deanna invited her mother and William to the Berkshires when Maddie fully recovered, and was visiting her mother every day. And Maddie told them she'd be spending time in Big Sur when she had a lull between shoots. William had become part of the family when he called to tell them their mother was alive. New bonds had formed and William was a warm addition to the group. He and Ben talked for hours, and hugged the moment they met, remembering William's call.

William came to sit quietly in Maddie's bedroom after he'd put Theo to bed in the room upstairs, and everyone had left. It had been a special evening, and they had plans for the weekend. Maddie looked tired but happy as she lay on her bed.

"You have great kids," William complimented her as he lay next to her. Her living through the hotel bombing had brought them all closer. "Thank you for letting Theo be here." It was an exciting visit for him, and he loved Deanna's girls.

"He fits right in." She smiled at William. And so did he. Even Deanna had hugged William warmly that night.

"I can't wait to get you to Big Sur after the **Vogue** shoot," he said and she agreed. She was recovering rapidly, but still tired from the trauma of what she'd been through.

By the time Theo left after his three weeks with his father, Maddie was on her feet again at full speed, and ready for the **Vogue** shoot. They were sorry to see Theo leave and he wanted to know how soon he could come back, and if they could spend Christmas in New York with Maddie and her family. Ben and Laura had promised to come for Christmas this year too. There was much to celebrate and share.

Penny had been booking shoots for October and November, after Maddie took two weeks off in Big Sur after shooting the **Vogue** cover. They were fully booked for the fall. And Maddie had informed her agent that she was giving up the high-risk assignments, which even he thought was smart, and long overdue. She didn't need them, even if she used to like them. It was time to let them go.

Once Theo left after Labor Day to go back to school, they settled into a routine. Life was getting back to normal, and William was working on his book upstairs. It was obvious to everyone that they were going to live together, alternating between Big Sur and New York, which was what William and Maddie had agreed to when they discussed it.

They were both surprised at how well living together worked for them. It already felt familiar and not like something new. They knew when to spend time together and when to leave each other alone. When she was busy getting ready for the **Vogue** shoot, he was in the room he used on the fourth floor, editing his book. It was almost as if they had lived there forever. It felt that way now. And they seemed to have found the perfect rhythm, in harmony with each other.

He had been upstairs working on his book one evening, and he came downstairs to find Maddie, to see if she wanted something to eat. He couldn't find her in her bedroom or her office. He heard noises in the studio and stuck his head in to see what she was up to. The **Vogue** shoot was in two days and she wanted everything to be perfect. She attended to every detail herself. He gasped when he saw her. She was perched at the top of a ladder adjusting a light that was at the wrong angle for the shot she wanted to start with. It had been bugging her all day.

She glanced over and saw him and looked sheepish as he crossed the studio in long strides to stand next to her and hold the ladder.

"I thought we had an agreement. You're not supposed to be up there."

"They didn't get it right today. It was driving me crazy."

"Why didn't you call me to help you?"

"You were working." She hated to interrupt him when he was writing. They respected each other's work habits, which was part of why they got along so well. Maddie never felt crowded or invaded by him. And he had the peace and private space he needed in the room upstairs.

"That's not a good excuse. Do you know what Deanna will do if you fall off a ladder again?"

"Yeah, she'll put me in assisted living with an alarm around my neck." She grinned at him.

"And kill me first. Can we make a deal? No more ladders unless I'm standing next to you to catch you."

"I promise," she said as she hopped down next to him. Her ankle was fine, and all the effects of the bombing had healed. It had been a month since she got back.

"Why is it that I don't believe you? You're a menace," he said, trying to look stern. "I don't want you to get hurt."

"I won't. I'm good at it. I've only fallen off a ladder once. And that was lucky. If I hadn't, I would never have run away, driven across the country, and met you in Big Sur. It all started when I fell off the ladder." She smiled at him so innocently that he couldn't be angry at her.

"You've got me now. Let's not do it again."

She was looking forward to spending two weeks

in Big Sur with him. She liked having two coasts and two homes for them to go back and forth between for a change of scene. Their lives had meshed incredibly well, better than either of them had expected. And she planned to see Ben and Milagra when she was there.

She went back upstairs with him then, after he put the ladder away, the light was at the right angle now. They had dinner in the kitchen, and he told her about what he had written that day. She loved hearing about his work. And he was fascinated by hers. The piece in **The New York Times Magazine** had come out by then and been well received. The photographs were extraordinary, including the ones she'd taken of the bombing as she fled.

The **Vogue** shoot went smoothly, she got great shots of the actress, and the editors were pleased. Two days later, they were on a plane to San Francisco. They were going to stay at The Fairmont that night. They were having dinner with Ben and Laura and their children, and going to Big Sur the next day. There was no sign left of the bombing. Maddie felt fine again and her grandchildren were thrilled to see her and William. He was great with them. They reminded him of Theo. Laura hugged Maddie and said in an emotional voice, "We're so grateful you're okay."

"So am I." She realized now, more than ever, how fortunate she had been, in so many ways.

They had a noisy, lively dinner with the children, sat and talked among the adults for a while afterwards, and then went back to the hotel. They wanted to get an early start the next day. William hadn't been home in a month, and he had a list of things he wanted to do.

"I had the gardeners hide all my ladders, by the way. I don't trust you," he told her on the drive down and she laughed.

"You're probably right," she admitted. She couldn't wait to get to the house and sit on the deck with him, overlooking the sea. He wanted to write while they were there. They had plenty to do when they arrived. And at sunset, Maddie and William sat on the deck and he poured them each a glass of wine. It was perfect. Somehow, miraculously, they had found each other, and fit together like two pieces of a puzzle. Everything had fallen into place. There was enough time together and enough time apart. He worked on his books, and she had her shoots and assignments, all lined up for the next few months. He was going to New Delhi with her in November.

It had all started with a box of old love letters

and a fall off a ladder. She had driven across the country in search of the past. She knew now that she had been looking for her lost youth. It was gone, swept away by the winds of time. But what she had found with William was even better, a grown-up love and shared life that served them well. She had found her womanhood in his arms, after having run away from it for so long. What they had made them both feel young again, which was the next best thing to being young. What they had was everything they needed for now, having discovered exactly what suited them. They couldn't ask for more than that. And they agreed that it had been worth the wait. Everything they had lived through before had been preparing them for this. It was a perfect moment in time.

The future was uncertain, the past a dim memory. Maddie and William had exactly what they wanted in each other. What they had found was a gift, and whatever they had lost didn't matter at all.

About the Author

DANIELLE STEEL has been hailed as one of the world's most popular authors, with almost a billion copies of her novels sold. Her many international bestsellers include **Blessing in Disguise, Silent Night, Turning Point, Beauchamp Hall, In His Father's Footsteps, The Good Fight, The Cast, Accidental Heroes, Fall from Grace,** and other highly acclaimed novels. She is also the author of **His Bright Light,** the story of her son Nick Traina's life and death; **A Gift of Hope,** a memoir of her work with the homeless; **Pure Joy,** about the dogs she and her family have loved; and the children's books **Pretty Minnie in Paris** and **Pretty Minnie in Hollywood.**

Daniellesteel.com
Facebook.com/DanielleSteelOfficial
Twitter: @daniellesteel

LIKE WHAT YOU'VE READ?

Try these titles by Danielle Steel,
also available in large print:

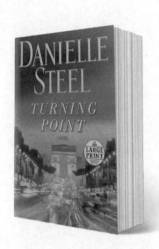

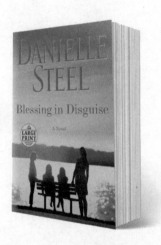

Silent Night
ISBN 978-1-9848-8457-2

Turning Point
ISBN 978-1-9848-2766-1

Blessing in Disguise
ISBN 978-1-9848-8456-5

For more information on large print titles, visit
www.penguinrandomhouse.com/large-print-format-books